# The Revenge Trail

## L.E. Luttrell

First Published in Great Britain in 2025
Copyright © L.E. Luttrell 2025
The moral right of L.E. Luttrell to be identified as the author of this work has been asserted in accordance with the Copyright, Designs and Patents Act 1988.



A CIP catalogue record for this book is available from the British Library.

ISBN 978-1-0685868-1-1
ebook – 978-1-0685868-2-8

Typeset in Great Britain by Designed Memories
Published by Woolloomooloo
Printed in Great Britain

Cover photograph: Outback scene, Australia - licenced by Shutterstock

This book is dedicated to Anna Bagi, friend and colleague
who left this earth suddenly last summer

Also by **L.E.Luttrell**

**India Hargreaves Series**
DRAWING DANGER
THE BREAKDOWN
SMALL SACRIFICES
THE PHOTOGRAPH

**Frank Bailey and Rachel Sharp Series**
A CONVENIENT ACCIDENT
THE REVENGE TRAIL

**Standalone Novel**
THE WAVE

# 1

**Newcastle, NSW**
**Thursday 17th November 2005**

Carrie Ross wasn't feeling too steady on her heels. Sober, she could just about manage to walk in them with dignity, but after several drinks was finding it difficult. She stopped, contemplating whether to take them off and walk in her bare feet. It was still a good few minutes' walk to her turning, then the struggle up a steep hill. Decision made, she shook first one, then the other shoe off. As she was bending over to pick them up, she felt something ram into her from behind and she fell face first to the ground. Confused she started to turn over when a large shape loomed over her and smashed a fist into the side of her head, knocking her unconscious.

# 2

**Police Area Command
Newcastle.
Friday Morning**

Detective Chief Inspector Frank Bailey hung up his phone, walked out of his office and called to Detective Senior Sergeant Rachel Sharp who was about to take a drink from the mug of coffee in her hand. It was only 7.30am and Frank hadn't even had time to make himself a coffee. 'We have another rape on our hands,' he said. 'I'm going to join you on this one. She's been taken to the Royal. Let's walk over there. This time the injuries are life threatening.'

Rachel's face clouded with concern. 'Did it happen in the same area?' she asked, after taking a quick sip of coffee and grabbing her bag.

'Not far off. The young woman was found in the park opposite the college.'

Frank had put Rachel in charge of a rape case that had been reported the previous week. The victim was a street prostitute and he was confident Rachel would investigate the case with the diligence and respect due to the woman –

whereas he knew many of the male detectives on his squad held low opinions of street girls and would be unlikely to take the case too seriously. Rachel and Detective Senior Constable Ayesha Patel had spent the past five days gathering as much information as they could, but so far, they had little in the way of evidence or leads that even began to point to the perpetrator.

'Another street girl?' Rachel asked Frank once they were on their way to the hospital.

'I don't know. I don't have the full information as yet. But a second rape in less than a week in a similar area is worrying. We might have a serial rapist on our hands.'

At the hospital Frank and Rachel were shown to the critical care unit where they were greeted by the uniformed sergeant who was sitting on a chair outside the woman's private room while a young constable stood sentry at her door.

'Sergeant Rooney,' Frank said greeting him. 'You know Detective Senior Sergeant Sharp I believe?'

Rooney and Rachel nodded at each other.

'What have you discovered so far?' he asked Rooney.

'The woman's name is Carrie Ross. Twenty-four years old. She lives in Bryant Street, Tighes Hill. We found her address on a driving licence in her handbag. I sent some uniforms round to her address and a young woman answered the door. It's a shared rental house. She told them Carrie got all dolled up to go to a party somewhere in Islington last night, but the housemate didn't know where. They share the house but aren't close chums apparently. Miss Ross's family lives in Rutherford - I've had them tracked down, they've been notified and the parents are on their way in now. Miss Ross works for a firm of accountants in the city somewhere, the housemate said. Again, she didn't know the details.'

'So not a street girl, like our case last week,' Rachel said.

'No, but she could have been mistaken for a prostitute,' Rooney said. 'Judging by the way she was dressed.'

'What about where she was found? And who found her?' Rachel asked.

'It was an early morning dog walker who found her around five am and phoned it in. The young woman was unconscious. He thought she might be dead.'

'And, how is she?' Frank asked.

'She's still unconscious. She has a fractured skull and was beaten pretty badly. Her face is a bloody mess; it's swollen and I believe she's lost a few teeth. But the doctors think she'll pull through. If she hadn't been found so quickly it might have been a different story.'

Turning to Rachel, Frank said, 'Why don't you head off to the crime scene – or where she was found at least. Phone Ayesha and ask her to pick you up. You two check everything is being dealt with properly there and that the whole area has been cordoned off.'

Rachel nodded and turned away, pulling out her mobile phone to make the call.

Frank turned back to Rooney. 'Have you asked for the victim's clothes to be bagged up for forensics?'

'Yes, that's been dealt with – what there was of her clothes anyway. I believe they amounted to a skimpy dress and a bra. Her pants are missing.'

'And has anyone given you an indication of when Miss Ross might regain consciousness?'

'They don't know. She's heavily sedated at the moment, so it could be a while.'

'I'd like to take a quick look at her before the family arrives,' Frank said. He walked past the constable and opened the door. He could see the young woman was surrounded by machinery and her head was swathed in bandages. His stomach flipped and his heart started beating rapidly. He hesitated before moving towards the bed. Seeing Carrie Ross brought back memories of his wife Beth. Were they real memories or was he imagining this was what she looked like from her recounting of events years later? He paused and dredged up his memory of that day at the hospital back in 1975. He'd only been a young constable when he'd accompanied his sergeant to Maitland Hospital. He'd followed his sergeant into the private intensive care room where Beth lay unconscious. She was being kept alive by breathing apparatus following a serious accident. Perhaps his sergeant had realised how shocked he was because he immediately sent Frank off on another task. Yes, he was sure the memory was real as he recalled events that followed after leaving her room. Several weeks later, he and his sergeant had visited Beth as she was recovering in a ward. Her short spiky hair was beginning to grow back, having been shaved, but the stitches and bruises were still very evident on her face and skull. If you looked at Beth closely today, the scars from that incident were still there as a reminder of how close to death she had come – all because of the greed and evil actions of one man. It was to be another 25 years before he saw Beth again and several more years before they married.

Frank regained his composure and moved towards the unconscious young woman. Unlike Beth, Carrie Ross clearly hadn't lost all her hair. Dark brown strands were protruding from her bandages – so they hadn't completely shaved her. But here was yet another young woman brought close to death due to the callous actions of a man.

The prostitute who was raped last week was blond. If it was the same rapist, he wasn't going for a type. Not with a particular hair colour anyway. Last week's victim had been in her early twenties though. They had that in common.

Frank leaned over the young woman for a closer look. Her left eye was puffed up and showing the early stages of bruising. It was the same down the swollen left side of her face, indicating that her attacker was right-handed. Her lips were also swollen and split.

A commotion erupted outside the room. Thinking it was probably the young woman's family he retreated from the room to introduce himself.

Out in the corridor, Sergeant Rooney was talking to a middle-aged couple and a young woman he assumed might be another daughter as she looked to be a younger version of the woman she was standing beside.

After introducing himself to the family, the mother excused herself and rushed into her daughter's room.

'I wonder if you could fill in some gaps of information for me,' Frank said, pulling out his notebook.

'Tell him Carmen,' Mr. Ross said, turning to his other daughter.

'Carrie was going to a gathering at Finn's place last night. It was Finn's birthday.'

'Do you know Finn's last name, or his address?'

Carmen shook her head. 'I know he has a house in Hooker Street, Islington. But I don't know the number – nor do I know his last name. The company where Carrie works will be able to tell you. He's an accountant and works for the same firm.'

Hooker Street was an unfortunately named street, Frank thought, given that nearby Maitland Road was where a number of street prostitutes worked.

'Is Finn Carrie's boyfriend?' Frank asked.

'God no. He's just someone she works with. But they are good friends. Finn is *old*. He's in his mid-thirties,' Carmen said.

Frank raised an eyebrow at the girl's statement about Finn's age. He could see her father had done the same.

'Carmen's only twenty. She thinks *anyone* over the age of thirty is old,' Mr. Ross said with an apologetic look on his face.

'That's very helpful,' Frank said nodding at Carmen before turning back to Mr. Ross. 'I was going to ask you the name of the company where your daughter works and whether you have a contact phone number.'

'Yes,' he said. 'The company's called Healey and Phillips. They're located in King Street, near the junction of Union Street. Carrie works there as a receptionist and typist. She's been there a little over a year now. I have their number at home, but not on me. I do have a mobile phone with the number but I'm afraid I left that at home. I can't seem to remember to always carry it with me. Or charge it,' Ross added.

Frank was exactly the same. He'd plugged his mobile in to charge as soon as he arrived at the office this morning, but hadn't remembered to pick it up when he left. He was supposed to carry it on him at all times, but often forgot it – much to everyone's annoyance.

'I have their number,' Carmen said, pulling out a small mobile phone. She searched through her contacts and then held the phone out for Frank to note down.

'Okay thank you. Could I also have full details of yourself, your wife and Carmen in case we need to contact you for any reason?'

Ross nodded. 'My name is Michael Ross. My wife's name is Gemma. And you know Carmen's name. Ross then rattled off their home address and land line number. He also recited his mobile number, his wife's number, Carrie's number and Carmen's mobile number. Frank would bet that Carmen wouldn't be capable of doing that. Most young people didn't see the need to remember numbers these days as they had them listed in their phones. Frank's concern was that if you lost your phone, or it ran out of charge, you had no way of contacting people if you hadn't memorised numbers. It was frequently predicted that mobile phones would soon replace land lines altogether. He dreaded to think what that would be like; especially with police work. It would be impossible to function properly. He sighed and thanked the family before moving off to find one of the doctors who was treating Carrie Ross.

# 3

Rachel and Ayesha arrived at the edge of the park, pulling off the Maitland Road into a small side street. Carrie Ross had been found at the far end of the park between the road and the canal.

'This is an ideal place for a late-night attack,' Rachel said. 'What with the TAFE College over the road and commercial premises on this side closed. There's no residential housing so less likely to be witnesses.'

'I agree,' Ayesha said. 'The TAFE should have security cameras though that might show the attack – if we're lucky.'

'Yes, we'll pop over there after we've finished here.'

As they stepped over the cordoned off area Rachel could see Detective Sergeant Stuart Tyler talking to one of the uniformed officers. She turned to Ayesha who had raised her eyebrows. Tyler hadn't been assigned to this case so what was he doing here?

'Detective Tyler,' Rachel said. 'Can I have a word?'

She walked several paces away from Ayesha and the uniformed constable. Once they were out of earshot, she asked Tyler why he was there.

'I spotted the police cars and the tape cordon on my way in this morning and stopped to find out what had happened. It looks like another rape of a prossie,' he said smirking.

'You're wrong. The young woman who was attacked was an office worker on her way home from a birthday gathering.'

'Oh. Right. Well judging by the *fancy* high heeled shoes they found and the way they described her skimpy dress, I assumed she was another street girl.'

'It's not your case Stuart,' Rachel said, doing her best to remain civil. 'The Chief has decided to join me and Ayesha on this case. If he wants you involved, I'm sure he'll let you know. It's probably best if you head into Area Command now.'

'Right. I get the message. I'll be off then,' he said turning and walking away with attitude. Rachel grimaced. Thank goodness the Chief hadn't assigned Tyler to work with her and Ayesha on the earlier rape case. She hoped he wouldn't bring Tyler into this one either. The man had a scathing attitude towards prostitutes and, like several men in the force, believed that any violence the women encountered was their own fault. Even learning that their latest victim was an office worker probably wouldn't persuade him that she hadn't caused her own attack. He'd made it clear by the way he'd referred to how the woman was dressed. She'd often heard men from the squad talking in derogatory terms about the way some women dressed. 'She's just asking for it, dressed like that,' she'd heard bandied about. 'Asking for what?' she'd challenged them a couple of times. They simply turned away and mumbled among themselves.

From Rachel's experience of dealing with young women who'd been sexually assaulted over the years, most of them hadn't given a thought to how they dressed. They were simply wearing the latest fashions like all their mates. Wanting to look glamorous when they went out for the night; or be cool if the weather was particularly hot. They'd wear clothes that barely covered them in the hope of feeling more comfortable in the heat. It often shocked them that a man would think they were fair game. And Rachel agreed. Yes, their outfits might be considered 'provocative' by some men, but that didn't give them the right to attack a woman or young girl. Men stripped off to their bare chests in really hot weather and wore shorts. She'd yet to come across a woman who considered these stripped-down men were 'asking for it.'

She re-joined Ayesha who told her how the first officers on the scene had found a pair of high heels on the pavement.

'They've been bagged up. The techies found blood around the same area and evidence of drag marks where the victim had been dragged further into the park behind some bushes – that's where they found her pants. They've also found a couple of boot prints in the dry sandy soil – something we didn't have from Tessa Cooper's attack. They're combing every square inch of the place.'

Tessa Cooper had been attacked on Maitland Road last Saturday night and dragged into a tarmacked back alley. Little evidence had been found at the scene. The part of Throsby Park, where Carrie Ross was attacked, was also on Maitland Road and not far from where Tessa had been assaulted.

'Let's hope we'll have more to work on this time. Right, let's leave the techs to carry on; we can speak to the man who found Carrie Ross. Then we can visit the college.'

At the college (known commonly as TAFE) a disappointed Rachel was told that the crucial camera that was pointing towards the park opposite was out of action. They were waiting for someone to come and fix it.

'Why is it that nearly all security cameras we need to help solve crimes *always* seem to be broken,' Rachel complained on their way back to base. They'd checked with the small number of commercial premises further along on the other side of the road and collected recordings from them which might be helpful though. Ayesha didn't mind trawling through footage and volunteered to spend time going through it.

# 4

Soon after leaving the college, Rachel received an angry phone call from Tessa Cooper, their first rape victim.

'*That bastard has tattooed me,*' Tessa shouted down the phone.

'What do you mean he tattooed you? Where?'

Tessa had undergone a rape kit examination. And as far as Rachel knew she'd been checked carefully due to all of her injuries.

'*It's a bit embarrassing. On my bottom. Inside the crack. I was feeling a bit tender there and thought it was just because of the attack. But when it became really itchy, I spent ages performing gymnastic feats with mirrors to try and see what was going on. It looks like an amateur tattoo. I asked my friend to look at it and she confirmed it.*'

'What does the tattoo look like? Is it an image of something?' Rachel asked, wondering how the tattoo had been missed during Tessa's examination.

'*Not an image. It's a number two.*'

'Two?'

'*Yeah. The bastard must have already attacked someone else.*'

Not that they were aware of. Unless it happened outside

the Newcastle District.

'Do you mind if Ayesha and I come over and photograph the tattoo, Tessa?'

*'No, I don't mind. Just don't bring any of your male colleagues.'*

'He must have done it after knocking me out,' Tessa said when they arrived at her house. 'Otherwise, I would have been aware of what he'd done. I've had to buy some antiseptic cream as I think it's become infected,' she added.

'How are you, Tessa? I'm still not sure it was wise for you to discharge yourself from the hospital so soon.'

'I told you I needed to get home to my daughter.'

Rachel nodded and took a digital camera out of her bag. The doctors hadn't been happy about Tessa leaving the hospital less than 48 hours after she'd been admitted; they needed to continue monitoring her head injury. Tessa insisted she was fine and she did seem okay. Rachel knew she'd experienced a few beatings in the past from ex boyfriends and customers. She'd certainly bounced back with a fighting spirit; keen to help them find her attacker.

'Now promise you won't laugh,' Tessa said, removing her shorts and underpants ready for the shot.

'We won't,' Rachel assured her.

Tessa bent over and parted her bottom cheeks. 'Can you see it?'

'Yes, but not very clearly,' Rachel said. 'We need more light. How about over here closer to the window?'

'What and expose my bottom for the world to see? I know I take on paying customers, but that's a bit too much even for me,' Tessa joked.

'We don't need to pull back the muslin curtains,' Rachel said. 'I just think there'll be better light there.'

'Okay.'

Tessa moved over to the window and bent over again. Rachel crouched down and took close ups from different angles. It did feel surreal and she could feel laughter bubbling up. She swallowed and shook her head. She couldn't break her word. Although the home-made tattoo was looking red and angry, she could clearly see the shape of the number two.

'All done', she said after checking through the shots to make sure the images were clear.

Tessa re-dressed and flopped down on the couch, wincing as she did and holding her arm across her ribs. A couple of her ribs had been broken in the attack and the bruising on her eye and cheek were still very apparent. Rachel hoped she was going to allow herself time to recover. While visiting her at the hospital, Rachel had persuaded Tessa to complete some forms to claim benefits, thinking that might keep her off the streets. Maybe this brutal attack might prevent her from returning to her former work. She knew from questioning Tessa that there was no pimp involved in her transactions with customers. Nor was she a drug addict. It was simply that Tessa hadn't been able to get a job after being made redundant from her former job in a factory and had a school-aged child to support. She shared her house with a female friend (Rachel suspected the housemate was more than a friend) who worked during the day and Tessa went out onto the streets at night. A dangerous occupation.

'Catch this bastard, Detective Sharp,' Tessa said. 'I heard there was another attack last night. Was it the same guy? If so that makes three of us. You didn't tell me someone else was attacked before me.'

'We're not aware of a previous attack Tessa. None has been reported.'

'Well, there must have been if I'm number two,' she retorted.

'You haven't heard anything from other women working on the street, have you? We've been questioning them to see if they heard anything, but no-one's told us of a recent attack. Do you think that's something they might keep quiet about?'

'Who knows? I'm not exactly bosom buddies with any of them. I haven't heard anything.'

'Okay, well take it easy Tessa. We'll be in touch if we hear anything.'


Back at the station, Rachel and Ayesha called into Frank's office to update him.

'Number two you say?' Frank asked looking shocked. 'We've had no other reported attacks, have we?'

'No, Ayesha double checked when we returned from Tessa Cooper's place. I've uploaded the images and sent you one to see for yourself.'

'Okay, I'll look at it shortly. I'll get onto doctors at the hospital to see if Carrie Ross has a similar tattoo. If she has, we'll know for sure that it was the same perpetrator. I've been to Carrie's place of employment over in King Street. She works for a company called Healey and Phillips.'

'Oh, I know them. Andy used to work for them.'

'He no longer works there then?'

'No. He left about four years ago.'

'Okay. That's good, otherwise we might have had a conflict of interest. Carrie's sister told me Carrie had attended a birthday party last night in Islington – at the house of a colleague. A man called Finn Dunbar. He lives in Hooker Street.' He paused to see if they reacted to the street name. When they didn't, he carried on. 'Dunbar was in work as usual this morning. Two people who attended the gathering have not turned up for work. One of the accountants named Leon phoned in ill, and Carrie – who they hadn't heard from. They assumed Carrie had slept in or had a hangover. Dunbar told me she was a little under the weather when she left.'

'Why did they let her leave on her own then?'

'Dunbar offered her a bed for the night, but he thinks she took it the wrong way and insisted she'd walk home. She only had a ten-minute walk to her house. He claims he meant she could crash in his spare room. He told me he he's not interested in women. In other words, he's gay. Only he doesn't think Carrie is aware of that. Although they often go out for drinks, he's never mentioned it. He doesn't want people at work to know.'

'Okay. What about this Leon? When did he leave the party? And how many other people were there?' Ayesha asked.

'There were eight of them. A dinner party of sorts. Before Carrie left, only three of them remained. Finn Dunbar, Leon Asher and Carrie Ross. Asher was the last to leave. He left after Carrie but Dunbar can't recall what time either of them left. The other five left earlier, one shortly before Carrie. One of the guests, Harry Quinn, is another employee of the company. He attended with his wife. The other three were Dunbar's friends. I have all their names and I'd like you to follow up on them. These are their names and numbers,' he said passing Rachel a sheet of typed up details. 'You'll see there are addresses for a couple of them. Dunbar didn't know the exact addresses for the remainder, just the suburb they live in. The company gave me Leon Asher's address. I've spoken to Harry Quinn. He's the one who attended with his wife. They left about ten pm. His wife is in the early stages of pregnancy and was feeling tired. Quinn claims they went straight to bed when they returned home. You could verify that with the wife.'

'What about Carrie. Any word on when it might be possible to interview her?' Rachel asked.

'Maybe later this evening or tomorrow morning, a doctor told me. You go off and deal with these other guests who were at Finn Dunbar's, starting with Leon Asher. I'll let you know if, and when, I hear anything from the hospital. I'll also ask them to see if they noticed a tattoo.'

'It wouldn't be obvious if she has a similar tattoo to Tessa Cooper – hospital staff will need to examine her in the specific area.'

Rachel thought the chief looked highly embarrassed. He cleared his throat and said, 'Right. I'll tell them that.'

# 5

Leon Asher lived on the second floor of a modern apartment block in Hamilton. After being buzzed in they discovered there was no lift and had to climb the stairs. Rachel was surprised to see a tall, slim, but well-built black man who must have been at least 6ft 5 inches waiting for them on the landing. His eyes were very bloodshot. They squeezed past his fancy pushbike in the hallway and followed him into a living room which doubled up as a dining room. She could see through to a small galley kitchen. He indicated for them to take a seat on a large sofa.

'Now why would a couple of detectives be wanting to speak to me? How can I help you fine ladies?' he said. Rachel noticed a soft lilt to his accent. He certainly wasn't an indigenous Australian. He sounded more Caribbean.

'You weren't in work today. Can I ask why?'

'Why would you want to know that? Ah, I see, there's been some sort of crime committed at the office – and don't tell me, you're questioning anybody who was absent today? Am I right?'

'There was no crime committed at your office. We are questioning all the guests who were at Finn Dunbar's gathering last night.'

'Did something happen to Finn?' Asher asked looking concerned. 'He was fine when I left him.'

'Could you just answer the question Mr. Asher,' Rachel said.

'Ok, Ok,' he said holding up his hands. 'I was quite sick when I returned home last night. Something I ate obviously didn't agree with me. Or maybe it was the combination of rich food, too many coffees and too much alcohol. I was rushing to the bathroom until all hours and just felt drained this morning. It's not a crime to have a day off work, is it?' he smiled.

'No, it' not. We're investigating an assault on one of your work colleagues. She was attacked on her way home last night. We understand you were the last person to leave Mr. Dunbar's house after the birthday gathering.'

'Are you talking about Carrie?' Asher's eyes widened in alarm. He clearly hadn't heard anything about Carrie's attack.

'Why would you think the person attacked was Carrie, Mr. Asher?'

'Because the silly girl walked home; the only other females at the party left in taxis, as she should have done. Finn invited her to crash out at his place, but she wanted to go home. Is she okay? What happened?'

'We can't reveal the details, I'm afraid. We need to know your movements after Carrie left. We understand you left shortly after her.'

'About half an hour later. I stayed for another coffee with Finn before I headed back here. I also walked home.'

'What time was this?'

'I left before twelve thirty – probably more like twelve twenty and arrived home about fifteen minutes later.'

'Can anyone verify that?'

Asher thought about it for a moment.

'Well Finn could probably verify the time I left his place. I'm sure I passed a number of security cameras as I walked home. As to here? Unless someone spotted me entering the building, no one could confirm what time I arrived. I live alone.'

Rachel nodded.

'It was before midnight when Carrie left,' Asher added. 'You didn't answer me. Is she okay?'

'Her injuries are serious but it's hoped she will make a full recovery.'

'She wasn't … you know, like that other woman last week?'

'As I said, we can't reveal the details of her attack Mr. Asher. Can I ask you how well you know Carrie?'

'Not that well really. She joins a group of us for drinks after work some Friday nights. She quickly hit it off with Finn after she started working at the company. I think that was about a year ago. And she's close friends with Lilly – one of Finn's friends from outside work. Lilly joined Finn for drinks one night as she often did – I think it was the first time Carrie had joined us. Anyway, the two women gushed all over each other, saying they'd gone to the same school. Now when we go for drinks the two girls mainly chat together. So, I don't really know Carrie all that well. We work in the same company but don't talk that much at work. Just polite exchanges and a bit of friendly banter in the staff room. I know little about her personal life.'

From the list the Chief had given them Rachel knew a woman called Lilly was also at the dinner party. But had left soon after the Quinn couple. On the information the Chief had gathered from Healey and Phillips, she also knew Asher was 29 years old. And had been working in the company for two years.

'You've been at the company two years I believe,' Rachel said.

'This time around. Yes. I started working for Healey and Phillips about a month after I arrived in Australia.'

'When you say this time around … what do you mean? Had you worked with them before?'

'Yes. I came out to Australia on a work visa just after qualifying. Back in 2000. I toured around and then settled in Sydney for a time. Friends I made there subsequently moved to Newcastle and I came up here for a while. I liked it. I returned to London after about fifteen months and then decided to apply to immigrate here. I'd done some temporary work for a few months with Healey and Phillips when I was here previously and applied for a permanent job with them after moving here.'

When Asher worked at the company on his first trip to Australia, Andy might have still been working at the firm. Rachel couldn't recall him mentioning that they had someone from overseas working with them. But then he didn't talk about work too much. Neither of them talked about their work. Especially Rachel, as she was not able to discuss investigations except in general terms. She couldn't ask him about Asher now either.

'You're from London?' Rachel asked. His accent didn't sound like any London accents she'd heard on the news or in dramas she'd watched.

'My family is from what was once British Guyana. When I was a teenager, my parents moved to London as they were British Citizens. I completed my education and then training as an accountant there.'

Rachel nodded; her curiosity sated. She knew Guyana was on the east coast, near the top of South America, close to the Caribbean – and thought they must speak English with a Caribbean accent there.

'Are you aware of anyone who might have had a fixation on Carrie? Someone that she had rejected – maybe someone in one of the bars you drank in after work?' Rachel asked.

'I've seen a few guys try to chat up Carrie and Lilly when we've been out for drinks, but nothing that became antagonistic. No, nothing like that.'

'Is there a particular bar you always go to?' Ayesha asked.

'Yes and no. We often go to the lounge bar at the Grand Hotel. Not always. Sometimes it's the Oxford Bar on King Street, just a few doors from work. And occasionally we'd visit the Worker's Club to have a meal and a drink.'

'Okay, just one more question, Mr. Asher. What size shoe are you and what footwear were you wearing last night?'

Rachel had looked at his bare feet when they entered the apartment. He certainly had large feet.

'I'm size twelve. And I dropped home to change after work, wearing my trainers to Finn's place.'

Rachel nodded.

Ayesha had jotted down everything Asher had told

them. Signalling that she was done, Rachel turned to Asher and said, 'Well thank you for your time, Mr. Asher. We'll be in touch if there's any further questions we need to ask you.'

She stood and pulling a contact card out her skirt pocket, placed it on the coffee table. 'That's my card if you think of anything else that might be helpful. Don't hesitate to get in touch.'

Asher stood, towering over both women. 'Can I ask whether you're questioning everyone who was at Finn's dinner party? Or just me?'

'We're questioning *everyone* who was at the gathering last night.'

Asher nodded, smiled and walked them out to the door.


'Do you think Asher asked that last question about whether he was the only one being questioned because he was concerned about racist attitudes from us?' Rachel asked Ayesha.

'Maybe. I'm sure as a dark-skinned male who has lived in London, he will have experienced a considerable amount of racism – including perhaps from the police. But he may have also asked the question as he was the last person to leave Finn Dunbar's place.'

'Hmm. That's possible. Right let's head off to see Mrs. Quinn next.'

# 6

Frank's attention was diverted from the rape case when the body of a middle-aged woman was found in suspicious circumstances by her daughter when visiting her mother's flat. He set Detective Senior Sergeant Paul Lowry off to investigate.

'Take DS Tyler with you Paul. He seems to have little to do at the moment.'

After they'd gone Frank walked back over to the Royal hospital and spoke to one of the doctors about the tattoo issue. The doctor called in a female nurse and arranged with her to examine Carrie quietly if the opportunity arose. The problem was that the family were constantly by her bedside and they didn't think it appropriate to complete the examination with them present.

'Couldn't you ask them to leave the room? Tell them you need to examine Miss Ross in private,' Frank asked.

'We could do but what if the mother insists on staying?'

'Use us as an excuse – say you need to gather more evidence about her attack.'

'Okay we'll see what we can do,' the doctor promised.

Frank called into a sandwich shop on the way back to

pick up a coffee and a roll as he didn't think he'd have time to lunch at the canteen today. He'd not long arrived back at his desk when a call came through from the doctor confirming they'd carried out the examination.

*'There was a tattoo. She had the number five on her … .'*

'Five?' Frank said, cutting in when the doctor hesitated. 'Are you sure it wasn't a three?'

The doctor cleared his throat. *'No, it was clearly a five. Not a professional job by any means, but it was legible.'*

'Okay, thank you,' Frank said before ringing off.

*Five.* There'd been *four* earlier victims and they only knew about *one* of them? Tessa Cooper. Who'd only been attacked five days ago. Between Tessa Cooper and Carrie Ross last night there'd been two further attacks and no reports had come in. The perpetrator was attacking more frequently. They had no idea who victim one was or when she'd been assaulted. Were women being raped and not reporting it? He knew from estimated statistics that many rapes went unreported. Unreported rape cases were usually committed by someone known to the victim. Most rape cases in Frank's experience were committed by known perpetrators. Stranger rapes were rarer by comparison – but it looked like they had one operating in the Newcastle area at present. He needed to call Rachel and Ayesha back in. Where was his mobile phone? He knew he'd left it charging this morning but he could see it wasn't charging now. The lead was plugged into the wall next to his desk and now the lead – minus the phone, was dangling on the floor. He searched his desk and drawers to no avail. Damn. Why did he have such a mental block about the stupid thing? Then he realised it didn't matter anyway – he had everyone's mobile number written down on in his roll-a-desk file and he could call Rachel from the landline. He thought he probably knew Rachel's number anyway but preferred to make sure. He flipped the cards to Rachel's name and found he was right.

He dialled her number which after several rings went to answerphone. He left a message.

'I need you to come back to Area Command as soon as you get this message.' He decided not to leave any other details.


Rachel and Ayesha were sitting with Lilly Chen at her parents' Chinese restaurant in Beaumont Street, Hamilton. Lilly worked at a recruitment office further down the street and after Rachel had phoned her, she suggested they meet her at the restaurant while she was on a lunch break. She'd burst into tears, after learning of her friend's attack, but now wiped her eyes and looked up at Rachel.

'What do you want to know?'

'Can you tell us what time you left Finn Dunbar's place last night?'

'It was around ten thirty. I ordered a cab to take me home to East Maitland where I live with my parents. They don't like me coming in too late. Not that they're always there. But one of them, or my grandmother usually is.'

'How was Carrie when you left?'

'A bit tipsy, but okay. She shouldn't have walked home alone like that. Why didn't they call her a cab?'

'It's our understanding that she didn't want one. Finn did offer her a bed for the night but she elected to walk home,' Ayesha said.

'Well one of the men should have walked with her.'

Rachel nodded. She doubted it would have occurred to them to offer to do that.

'How do you know Finn Dunbar and Carrie Ross?' Rachel asked her. She wanted to know if the information Leon gave them about the women was accurate. She heard the faint vibration of her mobile in her bag but decided to leave it for now.

'Carrie was in my year at school. We weren't particular friends then, but we got on okay. I met up with her when I joined Finn and his mates for a drink one night. She'd just started working in Finn's firm. I met Finn when he came to our recruitment agency. We set him up for the job at Healey and Phillips about four years ago. I bumped into him here at my parents' restaurant a couple of times after that and we became friends from there. Finn's gay, but Carrie doesn't know that. I've never mentioned it because Finn said he didn't want people at work to know. When he offered her a bed for the night, she probably thought he wanted to sleep with her and that's the last thing she'd want to do.'

'Does Carrie have a boyfriend?'

'No. She hasn't had much luck with men. They've all turned out to be cheating bastards.'

'Anyone in particular you could name? Someone who might hold a grudge against her?'

'No, I think it would be the other way around. Carrie had reason to have a grudge against them. Her last boyfriend was a guy called Damien who she was seeing up in Maitland. Near where she used to work. Her sister

Carmen could probably tell you more about him. I think that's why she left that job and moved out of her parents' house so she didn't have to bump into him. He was two-timing her, having an affair with another woman. As far as I know Carrie hasn't gone out with anyone since she started working at Healey and Phillips.'

'Can you recall anyone at any of the bars you drink at who made an unsuccessful attempt to chat up Carrie? Someone she rejected?'

Lilly sat back and thought for a minute. 'There was a couple of guys tried to grab both of us on our way to the toilet one night. But that was ages ago. Just before Christmas last year. Otherwise no, I can't think of anyone.'

Rachel's phone buzzed again. She dug it out of her bag and saw it was Area Command calling. 'I'm sorry I have to take this,' she said standing. 'Thanks Lilly. Detective Patel, could you leave Lilly your card,' she added before moving away to answer her call.

'That was the chief on the phone,' Rachel said when Ayesha joined her outside the restaurant. 'We need to get back to Headquarters. Carrie Ross did have a tattoo. A number five.'

'*Five?*'

'Yes.'

'Shit!'

'Yeah, shit is right. Let's go.'

Frank updated them on their return to Area Command,

while they filled him in on their interviews with Leon Asher, Pippa Quinn and Lilly Chen.

'If Carrie Ross was victim five, then that means the rapist attacked two other women between Saturday night and Thursday night. If so, surely it must have happened elsewhere given that no reports have come in to us. I know not all rape victims report the crime, but these tattoos are suggesting that *three* victims haven't made a report. It doesn't seem realistic,' Rachel said.

'I agree. I called Area Command in Sydney and asked them to check their files on recent rape cases. Guess how many they are dealing with that have happened in the past two weeks?'

'Twenty?' Ayesha suggested.

'No. Thirty-nine.'

'Thirty-nine?' Rachel gasped.

'Yes. The majority separate, unrelated, incidents. They have three that they think is the work of the same man.'

'Any chance these three could be our missing cases?' Rachel asked.

'He's going to look into it. The Inspector said they're looking for a Lebanese man for those three particular rapes. He reckons this heatwave we've been having has escalated the problem. He said there's always more rape crimes during heatwaves and it seems to send the male residents of Sydney a little troppo when the humidity is so high. The Inspector is from Northern Queensland I learned.'

'What – he claims heatwaves make men a little crazy so they set out on raping sprees?' Rachel asked. 'I know we see more violent crimes in heatwaves, like fights and knife attacks but these are the first rape crimes that have been reported here for some time.'

'*Reported* rape crimes being the operative word,' Frank stressed. 'I've asked him to check whether any of their thirty-nine victims were tattooed with a number like our two. He's going to get back to me on that, and also make sure that the other Area Commands in the wider Sydney region have that information. I think we need to be doing the same across other Area Commands throughout New South Wales. Our perpetrator could be a truckie who moves around.'

'I can do that,' Ayesha said.

'You were going to go through the recordings we picked up,' Rachel said, turning to Ayesha. 'That still needs doing. Do you think you could assign someone else to look at the footage we've collected?' Rachel asked him.

'Sure. I'll get someone on to it.' Just then the phone on his desk rang. He signalled to the girls to hang on a moment while he answered it. He listened to the caller and then said, 'We'll be right over,' before hanging up. 'That was the hospital. Carrie Ross has regained consciousness. The doctor said we could have a few minutes with her. You come with me Rachel. Ayesha, you start on contacting the other New South Wales Area Commands.'

# 7

Rachel introduced herself and Frank to Carrie Ross saying they were going to ask her some questions but if at any time it became too difficult for her, she was to say. Frank had decided on their walk over to the hospital, that Rachel should do the questioning, while he took notes.

'Can you tell us what you remember from the moment you left Finn Dunbar's house?' Rachel asked.

The doctor had explained that Carrie might have some difficulty with speech with her jaw and lips so swollen and the loss of two of her front teeth. She cleared her throat before replying to Rachel.

'I crossed over the lights at Maitland Road and started walking beside the park. Just past the canal I stopped to take my shoes off. While I was bending over, I felt as though something had slammed into the back of me causing me to fall forwards. Then, when I turned to look behind me, I was hit on the head. I don't remember ... '

Frank could see the young woman's two upper front teeth were missing. Her words were a little slurred and were accompanied by a slight whistle sound as she spoke. He had to concentrate hard to pick up everything she was saying.

Tears started to trickle down Carrie's face. Rachel took her free left hand. 'You're doing really well Carrie. *Anything* you can tell us could be helpful.'

'I think I was unconscious for a while. When I came around, I was on my back and he … he was on top of me … I couldn't see … he was just a black shadow … he … I think … I think he was wearing a black singlet and I could feel his hairy legs rubbing against mine. And something else. Like shorts maybe? I could hear a clinking sound. I tried to fight him off but he started punching me and held one hand around my throat. It was difficult to breathe. When he took his hand away from my throat, I tried to lift my head but then he slammed me down onto something hard. I … I blacked out again. I'm sorry …'

'No, you've done brilliantly, Carrie.'

'I … I don't remember anything else. I'm sorry.'

'There's no need to be sorry. *We're* sorry to intrude on you so soon after … It's just that … we're going to do our best to catch the man who did this to you. Okay?'

Carrie made an attempt to nod and winced in pain.

Rachel turned to look at Frank who signalled it was time to leave the girl in peace.

'Thank you,' Frank said nodding at Carrie, then to the doctor and nurse who had remained in the room to monitor the interview.

'We'll come and see you again,' Rachel said before standing and following Frank out.

Carrie's parents approached them the minute they shut the door on their daughter's room.

'Was Carrie able to tell you anything helpful?' Michael

Ross asked him.

'Yes, a few things. But it's just the first interview. She may recall other things over time. You have to remember Carrie has only just regained consciousness.'

'You won't need to keep coming and asking her more questions, will you?' Gemma Ross asked him. 'Only I don't think Carrie could handle that. She's very distressed.'

'But the police need as much information as possible in order to catch the bastard who did this. *Of course,* they'll need to question her again,' Ross said to his wife. Turning back to Frank, he said, 'You will get the bastard, won't you?'

'We'll do our very best Mr. Ross.'


'I wonder if the clinking sound Carrie heard was a belt buckle,' Rachel said as they walked back to base.

'Yes, I was thinking that. He must have been wearing shorts and a singlet. He could well have been wearing a belt. Sounds a bit like the outfits tradies wear in summer. Didn't you tell me the techs picked up a couple of boot prints?'

'Yes. We'll need to get on to them to find out if they've been able to identify the make. I'm not sure that they've finished with the crime scene yet though.'

'Okay you follow up on that and see how Ayesha's getting on with her enquiries. You've still got a couple of people to question from Dunbar's party. Given what we've learned from Carrie Ross I suspect that will be a waste of time, but we need to be thorough. Once I've lined up a CCTV analyst to look at the footage you've collected, I need to check in with DSS Lowry about his case. I sent him and Tyler off to look at a suspicious death this morning.'

'It's security footage we've collected,' Rachel reminded him.

'Okay,' Frank nodded. As far as he was concerned it was all the same thing. Time lapsed distorted shots that could be helpful in tracing vehicles or of known people's movements but often pretty useless on positive identifications of complete strangers.

'Expect to be working some long hours over the weekend,' Frank added sighing. He and Beth had planned to drive down to Sydney tomorrow to stay with her father overnight. He'd now have to tell her he wouldn't be able to go.

'Yes, I was expecting that,' Rachel said with resignation in her voice.


'Okay what have you found out?' Frank asked Lowry when they met later.

'The victim is Rhonda Newland. A mixed-race indigenous woman aged forty-two. She lived in a one-bedroom flat in Georgetown. A housing complex for Aboriginal people. I'm sure you know the one. She was supposed to join her daughter in Taree on Wednesday for her granddaughter's second birthday but she didn't turn up. The daughter, Kay, last spoke to her mother around six pm on Tuesday evening when her mother confirmed she had booked and paid for a seat on the coach. Kay went to meet the coach even though her mother hadn't sent her usual message, saying she was on it. The driver confirmed

Rhonda hadn't boarded the coach. She didn't answer her phone when Kay tried to reach her. After still not being able to reach her mother for several days, Kay drove down from Taree this morning to find out what was going on. She has a key to her mother's place. Apparently, Rhonda Newland had a history of hitting the grog at times. She found her mother dead on the living room floor. It looked like she'd been badly beaten.'

'Cause of death?'

'Hale's not positive – she had a few blows to the head – he said we'd have to wait until the post-mortem for an accurate C-O-D but he's guessing strangulation at this stage. There were prominent marks around her throat. Looks like she was sexually assaulted also.'

Frank's head shot up at the mention of sexual assault. Could this woman be linked to their rapist? But then the other two victims were very young. Rhonda Newland was almost twice their age.

'She was raped?'

'Hale thinks so.'

'When does Hale think she died?'

'Sometime in the early hours of Wednesday morning. She'd been lying there for a couple of days.'

'When's the post-mortem?'

'Tomorrow morning at 9.30 am.'

'Okay. When Hale does it, can you ask him to check inside the cracks of the woman's bottom to see if there's a tattoo there.'

'A tattoo? What kind of tattoo'.

'A number.'

'What? Are you saying the rapist tattooed the two

victims we're investigating?'

'Yes. Saturday's victim was number two. Last night's victim was number five.'

Lowry whistled. 'I hadn't heard about this.'

'Saturday's victim, Tessa Cooper, only made the discovery this morning. We've had the hospital check on our new victim, only to learn she's number five. We've had no other reported cases. And we're *not* releasing that information to the press.'

'Understood,' Lowry said nodding. 'The other victims must have been attacked somewhere else then.'

'We're checking into it.'

'Rhonda Newland doesn't fit with the other cases though. She's quite a bit older.'

'I know, but as it's possible she was raped we need to make sure. If Hale finds a tattoo you need to phone me immediately. Okay?'

'Yes, of course. I'll ask him to look at that first.'

'Have the techs finished with the victim's place?'

'No. They're still working on it.'

'Okay. Have you questioned the neighbours?' If Frank's recollection of the flats Lowry was talking about was correct, the complex was single story – spread out in a horseshoe shape. It would be easy to spot visitors to a neighbour's flat.

'I've left Tyler doing that.'

Frank nodded. 'Okay, just make sure he visits every single one.'

'Don't worry I will,' Lowry said.

# 8

Roisin Murphy sat on the couch hugging herself and shivering despite the hot weather. Her sister Mairead had not accepted her story of falling down the stairs at work. Roisin had been avoiding her by shutting herself up in her room, but Mairead had arrived home just as she was coming out of the toilet and spotted her injuries.

'Come on Roisin, you need to tell me what really happened to you and don't give me any of this malarkey about falling down some stairs. I can see someone has beaten you. Was it Aiden? Did he return home earlier than planned?'

'No. Aiden's still away in Perth. Of course it wasn't him. I know you don't particularly like him but how could you even think that about Aiden?

Aiden wasn't due back for another three weeks and Roisin was hoping by then her bruises would have completely faded.

'And don't you dare tell him anything about this,' Roisin added.

'So, tell me.'

'I can't,' Roisin whispered.

'Of course you can. Aren't I your sister? Don't we tell each other everything? Remember when I told you about Fergal?'

Roisin shook her head and hugged herself even tighter, letting Mairead's voice fade into the background. Fergal was one of Mairead's ex boyfriends. He'd become angry when she wouldn't have sex with him and he had hit her. That was nothing like what had happened to her. Mairead had leaped out of his car and taken off. *She* hadn't been raped. Roisin knew if she revealed the truth everyone would look at her differently. Aiden would break off their engagement. She'd be an outcast. But maybe *she* should break off her engagement to Aiden. She couldn't ever let him see what the man had done to her. And the thought of Aiden touching her made her feel sick. She didn't want *anyone* touching her. Not after …

'Roisin. Look at me. You're not even listening. I can see you're in pain. I can see you're distressed. You haven't been to work for two days. You've shut yourself up in this house and barely come out of your room. I know you've been hiding from me. I think you should go to the hospital to let them see to your wounds. Because you don't look okay to me.'

'I'm fine. I don't need to go to the hospital. Or see a doctor.'

'I think you do. It happened on Wednesday, didn't it? When I stayed over at Conor's.'

Conor was their older brother and on Wednesday night Mairead, Conor, Cien her other brother, and a few of their mates were watching the replay of a game of rugby where Ireland had defeated Scotland. Roisin couldn't stand rugby or any sports for that matter. She'd elected to come home and have an early night. It was a hot evening so she'd opened the windows and had the fan going. Then she'd woken to find … no she couldn't think about it.

'What about allowing Aisling to examine you?'

Their older sister Aisling was a doctor. A practising GP. The idea of Aisling examining her was even worse.

'No. Definitely not,' she said shaking her head vehemently.

'Well, if you're not going to see a doctor or tell me what happened, then I've got no option other than to call Ma and ask her to come to Newcastle. Perhaps you'll tell *her*.'

'Don't you dare ring Ma and make her come all this way for nothing.'

After retiring last year, their parents, wanting to live in warmer climes, had moved up to the Gold Coast and lived just over the border in Queensland. They were all due to go up at Christmas but … no, Roisin couldn't tell Ma anything of what had happened to her. She'd rather die.

'It's not for nothing Roisin. Come on sweetheart. You're my baby sister. You know the family will support you no matter what happened.' Mairead reached out attempting to pull Roisin into her arms. 'My poor, poor baby,' she murmured. Roisin recoiled and pushed her away.

'Don't touch me. I don't want anyone to touch me,' she screeched, jumping up off the couch and fleeing back to her room as fast as her broken body would allow her to. After slamming the door, she grabbed a chair and wedged it hard under the door handle, to make sure Mairead couldn't get in and then lowered herself carefully onto the bed. Sure enough Mairead followed her and was rattling the door handle.

'Let me in, Roisin.'

'NO. GO AWAY. I don't want to talk to you.'

'Okay. Suit yourself. But we're going to get to the bottom of this, one way or another.'

Mairead retreated to the living room and picked up her mobile. She scrolled down to Conor's name, opened it and tapped out a message to him.

> Cancel any plans you have for tonight. We need an urgent family meeting. Someone has given Roisin a beating (not Aiden.) Can you contact Cien and Aisling and ask them to come to yours for 8pm? I'll grab a Chinese take-out on the way.

**9**

Ari Kahinu, who had attended Finn Dunbar's birthday meal, was the last person they had to see. He hadn't answered his phone until after finishing work for the day, apologising saying he had to have his phone switched off while he was at work. It was just gone 6.30 pm when Rachel and Ayesha pulled up at his house in Lambton.

He answered the door and ushered them down the hallway to the living room which was in the centre of the house. Rachel had come across old houses like this before where there were two bedrooms at the front with the living room and kitchen areas at the back with an add on bathroom and laundry behind them, making a strange layout.

'You want to speak to me about when I left Finn's place? Couldn't we have done this over the phone? Or couldn't Finn have told you?'

Kahinu had the most beautiful face that Rachel had ever seen. She was momentarily stunned into silence. He looked as though he was of Māori descent with another bloodline mixed in, as his skin was a light milky coffee colour. His accent was definitely that of a Kiwi.

'Mr. Dunbar doesn't recall the time most people left and we prefer face to face contact with people in our enquiries,' Ayesha said, pulling Rachel out of her reverie.

They liked to judge whether the person was telling the truth and that was often difficult to do over the phone.

'When you say 'our enquiries'. What exactly are you investigating? Did Finn have a break-in or something?'

She looked at Ayesha. Kahinu didn't know about Carrie's attack. Clearly no-one had been in touch with him. Rachel nodded at Ayesha to continue.

'Carrie Ross, one of Mr. Dunbar's other guests, was attacked while walking home from the party last night.'

Kahinu's eyes widened in shock. 'I heard something about a young woman being attacked when I was on my way home from work tonight. That was Carrie?'

'Yes.'

'Crikey. I didn't know. Is she okay?'

So, Finn Dunbar had kept his word and not made contact with anyone who had been at his birthday dinner.

'She's in hospital and is expected to recover from her physical injuries,' Ayesha told him.

Rachel noticed Ayesha had said 'physical injuries'. It would take a lot longer for Carrie to recover mentally from her attack. 'So, what time did you leave Mr. Dunbar's house, Mr. Kahinu?'

'About eleven. Are you asking me these questions because I'm a suspect in Carrie's attack?'

'It's just routine. We need to eliminate everyone who was at the party. How did you travel home?' Rachel said.

'I cycled. I probably shouldn't have but I'd only had a couple of beers and had eaten plenty of food.'

'What were you wearing last night?'

'What was I wearing? What has that got to do with anything? Ah I see. You know what the attacker was wearing. I was wearing a short sleeve Hawaiian style shirt, a pair of cream chinos and sandals. The sandals I'm wearing now. I can show you the clothes if you like. I threw them in the wash basket this morning. It was pretty hot last night and I got quite sweaty.'

'That won't be necessary,' Rachel said. 'Can anyone verify what time you arrived home?'

'Yes. My housemate. He was still up playing on his game console when I returned. But he's not in right now. I can give you his name and number if you like.'

Rachel nodded so Kahinu pulled out his mobile phone, scrolled through his contacts and passed it to Ayesha to make a note.

'How long have you known Mr. Dunbar?'

'We met at a bar a few years back. He was sitting with someone I knew. A mate from home. A New Zealander that is. I'm from Auckland and my mate, who'd been here quite a few years longer than me, knew Finn well. Finn and I became friends after that.'

'You mentioned that you couldn't have your phone on at work. What do you do Mr. Kahinu? And could we have the name and phone number of your employers.'

'Yes sure. I'm a designer.'

'Of clothes?'

'No toys. Mainly dolls.'

It was the last thing Rachel expected him to say. She battled to stifle a threatening laugh but couldn't help but smile.

'I know. It's a bit weird, isn't it? When I started at Reid's, they had me designing trucks, but then when one of the women messed up one of the doll designs and was off sick, they asked me to fix it. They then decided my creations were better and transferred me to doing that most of the time. I'm used to it now. You want Reid's phone number?'

He rattled off the number for his employers while Ayesha scribbled it down.

'Okay, thanks for your time, Mr. Kahinu. That's all we'll be needing from you.'

'No worries. I just hope Carrie is okay.'


'You reckon he's gay?' Ayesha asked as they climbed into the car.

'I suspect so. There'll be some lucky man out there who lands him. Wasn't he beautiful?'

'Mm. He was absolutely gorgeous! I noticed you went a bit weak at the knees when you laid eyes on him.'

Rachel laughed. 'Yes, I lost the power of speech for a minute. He's a bit too good-looking though. Imagine if he was your boyfriend or partner. Everywhere you went people would be staring at you.'

'Yeah, I guess. And making dolls. How creepy is that? I hated dolls when I was little. If anyone gave me a doll. I passed it on to my sister who, unlike me, couldn't get enough of them. I noticed you didn't ask him what size shoe he took.'

'No, I could see his feet were too small. When I phoned the techs earlier, they said we were looking for a size 11. I'd say Kahinu's about a size eight.'

'Right.'

'What about Robbie McDonald? What did you make of him?'

They'd interviewed McDonald in Mayfield before heading to Lambton to speak to Kahinu. McDonald had also been a guest at Dunbar's. They'd now covered everyone who'd been at the dinner party.

'I found him a bit off to be honest. Did you notice he had trouble looking us in the eye? I always find that worrying. And he left only a short time before Carrie. I didn't get the vibe that *he* was gay. Maybe I'm making unnecessary judgements here, but why is he still using the name 'Robbie' – even if it's his full name. Most males who'd been given that name would insist their mates call him 'Rob' or 'Bob' even. When he showed you his driving licence and you asked whether Robbie was short for Robert he said no, that Robbie was his full name and the name everyone knew him by. Don't you find it strange, and a little childish that he seems happy to be called 'Robbie'?

'Not really. Loads of men are called Bobby. I did notice he struggled to look at us though.'

'He said he was wearing shorts and a t-shirt. He might have had a singlet on underneath the t-shirt.'

'But he was wearing trainers, not boots, and the pattern on the bottom of them doesn't match the photo the techs sent me. Although the size matches. We'll have to check with Dunbar about the trainers. He did seem a sporty type so his story of meeting Dunbar at a tennis club is feasible. I was fascinated by his shade of red hair,' Rachel said. 'It was very striking.'

'Are you saying you found it attractive? I don't think I

could go out with someone who has red hair. They nearly always have *really* pale pink freckly skin. It would clash with my brown skin.'

'Not all redheads have pink skin. I've seen a few with smooth ivory freckle-less skin and others who tan. McDonald didn't have many freckles and he had a healthy glow to the skin on his arms. I'd say he tans. Do I detect a note of prejudice against people with very white skin? I'm quite pale skinned.'

'Ah but you're beige. Not pinkie white.'

'So, it's only people with pinkie white skin you're prejudice against?'

'Not prejudiced. Just don't *fancy* it on men.'

'Right.'

# 10

Back at headquarters Rachel and Ayesha filled Frank in on their interviews with the final two guests at the dinner party.

'Check with Dunbar concerning McDonald's and Asher's trainers,' Frank said. 'And see if anyone took any photos. I didn't think to ask him that. I've had the preliminary reports from the rape kit on Carrie Ross. No semen present but they've picked up some pubic hairs which don't belong to her.'

'That's good news. We had nothing like that with Tessa Cooper,' Rachel said. 'Will they be able to get some DNA from the pubic hairs?'

'That's the plan. But they won't know until they go for testing. It'll be some time before we have any results. I've also just had an update from the analyst I gave the footage to. There's nothing showing any single men passing either before or immediately after the time of Carrie Ross's attack. There's a couple showing small groups of people, but none wearing shorts. There's one dog walker who fits the description you gave me of the man who discovered Carrie Ross. It shows him heading towards the park and returning a short time after. Right about the time the attack would have taken place.'

'Ed Thorn – that's his name, did mention that he'd been there the night before. Claims he didn't hear anything although his dog barked a few times which he said is unusual. He thought the dog had detected another animal. Thorn walked down from Henry Street so he would have passed those commercial premises. Apparently, his dog is old and has a bladder problem. He can't be our man. He's small and wiry and definitely doesn't fit the shoe size. And he's in his early fifties,' Rachel added.

'I wouldn't be put off by his age. When is he coming in to give a statement?'

'Tomorrow morning at ten am. He had a hospital appointment today.'

'Okay. Well, I think the first port of call tomorrow morning should be the service station on the corner of Hubbard and Maitland Road. They're bound to have cameras.'

'We could go there now,' Rachel volunteered. 'We had planned to go there today but were distracted by Tessa Cooper's call.'

'No, I think you should go home now. It's been a long day and I suspect the weekend is going to be much the same. We need to follow up on the Sydney rape cases and you haven't finished making those calls to other Area Commands in New South Wales have you, Ayesha?'

'No, I'll get back onto that first thing, sir.'

'DSS Lowry is investigating the murder and rape of a forty-two-year-old woman from Georgetown,' Frank told them. 'The cases *could* be connected and we'll know after the post-mortem tomorrow morning.'

'How was the woman murdered and when did she die?' Rachel asked.

'Strangulation – probably. But she'd been beaten pretty badly like Carrie Ross and Tessa Cooper. Hale thinks she died in the early hours of Wednesday morning after being attacked Tuesday night.'

'If she is connected, then murder is an escalation of his MO,' Rachel said. 'He didn't murder either Tessa or Carrie. Although he made sure they couldn't identify him and Carrie said her attacker grabbed her throat when she came around and started to fight him off.'

'I know.'

'Perhaps he was disturbed by the dog barking during his attack on Carrie,' Ayesha suggested.

'Maybe. Well detectives, I think it's time you headed home. I'll see you bright and early tomorrow morning. I'll do the Maitland Road servo. It's on my way in.'

'Okay, if you're sure,' Rachel said.

'I'm sure. Now off you go.'

Frank waited until they'd closed his office door before picking up the phone to call his wife Beth.

# 11

Mairead Murphy arrived fifteen minutes late at her brother Conor's house. The others were all there waiting.

'Sorry there was a bit of a queue at the Chinese take-away. Let's eat first then I'll fill you in.'

Twenty minutes later Mairead described Roisin's wounds and told them how she had shut herself in her room since Wednesday evening.

'You think she might have been raped?' Aisling asked her.

'That's my guess. I looked at her bedroom window from the outside and saw that the fly screen seems to be held with two only screws on the left side. It would have been easy for someone to pull it aside to climb into Roisin's room. It's always been loose but now seems worse. I complained to the landlord about it but he's done nothing. There's also the air-con unit outside her window where someone could climb up to balance on before heaving themselves in the window.'

'But surely if someone climbed in her window, it would have woken her,' Cien said.

'Not Roisin. The house could be burning down around

her and she wouldn't wake up.'

'Yes, she's always been a heavy sleeper,' Aisling agreed nodding.

'Roisin's refused to be seen by a doctor or to go to the police. I wondered if you could do anything Aisling.'

With Aisling being a practicing GP, she was ideally placed to examine Roisin in Mairead's opinion.

'Did you suggest she could see me?'

'I did and she refused.'

'Then I don't see—'

'I meant without Roisin knowing. Drug her or something to knock her out first.'

'I can't do that! If Roisin reported me, I could be struck off.'

'Roisin is not going to report you. She wouldn't do that.'

'I don't know. If someone did that to me, I'd report them. Family or not,' Aisling said. 'It would be tantamount to being abused all over again.'

'If Roisin was raped, then that's the third attack since last Saturday,' Cien said. 'There was that prostitute who was raped last Saturday. Then another woman was attacked last night as she was walking home from a dinner party.'

'Another prostitute?'

'No. The girl works in an office somewhere in the city according to the news. I heard it on the radio on my way over here tonight.'

'Did they say whether they thought the two attacks were connected?' Conor asked.

'Yes, on the news they said the police were linking the cases and warned young women not to be walking around alone late at night.'

'But Roisin wasn't walking around in the night, was she?' Aisling asked.

'No. And it could have only happened on Wednesday when I stayed over here with Conor after the match. I saw Roisin on Wednesday evening before I came over here and she was fine. I went straight to work from here on Thursday morning. After work I met up with a few friends for a quick drink. When I arrived home, she was in her bedroom. She said – talking to me through her bedroom door, that she felt unwell and had been in bed all day. But she'd definitely had a bath. You know she prefers baths to showers and what she's like in the bathroom – leaves water everywhere as though a whale has beached itself in there. I'd say judging by the wet towels everywhere she'd had more than one bath. I was putting some rubbish out this morning and spotted a towel in the bin with blood on it along with sheets which I'm sure came from her bed. At first, I thought she had her … you know, monthlies. But when I saw the state of her this evening, I knew something else had happened. Her face is black and blue. Her lips swollen and cut. And I'm sure there's probably other bruises on her. I think she really should have medical attention.'

'I've been in fights where Ma and Pa just sorted out my face without going to a doctor. Maybe she doesn't need to see someone. We can deal with it ourselves if she'll let Aisling treat her,' Cien said.

'I went out to the bins after seeing her this evening and pulled out the bloody towel and sheets. I've bagged them up in case they're needed for evidence and I've hidden them in my wardrobe.'

'Shit. Look, I think the first thing we need to do is fix her window to make sure the bastard doesn't come back,' Cien said. 'Why didn't you say something to us about it before? What if she could identify the bloke? He might come back and finish her off. Or think he can get away with it again if he doesn't hear any reports about it.'

'Like I told you, she won't go to the police.'

'She's probably worried Aiden will dump her if she does,' Aisling said. 'Some men are funny like that if their woman has been raped. I've come across it before with patients.'

'Aiden wouldn't dump her surely?' Conor said.

'Do you know that for sure? Roisin said he's not due to return from Perth for another three weeks. I wondered if we could take it in turns to stay at the house day and night while Roisin is at home. She's not going to return to work while she looks like that. And if she doesn't provide a doctor's sick note, she'll probably lose her job. Perhaps you could give her a sick note Aisling,' Mairead said.

Roisin worked at the Hamilton library and Mairead didn't believe she'd ever let her colleagues see the state of her face, let alone the public.

'I could do that,' Aisling said. 'But I'd want to see her first. What did she say happened to her?'

'She gave me a cock and bull story about falling down some stairs at work but I could see that was a lie.'

'I could possibly put in for some time off,' Conor said. 'I'll tell them we have a family crisis. I'm owed quite a lot of holidays. The only problem is that I'd have to finish the job I'm on first. I'll need about another day and a half on it. If push came to shove and they're not happy about me having time off, I could work from home. You and Roisin would have to move in here though.'

'That might not be a bad idea,' Aisling said. 'It would be awkward for me with my surgery and the family.'

Aisling was the only one amongst the five siblings who was married with young children. Cien lived with his partner but was self-employed as a carpenter/joiner. Conor didn't have anyone in his life at the moment. Not after splitting with his previous girlfriend four months back. He was an editor at a local film production company. Mairead was a dental nurse in a one-man practice which would be awkward for her to take time off. She usually took her holidays when the dentist took his and closed the practice. But she could do every night. She currently had no ties.

'I could take a bit of time off,' Cien said. 'Not too much as I don't get paid if I don't work. I don't think Jess would be happy about carrying the costs for the two of us for weeks on end. I've got some savings though. I've got a job I have to finish tomorrow – then I can postpone the others I'm due to do. But I'll go over to yours first thing and fix that fly screen. I could free my days from Sunday to help out.'

'Who can do tomorrow morning? We have a half day on Saturdays. I can't take time off but I can be there every night,' Mairead said.

'I'll do tomorrow,' Aisling said. 'The surgery's closed and the family won't mind one day. Brian will just have to look after the kids. I'll see if I can persuade Roisin to let me examine her.'

'Great. Thanks everyone. That's a start then. I should get back – I don't want to leave Roisin on her own for too long.'

'We need to find out about how the police investigation is going,' Cien said. 'See what the police are doing, anyone they're questioning, or arrests they've made.'

'What would be the point of that?' Mairead asked.

'If the police arrest someone, it might make Roisin feel safer,' Aisling said. 'If she's been raped in her own home, she's going to feeling pretty traumatised. I'm surprised she hasn't wanted to move out.'

'I couldn't really see anything from the outside, but she has the window locked and the blackout blind down – which is unlike her. She usually has the window open. I'm sure she barricaded the door on me earlier. We don't have locks on our bedroom doors but I couldn't open it. I wouldn't be surprised if she's put something up against the window as well.'

'Shit, perhaps you need to sleep in the living room tonight to keep an ear out. I've got some barbed wire in my shed. Why don't I come over now and spread that over the air con unit as a temporary measure? That will stop any bastard trying to climb into her room,' Conor said.

# 12

**Saturday**

Frank called into the petrol station on Maitland Road at 7.10 am on his way to work. After producing his identification, he was shown through to the room where they kept the security tapes.

'I need you to give me any recordings you might have for late Thursday night and early Friday morning,' he said.

'I'll have to check with the boss first,' the employee, a young Asian man said. 'I'm sure he wouldn't mind you looking through them here, but I'm not sure about taking them away with you.'

'If I was to look at them here and find something crucial, I would need to take them anyway. Can you phone your boss then and get this sorted out? We are investigating a very serious crime here.'

'Yeah, I know. It's about the attack over the road, isn't it?'

'Yes.'

'Okay, I'll be back in a minute.'

When the young man returned, he said, 'The boss said

you can have it. It'll only be the one disc. I'll just find it for you. It's probably the one I took out yesterday.'

Five minutes later Frank was on his way to headquarters, worry lines creasing his brow. Why hadn't any other women come forward if Carrie Ross was victim five? He knew many women found it very difficult. Police*men* didn't have a good rep when it came to rape cases. As a young policeman he'd sat in on a couple of interviews with rape victims and the leading officer had not put the person at ease. In fact, in both cases, he'd almost accused the victim of lying. That was back in the seventies and as far as he could make out attitudes hadn't moved on a great deal since. What had tightened up was the strict protocols in place today which protect the victim. However, if a case made it to court the victim would often be subjected to a harrowing experience. He said/she said scenarios where the defence decimated the victim's testimony. At least today there were women on the force who were more sympathetic and sensitive with the women – or men for that matter, who contacted them about being raped. It wasn't only women who were raped. There'd been the occasional false allegations made against innocent parties. But the majority of cases he believed to be true – although sadly not *all* of them made it to court. They'd have to make sure they had airtight evidence against their perpetrator to ensure a conviction. Frank sighed as he pulled in to the car park at Area Command, hoping more evidence would be revealed today that would enable them to move forward with the case. The techs might have something positive for them and maybe the footage he had would produce results.

*****

Rachel and Ayesha were already sitting at their desks when Frank arrived. He headed straight to the kitchen to make himself a coffee, not wanting to be caught out again like yesterday. On the way to his office, he signalled for the women to follow him, loosening his tie as he went. The temperature was already 29° according to the thermometer in the kitchen. They were in for another scorcher.

'I've collected a disc from the service station that needs to be examined,' he told them. 'Have you anything to update me with?'

'I've been looking online at home-made tattoo kits,' Rachel said. 'eBay sells a range of them. The most common one being a 'hand poke and stick'. From what I can make out it's a needle with ink in it that you jab into the skin, rather than using a powered machine. Certainly, the tattoo we photographed on Tessa looked as though it was made with something like that. It's not very neat or smooth. I can't find any listings for shops in the Newcastle area where you might buy something like that – although I'm sure there's likely to be one somewhere.'

'It seems absurd that the perp would carry around a home-made tattooing kit with him,' Rachel said. 'The time it would take would put him at risk of being caught in the act.'

'I agree. But don't forget both of his victims were unconscious, leaving him time to do a quick one if no-one was around. What about tattoo artists? Do you think it's worth approaching one or two to see if they could point you in the right direction?' Frank asked.

'Maybe. It's possible professionals could have fixed some disastrous home-made jobs and might know where the customers bought their equipment. If our perp bought stuff off eBay, we stand little chance of picking up information on local customers who purchased them,' Rachel said.

'Yes, internet shopping has proved to be the bane of a policeman's life. Unless we can access their computers to show proof of purchase. Ayesha? Do you have any updates?'

'I've finished checking with other Area Commands for rape cases. The Oxley one has a couple of cases they're looking into for me. There's nothing anywhere else that looks feasible. Have you heard back from Sydney?'

'Yes. I spoke to Inspector Hall before I left last night. So far, none of their victims have a tattoo, according to him. He's got a team checking all their cases, but there's more to do. He said he'd get back to me this morning once they've completed all the checks.'

'I spoke to Dunbar last night,' Rachel said. 'He can't recall what McDonald had on his feet. Asher, he said, was definitely wearing trainers. He said Carrie Ross took a load of photos with her digital camera. No digital camera was listed among the items found in her bag at the scene. I checked this morning. The techs have everything itemised on the system.'

'Could she have left it at Dunbar's?'

'That's a possibility. I phoned him about five minutes ago but it went to voicemail. I've asked him to phone back before he leaves for work. Although he might already *be* at work. If he doesn't phone back soon, I'll contact him again – I have his mobile number.'

'If Carrie left the camera at Dunbar's, he might not have

even noticed it. We might have to wait until this evening to find out,' Ayesha said.

'Her attacker could have taken it, as a trophy,' Frank said. 'Didn't you say in your report that Tessa Cooper was complaining about her attacker taking a photograph she had of her and her daughter that was in her purse?'

'Yes,' Rachel said nodding. 'And there were bound to be photos of Carrie on the camera. Perhaps he wants to keep looking at his victims. I'll check with Dunbar though.'

'Do you want me to start looking at the footage you brought in from the servo?' Ayesha asked.

'Yes, that needs to be our next priority,' Frank said.

# 13

Ayesha found the footage from the Maitland Road service station very interesting, giving them a few possible suspects. First there was the couple who seemed to having a blazing row. The man climbed out of the passenger seat and began filling up the car. The woman jumped out and appeared to be screeching at him. Her arms were gesticulating all over the place, her face was screwed up and her mouth going non-stop. The man turned and said something to her while waving one arm around. As soon as he'd finished filling the car, she jumped into it and drove out of the forecourt, turning towards Mayfield, with the man shouting after her. Ayesha would bet there were some choice swear words being exchanged. After freezing the screen, she was able to get a clear view of the number plate on this car and wrote it down.

Once the woman had taken off, the man, wearing shorts and a short-sleeve shirt, went up to the window and paid. Unfortunately, with cash, so they wouldn't be able to trace the transaction. She made a note of the time. The man then stood in the garage forecourt, seemingly unsure what to do. After a few minutes he crossed the road and turned towards Hamilton, walking along the edge of the park until he disappeared from view. A minute later she saw the same man returning, as though he'd changed his mind and was walking in the direction of Mayfield. He was definitely a possible suspect.

Then there was a character who pulled in from Hubbard Street in a white pick-up and filled up. He clearly knew where all the cameras were and did his best to avoid them. He was wearing shorts, a dark singlet and work boots. The cap on his head hid his features and his head was turned away from the cameras so his face wasn't revealed at any time. Not while he was filling up, nor while he was paying at the night window. She could see that he paid in cash though. The pick-up then left the garage turning towards Mayfield. He was another possible suspect. Unfortunately, the number plate of his pick-up wasn't visible while he was filling up or when he pulled out. A car pulled across the rear of the pick-up at the crucial moment the plate might have been revealed. They could however look into CCTV on Maitland Road to see if the vehicle could be spotted elsewhere.

During the time the man in the pick-up was in the garage, Robbie McDonald appeared. He walked up to the night window and purchased two cans of drink. He also paid in cash. He proceeded to open one of the cans and guzzle the contents and then threw the empty can into a bin. She couldn't tell what type of drinks they were. He was wearing a sporty shirt but after stepping away from the window he stripped it off to reveal a dark singlet. *Gotcha!* McDonald had dropped the large rucksack he'd been carrying onto the ground, opened the top and shoved his shirt in there. The remaining can of drink he stashed in a front pocket of the rucksack. He kept looking back towards Hubbard Street before walking out onto the road and turning towards Mayfield, continuing to look back as he walked. She made a note of the time. Hopefully there would some CCTV on Maitland Road where they would be able to pick up shots of him before he turned off towards his street which was shortly after the TAFE.

Carrie Ross appeared a couple of minutes later at the traffic lights beside the garage. She crossed the road and turned left to walk along the park – only minutes from her attack. She wasn't walking too steadily. The section of the park where she was attacked was not covered by the garage's cameras.

Ayesha stopped the recording there and went to find Rachel, who she'd spotted coming back into the office a few minutes ago.

'I found Robbie McDonald on the garage's recordings. He stops there to buy some cans of drink. He is definitely wearing trainers. He was in shorts as he described and while he was at the garage, he stripped off his shirt to expose a dark singlet. The most interesting thing though is that he's carrying a heavy looking rucksack. He could have had some boots in there.'

'Hmm. A dark singlet? I don't understand why men wear singlets under a t-shirt or a shirt in hot weather. My father always does, claiming it's to soak up his perspiration, so it doesn't show so much. When I argued that the extra layer would make him feel hotter and cause him to 'perspire' more – I say 'perspire' because my father won't use the word 'sweat' – he thinks it's too common. Anyway, he thought my theory was nonsense, insisting men 'perspire' more than women. With the humidity we've been having over the past weeks I'm not sure that's right. Going back to McDonald – why would he be carrying a heavy rucksack? He works as an IT technician for a bank.'

'The other thing is he kept looking back towards Hubbard Street as though waiting for someone. Then he continued to turn and look behind him as he walked along Maitland Road.'

'Okay. That's certainly suspicious. I've just returned from Finn Dunbar's. Dunbar returned to the house and helped me search the place. There's no sign of Carrie's camera there. She must have had it with her. In view of what you've told me, I think we need to question McDonald again. We could pay McDonald another visit right away but I think we need to get a warrant in case he doesn't co-operate. First, I need a glass of water. It's bloody hot out there again today.'

'Sure, but before we go, I need to tell you I spotted a couple of other potential suspects and there's things we need to follow up on them.'

'Okay. Tell me in the kitchen while I drink my water.'


'I played a game of tennis straight after work. That's why I had my rucksack with me,' Robbie McDonald told them.

They were sitting in McDonald's kitchen at the small table he had there. His lodger was in the living room playing a noisy game on the television screen. What is it with all these young men? Rachel was so thankful that Andy wasn't interested in playing games on the television screen. Before arriving, the women had agreed that Ayesha would ask the questions while Rachel made notes.

'Where and when did you play this match?'

'At the tennis club in Broadmeadow. My match was at 5.30. I didn't have time to go home before going to Finn's. I showered and changed at the club. My tennis clothes and work clothes were in the rucksack.'

'Okay. Can you explain why you were looking back along Hubbard Street as you walked into the garage – and why you continued to look back along Maitland Road when you left it?' Ayesha asked him.

McDonald's head shot up and he made eye contact with them for the first time since they'd entered his house, his eyes darting in startled surprise between them.

'What?'

'You kept looking back along Hubbard Street as you went into the garage. Were you waiting for Carrie Ross?'

'I don't … ah I know why I was looking back. My rucksack was pretty heavy and I was hoping to pick up a cab. There's often cabs come from the Clyde Street railway crossing and then weave around through Hubbard Street to join Maitland Road. None came though. Then when I left the garage, I kept looking for a cab as I walked along. They don't usually come along empty heading *towards* Mayfield though and I was out of luck. I had to lug my bag all the way home.'

'Why didn't you call a cab from Finn Dunbar's place?'

'As you know my house isn't that far from Finn's. I thought I could walk it, but forgot how heavy my bag was. I almost turned back to Finn's but decided against it in the end. I wish I had now. I could have offered to walk Carrie home. I assumed Finn would call her a cab.'

He'd mentioned the bit about Finn calling Carrie a cab

or walking her home when they'd spoken to him the day before.

'Did you notice before you left Dunbar's what Carrie Ross did with her camera?'

'No,' he said shaking his head. 'She was taking loads of shots throughout the evening. I remember seeing her walk out into the entrance hall with Lilly and place it on a small stand there. I can't recall seeing it there when I left though so she must have put it in her bag. My rucksack was beside the stand.'

'Have you laundered all the dirty clothes you were wearing on Thursday night or any clothes you had in your rucksack yet?'

'What? Why are you asking me that?'

'Can you just answer the question Mr. McDonald?'

'Well no, I haven't washed them as it happens. It was too late when I arrived home Thursday night and I dumped the rucksack in my room. I slept in Friday morning so after showering, I didn't have time to sort anything. I just grabbed my work shoes from the rucksack before I dressed for work. I meant to do it last night after you'd called at my place. But a friend called me and I went out to meet up with him for a meal in Mayfield and forgot all about it. I was about to put a wash on when you arrived.'

Ayesha and Rachel exchanged glances. On the way to McDonald's, they'd agreed they'd like to examine the rucksack, but didn't think it would still hold the same contents as it had on Thursday night.

'Can you show us your laundry basket and the rucksack Mr. McDonald?'

'I don't know why you'd want to see them. They only

have a bunch of smelly, dirty clothes in them.'

'Nevertheless, we'd like to see for ourselves,' Rachel said. 'Detective Patel will escort you to your room while you bring the rucksack out. We can look at the rucksack in the laundry which I can see is right off your kitchen here.'

Ayesha returned with McDonald a minute or so later. McDonald dumped the rucksack on top of a top loader washing machine. Rachel asked McDonald to step back into the kitchen. Ayesha donned a pair of gloves before opening the rucksack. Rachel could tell the smell that greeted Ayesha was unpleasant by the grimace on her face and the way she leaned back. She pulled the items out one by one, examining them before dumping them on the floor. On top of everything was a sports style shirt. This was likely to be the one she'd seen him remove and place in the rucksack. Next was a navy-blue cap with a carrier bag underneath which contained a damp towel and a wash bag. Then some black trousers and a smart short sleeved pale blue shirt – presumably the clothes he wore to work on Thursday. Next came a white tennis shirt and a pair of white shorts. Then white socks and black socks, followed by a pair of boxer undies. Finally, she pulled out another carrier bag which contained his tennis shoes. She shook her head, looking at Rachel, meaning there were no boots. They'd examined the sole of his trainers on their previous visit and they didn't match the pattern found at the site of Carrie Ross's attack.

'There's nothing else in here, but there are some compartments at the front to check,' Ayesha said. She opened the large zipped compartment to find one can of drink in there. It was one of those so-called sports drinks.

After pulling it out Ayesha dipped her hand deeper into the pocket and pulled out a digital camera.

'What's this Mr. McDonald?'

'I don't know. That's not mine. I don't how it got in there,' he said shaking his head.

'Is that Carrie Ross's camera?' Rachel asked him.

'It looks like the one she was using. But I didn't put it in there. I swear! One of the other guests must have.'

'Why would they put it in your rucksack Mr. McDonald?'

'I really don't know.'

He seemed to think about it for a minute and then shook his head again. He certainly looked puzzled by the camera's presence.

'We'll need to take this with us. And your clothes and the rucksack with some of the contents to have them examined by forensics.'

'You can't do that. Not without a warrant,' McDonald said.

'Ah, well, you see, we do have a warrant Mr. McDonald,' Rachel said. 'I didn't mention it when we arrived as I wanted to see if you would co-operate with us first.' She opened her bag and passed the warrant to him.

Rachel then turned to Ayesha who picked up the message that they'd need evidence bags and a DNA kit. 'I'll just pop out to the car to get some supplies,' she said.

She and McDonald sat in silence, McDonald busily scanning the warrant, until Ayesha returned. 'Would you be willing to give us a DNA sample Mr. McDonald?'

'A DNA sample? What for?'

'To see if you've had any close contact with Carrie

Ross.'

'No. No, I'm not doing that. You're not going to dump Carrie's attack onto me.'

'Well a DNA sample would clear you.'

McDonald shook his head. 'Carrie … Carrie came on to me as I was coming back from the bathroom not long before I left Finn's. She grabbed me and tried to kiss me. I pushed her away as I could tell she was a bit drunk. I … my DNA is probably on her clothes, but I didn't attack her.'

'We can check that with her.'

'If she remembers. Look, I'm not giving you a sample. The attacker's DNA is bound to be on her. You need to find him, not go after people like me. I'm not going to be stitched up for this. Not again. Why would I need to attack her? I told you she came onto me. I could have gone back to her place with her or brought her here to mine. But I could tell she was drunk. I wasn't. I would never take advantage of a woman in her state. Not after … It could lead to complications and regrets. And potentially false allegations. I prefer to make love to a woman while we're both sober.'

'What did you mean when you said 'not again'?' Rachel asked him. 'Have you been accused of something similar in the past?'

McDonald shook his head and wouldn't answer the question.

'We will find out if that's the case. There will be records.'

McDonald continued shaking his head. 'I'm not saying another word. Not without a lawyer present.'

'It may come to that.'

Rachel waited until Ayesha had placed the rucksack, its contents and the camera in evidence bags.

'Now we'll need the clothes you were wearing at Mr. Dunbar's'.

'You've already got the sports shirt I was wearing.'

'What about the singlet you had on underneath the t-shirt?' Ayesha asked him. 'Where is that?'

McDonald seemed surprised that Ayesha knew he'd been wearing a singlet, but then nodded as though realising something.

'It's in the basket there,' he said pointing to a wicker basket in the corner of the laundry.

Ayesha tipped the contents out onto the floor. There was another pair of boxer undies, socks, and a navy-blue singlet. She bagged the vest and boxer undies.

'Where are the shorts you were wearing that night Mr. McDonald?'

'They're in my room, I was going to wear them again today, but changed my mind.'

'Do you wear a belt with the shorts?'

'Sometimes. Not usually. I wasn't wearing one that night.'

'Detective Patel will escort you while you collect the shorts. And could you dig out the belt you might wear with these shorts *sometimes*?'

Ayesha returned with the shorts and belt in evidence bags. They collected everything they'd bagged up ready to go. 'Thank you for your co-operation, Mr. McDonald. We'll be in touch,' Rachel said.

***

'You think he's our man?' Ayesha asked her once they were in the car.

'I don't know. He seemed genuinely surprised about the camera being in his rucksack. We'll need to ask all the guests whether they put it in there. He's hiding something though. Something from the past. We need to look deeper into his history. I checked our records as I did with all the guests and he's not in the system, but there must be something. Maybe an incident involving a woman where he was never formally charged.'

'At work? Or university? In his bedroom he had a photograph of himself on what looked like his graduation day. I asked him and he said he did a degree in IT at Newcastle Uni.'

'Should be easy enough to find out.'

'Next to his graduation photograph there was one of a very attractive red-headed woman. The photos were in frames on the top of a small bookcase. I asked him whether the young woman was his girlfriend; he shook his head and looked angry for a moment. Then his shoulders seemed to slump. He said it was his sister Karen. After a pause he added that she'd died in an accident last year.'

'Did he say what kind of accident?'

'No, and I decided not to probe any further – I did the usual – "sorry for your loss". We could do a search on her name and find out how she died if you think it might be important.'

'Hmm. We can ask the chief. I get the impression he doesn't have a girlfriend at the moment. There was no trace of a female presence anywhere in the house. Oh well, let's get these items dropped off at the lab, then we can take a look at the other suspicious characters you picked up from the servo's security footage.'

# 14

Aisling was attempting to coax her sister to leave her bedroom, or at least to open her door. She was sitting on the floor outside Roisin's room.

'Roisin darlin', you need to trust me. You can't do this alone. I know. I've had many patients who've been through what I think you've been through. It's hard. Let me in. I promise I won't force you to let me examine you. I just need to make sure you're alright.'

She was greeted by silence. 'Roisin? There's no one else here. Cien has fixed your fly screen and he's gone. Mairead's at work. It's just us darlin'.'

Aisling heard movement and scrambled to her feet in anticipation. A chair scraped across the floor and she saw the handle of the door turn. Roisin opened it a crack and then scurried back to bed.

'I'm coming in now,' Aisling announced. She was assailed by the smell of blood and sweat as she walked towards the bed where Roisin was laying, a sheet drawn up to her chin. Roisin's left eye and cheek were heavily bruised, her mouth was swollen and Aisling could see her lips had at one point, been split and bleeding. Aisling's first reaction was to take Roisin in her arms and whisper endearments to her. But she knew from her experience of treating rape victims, that was not something they wanted. Not yet anyway. She held her emotions in check and decided to revert to her role as a doctor.

'Can I feel your cheek? I want to see if anything is broken.'

Roisin nodded and so she carefully felt down the angry bruise, pressing a little harder around the bone joints. Roisin winced and tried to pull back.

'I don't think anything is dislocated or broken. It's just a nasty bruise which will heal in time. Do you have any loose teeth or have you lost any?'

'No.'

'Do you have any other injuries?'

Roisin nodded.

'Show me.'

Roisin pushed the top sheet down and pulled up the summer pyjama top she was wearing. There were several purple bruises down the left side of Roisin's abdomen, indicating she had been thumped with a right hand. The bruises went as high as the ribs. Aisling could see bruising around Roisin's neck too. It was a wonder her attacker hadn't killed her.

'Describe the pain you're feeling from these bruises. Were you punched?'

Roisin nodded. 'It *really* hurts up here when I move, or cough,' she said pointing to her ribs.

'What about lower down?'

She shook her head. 'It did at first but it's okay now.'

'You might have a couple of broken ribs but you'd need

an x-ray to confirm that. If they are broken, they'll take a while to heal. From what I can see and what you're saying, I don't think the other punches have done much damage. Are you menstruating right now?'

Roisin gave an embarrassed nod.

'Were your periods due or are you bleeding because …'

'They were due, but not until tomorrow. They came on all of a sudden after …'

That was one thing to be grateful for at least, Aisling thought. There'd be no pregnancy resulting from the rape. In the past, a number of her fellow doctors, male ones especially, used to be under the misguided belief that a woman couldn't fall pregnant from being raped and if a woman did fall pregnant after claiming to be raped, then no rape occurred. However, when she'd administered rape kits while on rotation at the John Hunter Hospital during her training, she'd seen clear evidence of rape from the damage to the bodies of a couple of women and later learned that a pregnancy resulted. She often wondered if those same doctors still carried that belief after being confronted with the statistics. She'd also come across pregnant women who confessed they'd been raped by a family friend but hadn't reported it. The question now was whether she could persuade Roisin to report her rape. She could see Roisin was in a very fragile state. Aisling didn't think she would be up to dealing with police and strangers examining her. And a rape kit would yield little if Roisin had bathed several times since the attack. At least she was admitting she'd been raped. It was a start.

'He punched me in the head a few times as well. Here,'

she said touching the side of her head.

'Did you lose consciousness at all?'

'Not fully. But I was so dazed I wasn't able to do anything.'

Aisling ran her hands gently over Roisin's head. There was minor swelling but she could see no skin had been broken on the scalp.

'Are you up to telling me what happened on Wednesday night?'

Roisin turned her head to the side again and Aisling could see tears sliding down her face.

'Take your time. I'm here all day for you.'

'No, I want to tell you. I need to tell someone – it's just …'

'I know.'

Just then Roisin's body started heaving and she grabbed the bowl that was sitting on the stand at the side of her bed and brought up bile.

'How long since you've eaten anything,' Aisling asked her when she placed the bowl back on the stand.

'Nothing since Wednesday evening. I tried a bit of toast on Thursday but brought it straight up again.'

'That's three days Roisin. What about fluids. Have you drunk anything?'

'One cup of tea and some water.'

'You need to keep up your fluids or you'll become dehydrated in this hot weather. And it's like a furnace in here, even with the fan on. I know you don't like the air conditioning on, but you can at least open the window now Cien has fixed the security fly screen. There's a slight breeze today. But we'd have to move this wardrobe. Did you move that over to block the window?'

'Yes, and I don't want the window open,' Roisin said raising her voice in panic.

'Okay. Fine. But how about you tell me what happened. Once you've voiced the horror of your attack, I'm sure you'll be able to start eating and drinking again. It's because you've been bottling it all up and trying to deal with it on your own. Why don't we go and sit in the lounge?'

'Okay,' Roisin said after hesitating. 'Just give me a few minutes.'

# 15

DSS Paul Lowry phoned Frank from the Morgue. *'Rhonda Newland had a tattoo in the place you mentioned,'* he told Frank.

So, she was a victim of the same rapist – now rapist *and* murderer.

'What number?'

*'Three.'*

'Okay. Has Hale ascertained cause of death?'

*'Yes, from internal bleeding after a brutal beating.'*

'Not strangulation or head injuries?'

*'No. There's evidence of blows to the head which may have caused her to lose consciousness and further evidence that the attacker attempted to strangle her at some point, but that's not what caused her death. Hale said that she would have taken many hours to die and it's possible that if she'd been found and treated soon after her attack, she might have survived.'*

Frank groaned. 'Okay, thanks Paul. Ask Hale to get the autopsy report over to me as soon as he can,' he said before terminating the call.

He stood and walked out into the squad room where Rachel and Ayesha were back at their desks.

'Could you both come into my office for a minute – I have an update to give you.'

The women followed him back to his office and he waited until Ayesha closed the door before speaking. He was wary of talking about cases with others around who weren't involved. There had been some leaks to the press about a few cases which he was sure had come from someone in his team. He had his suspicions, but that's all they were. And it didn't involve the two women standing before him.

'Take a seat,' he said. 'I've just heard from Paul Lowry at the morgue. We've now identified victim number three. It was the forty-two-year-old woman found dead at Georgetown.'

'What?' Rachel exclaimed, looking shocked.

'Yes, I know. She doesn't fit with the other two attacks we know about.'

'Shit – that means – sorry sir – that means women of all ages are vulnerable to this rapist. And he *murdered* her?'

Rachel knew Frank didn't like members of his team constantly using four letter words. He was on a losing battle attempting to stamp it out in the squad room. It wasn't often he heard a swear word from Rachel or Ayesha though – which was one of the reasons he enjoyed working with them.

'I'm not sure if he *intended* to murder her, she died from internal bleeding.'

He filled them in on all that he'd learned from Paul Lowry since the woman had been found.

'Carrie Ross might have died from her wounds if she hadn't been found. And the attacker could have been disturbed by the dog barking which prevented him from finishing her off. We could have had two deaths on our hands,' Rachel reminded him.

'Yes, but the question is, did he intend to silence them permanently or did he not realise how brutal his attacks were and that they could lead to someone's death? From the preliminary reports from forensics, I've been told that it's likely that the back of Carrie Ross's head was bashed against a rock during the attack. They found blood and hair on a rock where she was found that they're still testing to see if it's hers. What worries me is that victims one and four could be lying out there somewhere undiscovered like Rhonda Newland.'

'Are we going to take over the investigation of her death?' Rachel asked him.

'I think we're going to need all hands involved with these cases. We'll merge them. So, what have you discovered this morning?'

The two women updated him on their inquiries so far that day.

'Let's wait and see what the labs come up with on McDonald's clothes. At some point we'll need to question Carrie Ross again, to see whether she backs up McDonald's story. The camera's a tricky one. You'll have to question all the guests again. Check out his story on the sister as well.'

Rachel nodded. 'I doubt we'll be able to find out anything from Newcastle University until Monday.'

'Hmm. Okay. In the meantime, go and see this woman whose car you spotted on the service station recordings and get the name of the man she was with. It's strange that he wasn't picked up by the security footage we have from the shops. Our analyst said the only man walking alone past the shops was the dog walker. Did he come in to make his statement this morning?'

'Yes, I asked DC Chris Walker to deal with it,' Rachel said.

'Just before you called us in, I heard back from Oxley Area Command. None of their victims have a tattoo,' Ayesha said.

'Yes, I've heard back from Sydney also. No tattoos there. So, it seems to be largely in this area our perp is operating. Unless he travels interstate. Let's hope not. I'm calling a team meeting for 5pm. I'd like you both to return by then.'

A young woman with artificial looking dyed black hair, pale skin and a scowl on her face answered the door to them at a modern house in Warabrook. Ayesha recognised her from the service station footage.

'Yeah, whadda ya want?' the woman said. 'If you're selling anythin', I'm not interested.'

They produced their identification.

'Two female cops eh.'

'We need to ask you some questions,' Ayesha said.

'Yeah, about what?'

'Do you mind if we come in?'

'I do actually. Just tell me what you wanna know?'

'You were caught on camera at the service station on Maitland Road in Islington on Thursday night.'

'Yeah, so what?'

'We'd like the name and address of the man you were with?'

'He don't live here.'

'Can you tell us where he does live?'

'Why – he paid for the petrol, didn't he?'

'Yes, that's not why we want to speak to him. We believe he may be able to help us with a case we're investigating. A brutal attack that happened shortly after he left the garage.'

'You mean you think he might've done the attack. Nah, he wouldn't't've. Are ya talkin' about the one in Throsby Park?'

'I'm afraid we can't give you any details. Can you tell us his name and where he lives?'

'Alright, but I think you're barkin' up the wrong tree with 'im. He might be a pain in the arse but he's not violent. He's me ex. We broke up that night. I'd had 'nuff of him. His name's Sam Fisher. He lives in Carrington. In Forbes Street. I remember the name of the street cos it's the same as my last name innit? Couldn't tell ya the number. But it's a manky white weatherboard with a dark blue door. A few houses down on the left if ya turn in from Young Street.'

'Okay, thank you, Miss Forbes,' Ayesha said as the door slammed in their faces.

'Charming young woman,' Rachel said smiling at Ayesha.

'At least we have his name.'


They found the house the Forbes' woman described and managed to park outside. The neighbour's dog ran out and started barking at them over the adjoining fence as they walked up the path to the front door.

A tall sleepy looking man with chestnut brown hair answered their knock, keeping the fly screen door closed. He was wearing just a pair of shorts with nothing on his feet. Rachel could tell by the man's eyes and the smell emanating from the house that he'd been smoking a joint.

'Mr. Fisher?'

'Yes.'

Rachel introduced them and showed him her ID. 'We'd like to ask you a few questions if you could give us a minute?'

'Er, what about?'

The dog was still barking which meant she had to raise her voice.

'Can we come inside? It's a bit difficult to have a conversation with that dog barking.'

'Um ...' Fisher looked behind him. 'If you'll just give me a minute to get dressed, then you can come in,' he said disappearing and closing the door a little. Ayesha rolled her eyes as they waited for Fisher to return. Rachel thought he was no doubt clearing up the evidence of his joints. He re-appeared a few minutes later wearing a t-shirt and unlocked the screen door. The dog was still barking and no-one had come out to quieten it or take it inside. Perhaps the owners had gone out and left it in the yard to guard the house.

Fisher had liberally sprayed air freshener about the place as it now smelled of lemons. He showed them through to an enclosed veranda at the rear of the house. It had no glass windows – only metal fly screens where they would have been and clear plastic blinds which could be lowered in rainy weather.

'Take a pew,' he said.

Several couches and chairs were dotted around the veranda, some covered with Indian style bedspreads. Once seated, Rachel explained why they were there.

'Can you tell us why, on the night Miss Forbes left you at the garage, you began you walking towards Hamilton and then turned back towards Mayfield? What changed your mind and where did you go?'

'Why do you want to know?'

'A serious attack took place in the park shortly after you were seen there. We'd like to know if there was anything you noticed as you walked along there. We can then, hopefully, eliminate you from our enquiries.'

'Okaaay,' he said dragging the word out. 'Well, I was so pissed off with Casey I decided to go home. I started walking towards Hamilton then I thought about it and stopped. I decided I really should go to her place and attempt to make it up with her. She'd had a go at me at the bar earlier and she was still going on at me when we pulled into the servo. I can't stand rows and I think it drove her mad that I didn't get into a slanging match with her. I can't even remember what triggered her anger now. Not that it matters. We're finished. Anyway, I turned back towards hers hoping I might pick up a cab on the way. I'd almost passed the park when an available cab came along from the direction of Mayfield. I hailed it with the original intention of asking the driver to turn around and head to Casey's, but then I thought stuff it, and stuff her and decided I'd rather come home instead.'

'Can you remember any details of the cab company?'

'It was white. That's all I know.'

'How did you pay for the cab?'

'By card. I realised I'd used almost the last of my cash paying for Casey's petrol. I tipped the driver in cash of course.'

This was great news. They'd be able to verify the transaction and the time.

'You must have been given a receipt then?'

'Oh, yeah I was. It's probably in my wallet or the pocket of the shorts I was wearing.'

'As you were walking beside the park did you notice anyone else there?'

'Not in the park. No. But a bloke walked past as I was about to hail the cab. It was near the end of the park – just past the creek.'

'Can you describe him at all?'

'Vaguely. He was a big bloke. Taller than me. I know he was wearing shorts and heavy boots as my eyes flicked over the bottom half of him as I turned to look back along the road and spotted the cab. Oh, and he was carrying a bag. Sorry, I don't remember anything else.'

'You don't recall anything about his face – for example was he clean shaven or did he have a beard? The colour of his hair?'

'No, he was wearing a cap. That's something else I noticed when I first spotted him. The cap I mean. I couldn't tell you if he was clean shaven. I didn't really look at him closely. You have to be careful looking at blokes like that late at night. They might get the wrong idea.'

'The wrong idea?'

'You know, they might think you're trying to pick them

up or something. Especially as we were near a park. The bloke could have turned nasty on me if he thought I was doing that. You must know what I mean?'

Rachel nodded.

'Okay. This has all been very helpful Mr. Fisher. Now do you think you could dig out that receipt for us?'

# 16

Roisin winced as she sat on the couch. Aisling had made them a cup of tea and some toast. She didn't think she could stomach having any of it.

'See if you can get some of this down you,' Aisling said gently. 'Have a nibble on the toast and sip at the tea.'

'Maybe in a bit.'

'I noticed you're having difficulty walking. Is that because of your ribs or …'

'It's because of what he did to me down *there*,' Roisin blurted out. 'He's *ruined* me! I can never marry Aiden now. I can't ever marry anyone.'

Aisling blinked at Roisin looking startled.

'Just exactly what did he do to you Roisin?'

Aisling listened to Roisin describing events as they unfolded on Wednesday night. She did her best to retain a neutral face but her heart was beating wildly. She had always been able to manage it with patients, but this was her much-loved young sister.

When Roisin finished the telling, involuntary tears slid

down her face; Roisin was holding her tears back, her face screwed up with fury.

'He left my room and must have just walked out the front door as though he'd been visiting as a bloody guest!' she added.

That meant someone might have seen him. They could ask the neighbours – pretending the house had been burgled. The problem with asking around was they'd have to have a plausible excuse as to why the crime hadn't been reported to the police. But perhaps that's what they could do. Report a *burglary* to the police. Not the rape. But they couldn't let them see Roisin if that was the case. And would the police take a burglary seriously? What could they say had been taken? A photo out of frame? No, they'd laugh at that. It would have to be something more substantial.

Aisling desperately wanted to take Roisin in her arms and hold her. But she needed to tread warily.

She moved her hand across and gently touched Roisin's hand. 'Do you think you could handle a hug? I think you need one.'

Roisin nodded and so Aisling shifted across the couch and placed her arms around her, pulling her close. Roisin succumbed to her grief and Aisling felt her body convulse with sobs. After several minutes she pulled away and reached for a couple of tissues from the box on the coffee table.

After blowing her nose and wiping her eyes, Roisin said, 'You can't tell anyone about the tattoo, Aisling. Promise me you won't.'

# 17

At five pm Frank assembled his full team in the squad room. There was DC Chris Walker, DSC Phil Rogers, DSC Ayesha Patel, DS Stuart Tyler, DSS Paul Lowry and DSS Rachel Sharp. There was no DI postholder at the moment due to budget cuts and a freeze on promotions. That meant Frank had to be more hands on – which suited him.

He asked Rachel to outline the attacks on Tessa Cooper and Carrie Ross. Using the map on the board she attached a photo of each victim to the site of their attack and then took the team through the two assaults she'd been dealing with. From Carrie Ross's camera they'd been able to print out photographs of all the dinner party guests and they were pinned up on the board linked to Carrie Ross with an arrow.

'The techs have now matched the boot imprints they found to a size eleven pair of Mongrel steel toe-capped high-leg work boots,' she added.

Frank thanked her then asked Lowry to summarise his case on Rhonda Newland. When he finished Frank took over.

'You can see from the map that all three victims were

attacked within a small radius. We don't know about victims one and four. No one's come forward. Tessa Cooper was attacked on Saturday night. She was victim two. Rhonda Newland who was victim three, on Tuesday night. We don't know about victim four but have to assume it was Wednesday. Carrie Ross, victim five, was attacked on Thursday night. Our perpetrator seemed to have the previous Sunday and Monday off, then resumed his attacks from Tuesday to Thursday, escalating to nightly attacks. Going on that principle, there should have been a further case reported from last night which hasn't happened. He may well have left victims one, four and possibly six, lying fatally injured in their homes as he did with Rhonda Newland and they haven't been discovered yet. We know he knocks them out first – presumably to stop them from screaming and attracting attention. When, and if, they come around, he beats them and half strangles them. As you heard from Paul, the beatings are savage and caused the death of Rhonda Newland. I've asked for extra patrol cars to police the area within the drawn circle on the map every night until we find this man.

'We could surmise that Tessa Cooper and Carrie Ross were random victims – plucked off the street. Rhonda Newland is a different scenario. She was attacked in her home. Did she know her attacker and let him in?' Frank said.

'According to her daughter Kay, Rhonda didn't mention that she was expecting to see anyone on Tuesday night. But that doesn't mean she didn't have an arrangement with him, or that he didn't just turn up at her place unexpectedly. As I said in my summary, there was no sign of a break-in,' Lowry said.

'So how does he choose his victims? We don't have a clear pattern to these attacks as yet. Two of the victims are of a similar age but dissimilar in appearance. Rhonda Newland was much older. If it wasn't for the tattoo calling card and the brutality of her attack which was similar to the other two, I'd say they were different perpetrators. But I don't think we're looking for two men. Just the one – and we need to find him before he kills anyone else. I'd like you to split into two sub teams to carry on with the investigation but to meet each day and provide updates. Paul will lead one team with Stuart and Phil. Rachel the other with Ayesha and Chris. Team leaders will allocate tasks.

'Paul – what feedback do you have after questioning the neighbours in Rhonda Newland's complex?'

'I haven't received the full update on that. I'll let Stu tell you.'

Rachel watched with interest as Tyler started to give his findings while remaining seated. She would have expected him or Lowry to attach a photo of the complex where Rhonda Newland lived. Lowry had pinned up a photo of the inside of her flat showing where the woman's body had been lying – stained carpets and all.

'I haven't been able to speak to *all* the residents as yet. Of the one's I've spoken to, none of them saw anyone entering Rhonda Newland's flat. I managed to catch up with one man today who wasn't home the night of the attack; he'd been drinking at a friend's place. I've verified that by visiting the friend in question. Some residents were home alone watching TV and they were able to recount details of the shows they watched. One of the male residents I visited didn't have a contact number for a male visitor he'd had that night. He was due to make some calls to get me a number. When I returned to see him today there was no answer. His neighbour told me he was taken to the John Hunter hospital. He'd told me the day before he was dying of cancer and when I checked with the hospital, I was told he's in a coma. He's not expected to last the night.'

'Why didn't this resident have contact details for his visitor?' Rachel asked.

'He'd turned up unexpectedly. Someone he hadn't seen for some years. A mutual friend had told him about his illness and he'd dropped by to see him.'

'Okay Stuart, I'd like you to keep returning to the flats until you have statements from *all* the residents,' the Chief said. 'Do you know whether the unexpected visitor arrived by car?'

'I asked that of the man who is now in hospital. He didn't know.'

'Check with all the neighbours. Someone could have seen him.'

'I've asked everyone who I've managed to speak with. No one saw anyone near Rhonda Newland's place or visiting our dying resident.'

'Okay, keep at it until you've spoken to everyone. I want *detailed* reports of those visits entered into the system so everyone has access to them. The same goes for all your visits Rachel,' the chief said.

'Yes sir. The ones we did yesterday are all in the system. There's just the ones from today to do.'

'Have you solved the mystery of Carrie Ross's camera?' the Chief asked.

'Yes. After phoning around the dinner party guests who left before McDonald, I was able to discover that Ari Kahinu had put Carrie Ross's camera into McDonald's rucksack. He'd tripped as he was wheeling his bike towards the front door and the bike fell onto McDonald's rucksack. When he bent down to pick the bike up, he noticed the camera lying next to the rucksack and thought it must have fallen out of an unzipped compartment, not realising it had been knocked off the side table. He put it in the front pocket and zipped it up so it couldn't happen again. It seems McDonald was telling the truth about being unaware it was in his bag. Whether he was telling the truth about his movements that night is a different matter. We're still looking into that and waiting for a report from forensics. There's one other thing we need to report back on. Ayesha spoke to a couple of tattoo artists. They don't know of any shops that sell home-made tattoo kits in Newcastle. They said as far as they knew, those items were only available from on-line outlets like eBay.'

'Did you find out anything about McDonald's sister's death?'

'Yes, it seems she died in a car accident on the New England Highway near Singleton last year. A truck carrying coal rammed into her vehicle.'

'Okay, well that's not relevant. Thanks Rachel.' He then turned to address the whole team. 'As Rachel mentioned in her outline of Tessa Cooper's case, a photograph of

Tessa was missing from her purse. We think it was taken by the perpetrator. Paul, you'll need to check with Rhonda Newland's daughter to see whether any photographs of her mother are missing from her flat. I know she lives in Taree; I'd like you to get her down here as soon as you can once forensics have finished there.'

Lowry nodded

'Rachel and I are going back to interview Carrie Ross again tomorrow. We know from forensics list of the contents of her bag and purse that she had no photos on her. What we need to ascertain from Carrie is whether one was stolen. I'm going to speak to forensics and see what they've found at Rhonda Newland's place so far. You said they're still working there Paul?'

'Yes,' Lowry said.

'I'll also be checking with them to see if they've finished their report on the search at the park. I know uniforms were helping with that. And one more thing. As you know, the fact that the victims were given a crude tattoo has not been released to the press. Those who do know i.e. doctors, nurses and pathology have given their word to keep quiet about it. If I come across any mention of it in the media there'll be hell to pay,' the chief said looking around the room. 'I'm expecting all of you to work tomorrow. I'd like you here by nine am. There'll be no days off until we catch this man. That's all. Thank you everyone. We'll meet again same time tomorrow evening.'


Frank could hear his desk phone ringing as he walked towards his office. He picked it up and listened. He felt his body slump with weariness from the news that had been imparted.

'Okay, I'll come down with someone now.'

He immediately walked back into the squad room and raised his voice. 'Listen up everyone.' He waited until everyone stopped talking. 'There's someone just come in with a relative claiming they were raped last night. This might be victim number six. Rachel, can you come with me. Ayesha, can you see to it that the visitor's room is ready to receive them and put the kettle on. I want you and Rachel to interview her.'

In the reception area two small plump women, who Rachel assessed were slightly under five feet tall, were waiting for them. One looked to be in her late forties; it was difficult to gauge the age of the other woman. She had a very young face but her long light brown hair had streaks of silvery grey threading through it. She was clearly the victim as she was sporting a black eye – but there were no other marks on her face. Perhaps she wasn't a victim of their serial rapist.

'Good afternoon,' Frank said. 'I'm Detective Chief Inspector Frank Bailey and this is Detective Senior Sergeant Rachel Sharp. I believe you are waiting to see us?'

'No men, no men,' the younger woman said, clinging to the arm of her companion.

'My sister won't talk to a man. My name is Lisa Tomlinson and this is my sister Melody Hudson. She was raped last night by an intruder who broke into our house while we were both asleep in bed.'

That made little sense to Rachel. How could the rape of one woman take place while her sister was in the same house without her knowing about it?

'I'm afraid Melody might have destroyed some crucial evidence. She didn't realise, did you love,' she said turning to her sister, who shook her head. 'She felt dirty you see and took a very long bath after he'd gone, then stripped her bedding and put it through a wash cycle. I didn't know she'd done any of that until this morning and it's taken me the better part of the day to persuade her to come here and report it.'

'I needed to sleep,' Melody whined.

'I see,' Frank said. 'Well don't worry, I won't be sitting in on the interview. Detective Sharp will take you upstairs to a comfortable room where another of our female detectives is waiting for you and you can give them all the details.'

'That's okay then, isn't it, Melody love. Two female detectives are going to interview us.'

Melody nodded and smiled.

# 18

Rachel showed the women into the visitor's room where Ayesha was waiting for them. After introducing Ayesha, the woman called Lisa asked to have a private word with Rachel out in the corridor.

'I need to give you some background on Melody. My sister has some learning difficulties. She operates at about the age of a young adolescent – about twelve years old. She's not stupid though and has a part time job working in a warehouse assembling boxes. She can follow basic instructions and can just about function around the house but she's not capable of running her own household. When our mother passed away three years ago, Melody came to live with me and my husband, Nick. Our father had died ten years prior to that. Nick couldn't stand Melody being in the house. We never had children, and so he wasn't used to the equivalent of a kid being there. Our place isn't that large you see, and Melody likes to watch all these silly shows on television with the volume quite loud. He walked out on us about six months later saying it was either her or him. I couldn't put Melody in a home – it wouldn't have been right. So, he left.'

'How old is Melody?'

'She's forty-one. I'm forty-nine. Dad was fifty, mum thirty-nine when I was born. Back then that was considered quite old. Eight years later, Melody was an accident and there were difficulties at her birth. My mother was forty-seven when she had her. Melody almost didn't make it. My mother always claimed the doctor was at fault – she was delivered by forceps you see, which Mum believed caused brain damage.'

'Right.'

'I don't sleep too well, so take sleeping tablets most nights. I took one last night and didn't hear a thing. I was so shocked to see Melody's black eye this morning and then hear about the rape. I'll let Melody tell you what happened, but I might have to help her at times.'

'Okay, thanks for filling me in. Before we go in, could you tell me whether Melody was a virgin prior to this rape?'

'No, she wasn't. When Melody started working at the factory, she was only nineteen. Soon after she had a relationship with another young man there. He was twenty and had some learning difficulties also. They talked about getting married because they'd had sex a couple of times and both believed that meant she would have a baby. When they spoke to our parents about it, my father went crazy and as a result the young man lost his job. They'd been sneaking into a cupboard during their lunch break to have sex. Melody was supervised more closely after that. Thankfully she wasn't pregnant. She hasn't had a boyfriend since, nor any further sex as far as I know. She said she didn't like it and that Vinnie had bullied her into doing it – which is another reason why my father was so angry. She flirts with men sometimes when we go out for a walk. Although if I see her doing it, I tell her off. It always worries me if she does her little coquettish stunts while we're walking near the oval, as I know she'll give men the wrong impression. I have fears of men dragging her in there and attacking her. That's why I never let her walk out there alone and why she only works part-time so she can be home before it gets dark. And my school is very understanding about Melody. I'm straight out the door at the end of the day so I can be home in time for her.'

'Okay that's all very useful to know. Shall we get started?'

From details the women had given on arrival, Rachel knew they lived in a Close that backed onto an oval in Mayfield East. The oval was used by many people for sports. She was familiar with the area and knew there weren't many houses there; it was going to be tricky to find witnesses.

Ayesha had made a large pot of tea and had mugs and biscuits laid out on the coffee table. As Lisa and Rachel entered the room, she heard Melody ask her whether she had any Pepsi cola.

'You know you're not allowed to drink fizzy drinks Melody. You can have a nice cup of tea instead.'

Melody pulled a sulky face but accepted the mug Ayesha pushed towards her. She pulled the sugar bowl towards her and put two heaped teaspoons in until Lisa shouted, 'enough!'

'Hi Melody,' Rachel interjected. Melody looked as if she was on the verge of a tantrum and she needed to avoid that. 'Can you tell us about the man who came into your room last night?'

'He put his *thing* in me. I didn't like it and told him to stop but he said he would kill me if I made any noise or fuss. He punched me in the eye to show me he meant business, then put a hand over my mouth. I kept quiet like a good girl. He said I *had* been a good girl when he left but he hurt me. And he did some funny things with my bottom.'

'What do you mean he did funny things with your bottom?' Lisa asked her. 'You didn't tell me this.'

'I forgot until just now. He didn't put his thing there. He kept pricking me.'

Rachel and Ayesha looked at each other. It sounded as though he was marking her with a tattoo.

'Melody, has anyone else put their 'thing' as you call it, into you recently? Or even the same man?'

She needed to check that this rape wasn't a continuation of something that had occurred at work like the incident in the past.

'No!' Melody said, her face her face screwed up with revulsion. 'I wouldn't let them. It's *horrible.*'

Rachel understood what Melody meant. Between the ages of 17 and 18 she'd had sex with a couple of boys who fundamentally just wanted to screw her. Prior to persuading her to participate in sex, they'd pretended to care about her, lavished kisses on her and whispered sweet nothings in her ear. Once her pants came off and they jumped on her, it was horrible. There was no further pretence of caring. She no longer existed except as a body for them to use to satisfy their own needs. She could have been anyone. Is that how the perp viewed the women he raped? It could be why the victims varied so much?

'Do you know how the man came into the house?'

'No,' both Lisa and Melody said together.

'Well, I'm not entirely sure,' Lisa added. 'Our house is only a single storey but there's no windows he could have climbed through. They all have security screens on them. I think he managed to pick the lock on the back door. It looked like someone had messed with it. I called a locksmith out this morning and it now has extra locks on it like the front door. Don't worry, I kept the old lock for you to see.'

But destroyed other potential evidence on the door, Rachel thought.

'We will still need to get our technicians to examine the door and look at Melody's bedroom.'

'That's okay,' Lisa said. 'Will they come this evening?'

'They're likely to. It might be better if we put you up in a hotel or motel for the night.'

'I'd need to get some stuff for us from the house first. And there's my cat to consider. If we're away for more than one day, I normally organise for a neighbour to feed him.'

'We can't have any neighbours entering the premises. I'll arrange for the techs to feed him,' Rachel said. Turning back to Melody, she added, 'Can you remember anything about the man? Did you see him?'

Melody nodded. 'Only for a second. I have a touch lamp by my bed. When I woke up 'cos he was on top of me, I touched the lamp to see what was going on. I didn't know if I was dreaming. He had a funny thing over his head and mouth, but I could see a little bit of hair peeping through the side near his eyes up here,' she said pointing to the side of her black eye.

'Did you see what colour his hair was?' Rachel asked her.

'Like sand you see at some beaches.'

'Like this?' Ayesha said, standing and pointing to a large framed photograph of Nobby's beach in Newcastle.

'No that's too creamy. Sandier than that.'

'Do you mean white sand?'

'No. *Sandy* coloured. Like Sandy at school,' Melody said turning to her sister.

'Ah. Melody had a friend at school called Sandy,' Lisa explained. 'Short for Sandra. She had pale reddish hair.'

Rachel froze, her pen poised mid-air. They had a possible suspect with red hair. McDonald. She wouldn't call his hair pale red though. It was a *striking* red. She made a note of 'pale reddish hair'.

'He broke my lamp, knocking it onto the floor so I couldn't see him properly again after that. I only heard his voice or saw his shape once my eyes got used to the dark.'

This was more than their other victims had experienced. Was he aware that Melody had some learning difficulties and thought he could easily manipulate her?

'Was there anything distinctive about his voice?' Ayesha asked.

'Whadya mean?'

'Did he sound like anyone you've met before – or maybe heard on a television show?'

Melody sat and thought about this for a moment. 'Nah, I don't think so. He didn't talk properly. He either growled at me or spoke in a whispery, snarly type of voice.'

'Is there anything else you remember? Have you noticed, for example whether any photographs of you are missing, Melody?' Rachel asked.

'How did you know that? They're clever aren't they Lisa?' Melody said turning to her sister.

'I had a lovely framed photo of Melody on the sideboard – a picture that was taken last year when we were on holiday in New Zealand. The frame is still there but the photo has been removed,' Lisa said.

He *is* taking photos as souvenirs or trophies from all the victims, Rachel thought.

'Melody, we really need a doctor to examine you to make sure you're okay down there and on your bottom. Are you okay with that?'

'Sure,' she shrugged. 'As long as it's a woman doctor and I can get home in time to see Water Rats.'

Rachel knew Water Rats was a series involving water police set around Sydney Harbour. Repeats were currently being screened. The majority of shows the television stations aired from early November until late February were re-runs of old shows or ancient films.

'We could always arrange for you to see the show at the hospital.'

'Okay then. Let's go,' Melody said standing as though the idea of being examined was going to be an adventure.

'We'll need more details from you first; telephone numbers and places of employment. Detective Patel will take those down while I organise the hospital examination.'

***

When Rachel returned to Frank's office he'd just finished talking to the hospital and had arranged for Melody Hudson to be examined with a rape kit.

'Ah, you've beaten me to it, thanks.' Rachel said after he told her.

'I thought I should organise one even if you didn't think she'd been raped; we need to ensure we've fully supported her, especially as she is adamant she was raped.'

'Oh, I believe she was raped. Only this time as a more co-operative victim, which is why she's not so badly injured. And I'd say the perp knew about her learning difficulty and saw her as an easy target.'

'But where does he know her from – that's the question?'

'Possibly her place of employment? She's been targeted there in the past. Or her neighbourhood. The sister told me they go out for local walks.'

Rachel filled him in on what Lisa Tomlinson told her about Melody's past sexual encounter at work and Melody's statement about her experience with the rapist.

'With regard to the historical incident. I suspect neither the father nor the employers would have made a report to the police about it because both young people had learning difficulties and even if the young woman was bullied into it, she went willingly with him into that cupboard from everything the sister told you.'

'Hmm. Yes, I suspect you're right.'

'With this rape varying yet again from his previous approaches, it begs the question whether this guy gets off on the violence he inflicts or whether it's the penetration he's after to relieve an urge; the violence maybe has become the necessary means to achieve coition. He's clearly a man who is not socially capable of having a normal relationship with a woman.'

'Hmm. Rape is about power as well. Is he a man who believes he has had insufficient power in his life? Especially when it comes to women,' Rachel said.

'We need to focus on Rhonda Newland and Melody Hudson. Our rapist must have a connection with them as he attacked them in their homes. I don't think they were random. They must have been targeted.'

'Yes, that's likely. As well as checking with Melody's employers, I'll need to question Lisa Tomlinson a bit further to see if they've had any handymen in to do jobs around the house. We can also check with the management company of the flats. See if anyone has been carrying out any repairs at Rhonda Newland's place. At least with Melody's clue about the pale reddish hair we now have something tangible to go on.'

'Doesn't McDonald have red hair?'

'Yes. Not pale reddish hair though. He's still in the frame so we'll see if we can connect him to the sisters.'

'Poor lighting in the room might have altered the appearance of the hair colour. Apart from the black eye, does she have any other injuries?' Frank asked.

'Not that she mentioned. We will ask them to check her thoroughly at the hospital. It sounds as if he tattooed her. And he stole a photograph.'

Frank nodded. 'The photographs seem to be a common theme with our rapist. While Miss Hudson is being examined, we can check in with Carrie Ross and ask whether she was carrying any photos on her and whether she had any close encounters with McDonald at Dunbar's.

I'm sorry Rachel, it's going to be another late night.'

'That's okay, I've warned Andy but I wouldn't mind getting something to eat at some point. I haven't had anything since breakfast.'

# 19

Aisling gave a brief summary to her brothers of Roisin's attack. She wasn't willing to give them the full details that Roisin had revealed to her; all they needed to know was that she was raped and brutally beaten.

'Should we consider reporting the break-in without mentioning Roisin's attack or rape?' Aisling asked them.

'I can't see any point in getting the police involved. It might be better if we talked to the families of other victims,' Conor said.

'How could that help us?' Aisling asked.

'The police will tell them at least some of the things going on in their investigation. For example, they will probably tell them if they arrest a suspect.'

'And that can help us how?' Aisling persisted. She couldn't understand why Conor would be suggesting this.

'Well, we'd know that the bastard who attacked Roisin is in custody at least. And we could tell her she's safe at home.'

'I don't think Roisin will ever feel safe in that house again. You should have seen what she'd done with her bedroom. She'd dragged her wardrobe across the window and she had a chair barricading the door. Mairead said the landlord is going to go crazy when he sees how she's scratched the wooden floor. Anyway, Roisin told me she wants to move.'

'I've already said she can move in with me for now,' Conor said. 'My second bedroom has a large bed in it that can be split into two single beds – one for her and one for Mairead. It has its own bathroom. They'd have to store quite a bit of their stuff, there's no room for it all here. I could probably fit quite a bit of it in the garage though.'

'When I mentioned to Mairead that Roisin wants to move she said they're tied into a lease until next April. The landlord renews the lease once a year. They're on their second year now.'

'We can tell the landlord that his house was broken into because he didn't fix the bloody security screen. And that I had to fix it for him because my sisters were so scared. And because there's a serial rapist out there they want to move in with family. All of that's true anyway,' Cien said.

'I suspect the landlord would want to see a police report about the break in,' Aisling said. 'Otherwise, they'd be expected to pay the full rent up until next April.'

'Okay, so talk to Mairead. See if she will go to the police. Perhaps she can claim she heard someone breaking in and scared off a man who was about to climb in the window. She can say Roisin was staying over here at Conor's the night it happened or something.'

'What if they want to talk to Roisin to verify that? Roisin won't talk to them, or let anyone see her.'

'Oh, for feck's sake. I don't bloody know then. You come up with a better idea!' Cien shouted.

***

At Melody's insistence, Ayesha remained with her while she was being examined. She didn't want her sister Lisa with her. Rachel and Frank left Lisa in the relative's waiting area while they went to visit Carrie Ross.

Carrie's mother was by her bedside. 'How are you today, Carrie?' Frank asked.

'How do you think she is?' her mother snarled. 'Have you caught the scumbag who did this to Carrie?'

'We have a team working hard on the case.'

'No, I didn't think so, so—

'Mum, stop. Don't have a go at them. It's not their fault,' Carrie said.

'Hmph.'

'Carrie, we wanted to ask whether you were carrying any photos of yourself in your purse or handbag,' Frank said.

'Well there was my digital camera. I think that was in my bag.'

'No. You didn't have that with you. We have your camera.'

'Oh, I left that at Finn's place, did I?'

Frank looked at Rachel and shook his head slightly. He didn't think they needed to mention how the camera ended up in McDonald's rucksack.

'Did you have any photos in your purse?'

'Umm. I don't think so. Oh, hang on. Yes, there was a photo of me with Carmen. One of those booth type ones. Taken a couple of years back. That was in the wallet compartment of my purse.'

Not anymore, Frank thought. So, the perp was consistently stealing photos of his victims. That would take time to do. If Carrie's attacker was disturbed by the dog, then that must have been one of the first things he did.

'I can't show you the photo because my bag hasn't been returned to me.'

'No, it's still with our forensic technicians. Have you remembered anything else about your attack?'

Carrie shook her head. 'Only what I've already told you.'

'Can I take you back to when you were still at Finn Dunbar's place,' Rachel said. 'Do you recall bumping into Robbie McDonald outside the bathroom?'

Carrie's face reddened and looked downwards. 'I … I don't remember.'

'Just what are you trying to imply?' Gemma Ross asked, in her usual aggressive tone.

'Nothing,' Frank said. 'We're simply attempting to ascertain how different guest's DNA could possibly be on Carrie's clothes.'

'You found this man's DNA on Carrie's clothes? So, he might be her attacker?'

'No, I didn't say that,' Frank said. 'We are looking at all the events from the dinner party. It may be that Carrie picked up some DNA from *different* guests. For example, did you give Lilly a hug when she left? That might have left DNA traces on your clothing.'

'Yes,' Carrie said nodding, before realising that wasn't wise with her injury and winced. 'I did hug her when she left. I definitely gave Finn a hug too. I've got a clear memory of the smell of his aftershave. And I might have hugged some of the others as well. I … just don't remember'

'Okay. Thanks Carrie. Sorry to have disturbed you. We'll leave you in peace.'

'Good save,' Rachel whispered as they left Carrie's room.

In the corridor Mr. Ross appeared carrying a tray of hot drinks.

'How is the investigation going? On the news we heard there was another victim who died this time.'

'Yes. Sadly, she wasn't found in time.'

'Have there been any further attacks?'

'I'm afraid we can't discuss—'

'So that's a yes, then. There *have* been further attacks.'

Frank shook his head. 'No, we have no confirmed new cases, although I suspect we will.' This was technically correct. Melody Hudson's allegation had not been corroborated.

'What are you doing to find this bastard? How many more women are going to die or be murdered—'

'As I just told your wife, we have a team working hard on the case,' Frank said cutting Ross off. 'We also have many extra patrol cars on alert. They're—'

'Alright. Alright. I'm sure you're doing your best. Let me know as soon as you've made an arrest,' Ross said walking off.

'We'll keep you posted,' Frank said, calling after him. He took a deep breath. He had the distinct impression the Ross couple didn't have a great deal of faith in them – and certainly no patience.

Turning to Rachel he said, 'Did you … oh never mind.

We'd better take Lisa Tomlinson over to her house to pack a bag under tech supervision. They won't want her damaging the crime scene. I'd be interested to know if they've found anything. Ayesha will let us know how the examination went. I've asked her to message me if there's confirmation of a tattoo. I need to get back to Area Command. The Chief Super and Detective Superintendent Jenkins want a meeting with me to give them an update.'

# 20

'Okay you've had a few mouthfuls now, which should keep you going – fill me in,' Rachel demanded.

Ayesha had pounced on the pizza when she returned to the office, claiming she was ravenous. Like Rachel, she hadn't eaten since breakfast either.

'Melody Hudson had a number six tattoo,' Ayesha said, wiping her mouth. 'I sent the chief confirmation of that as he requested. There were definite signs of rough penetration. No forensic evidence to gather of course as she had bathed. Have you heard back from forensics working at the house?'

'We called over there with Lisa to pack a small bag before dropping her back at the hospital,' Rachel told her. 'They've only found two sets of fingerprints in the house which belong to the women. They took Lisa's fingerprints while we were there. It is assumed the other prints were Melody's due to the small size of the hands. Our perp is obviously clued up enough to be careful about leaving any evidence.'

'What about the pubic hairs they'd collected previously from Carrie? Any DNA?'

'No. They weren't able to get any DNA off them. But they are a light reddish-brown colour which backs up Melody's claim of the hair colour. If they find similar hair, they'll be able to match it.'

'I've settled the two women into the motel in Hamilton and told them not to open the door to anyone other than us,' Ayesha said. 'The chief arranged for a couple of uniforms to park outside their room overnight. With the manager's agreement, uniforms will have access to a bathroom and coffee facilities in the reception area.'

'Right. The Chief wants someone watching them in case the perp followed them. He's got a couple at the house as well. Once the two women return home tomorrow the surveillance will continue; he's concerned the perp may return seeing as how Melody was so compliant. How was she after her examination?'

'She seemed fine. Once they stepped foot in the motel room, she immediately put the TV on. When their food order was delivered – a Chinese meal, she attacked it with gusto, whereas Lisa just picked at hers. I felt like saying, "I'll eat yours if you don't want it". If you hadn't sent me a message saying you were ordering in pizzas I might have. Unlike our other victims, Melody doesn't seem to be too affected by her attack. As far as she is concerned it was just an unpleasant experience she'd rather forget. I don't think Lisa is going to have much peace and quiet while they're there. What else has been going on? Who's been doing what?'

'I think Tyler went back to the flats in Georgetown. The Chief sent Lowry and Rogers over to Lisa Tomlinson's place. We left Rogers there but Lowry was then sent home as he's heading up to Taree first thing in the morning. I've just sent Chris Walker home but earlier I had him looking into CCTV to see if there's any sign of McDonald before his street turning,' Rachel said. 'There's a camera on the corner of Carrington Street and Maitland Road. McDonald wasn't caught on that camera, nor was he picked up on the electrical shop's security cameras which I find puzzling. I've also had Chris looking for the white pick-up that you saw in the servo with the dodgy bloke who avoided the cameras. He didn't spot his vehicle on the CCTV either. Nor does the pick-up pass the electrical store's security cameras; leaving only one right turn he could have made after leaving the servo.'

'Interesting. He might live around there or he perhaps he used the turning to cut through to other streets.'

'It might be useful to swing around some of those streets in Tighes Hill if we get a chance. Tomorrow being Sunday, the evening might be a good time to catch people at home. We could be looking for a needle in a haystack if, as you say, he turned there to head in another direction. Maybe back to Maryville. I'm more interested in why Robbie McDonald wasn't picked up on any cameras. If he went straight home as he claims.'

'Do you want to pop around to his now?'

'Yes, I think it would be good to find out how he managed to evade the CCTV cameras. If you've had enough to eat that is.'

'I'll save some to take home for later.'

McDonald was home alone and seemed reluctant to let

them in. 'We just have a few more questions we'd like to ask you Mr. McDonald,' Rachel said.

'Such as?'

'It would be better if we could do this inside.'

McDonald sighed and unlocked the screen door. They followed him into the lounge where the TV had been frozen on something he had been watching. A DVD maybe.

'What do you want to know?' he asked them while they all stood standing. He made no attempt to suggest they sat.

'Can you give us the exact route you took when walking home on Thursday night? We couldn't find you on any CCTV on Maitland Road.'

'I walked along the storm water canal and cut through Lichfield Park,' McDonald said. 'I always do that if the canal's empty of water and I'm walking – seeing as my house is only a few doors from the park. It was a clear night and the moon was bright enough for me to see my way. Didn't the cameras at the TAFE pick me up as I walked past?'

'They're not working,' Rachel said.

'The park might have some. Check there.'

Rachel nodded. 'While we're here, I'd like to raise the matter of taking your DNA again.'

'I told you I'm not giving you a sample. I don't have to.'

'You're right, you don't. We're asking Lilly Chen and Finn Dunbar to give us samples too, as they had close physical contact with Carrie Ross. We need the samples for elimination purposes so that if further DNA is found on Carrie's clothing, we will know it belongs to her attacker.'

'You're asking for Lilly and Finn's DNA to eliminate

*them*. You're asking me because you think I might have attacked her. That's different. I'm not going to be stitched up for her attack or the other attacks that have been reported in the news.'

'You could give us details of your movements when the other attacks occurred. That would soon eliminate you. For example, you mentioned you met up with a friend in Mayfield for a meal on Friday night. What time did you return home from there? And could you give us the name of the friend you met.'

'I've no idea what time I returned home and I'm not prepared to give you my friend's name. I don't want people finding out that I'm being questioned as a possible *suspect* for these attacks. Was there another attack on Friday night? If that's the case, I'm not prepared to give you any further information on my whereabouts without a lawyer being present.'

Rachel nodded. 'I was under the impression from the last time we saw you that you had an allegation made against you in the past. There's nothing in police records. Why don't you tell us about it?'

McDonald looked angry. 'Why, so you can say, "well he's done it before so it's got to be him". Isn't that how it goes?'

'No, I'm asking you to talk to us about your experience so that we can understand why you're so reluctant to give us your DNA,' Rachel said.

McDonald sighed and slumped onto the lounge chair he'd clearly been sitting on before they arrived. There were a couple of empty tinnies on the side table beside it.

'Okay. I may as well. I know you're going to find out

anyway. Sit down.'

He waited until they both sat on the couch before starting.

'It was something which happened towards the end of my first year at Uni just before the term ended. I was living in a shared house and we decided to throw a party. My mates and I knew a particular group of girls from the canteen – we often had lunch with them and we invited them all to the party. None of them were on our courses but we'd become pally with them. I got together with one of the girls. The two of us had been dancing together on and off through the night – including some slow close numbers and we'd shared a couple of spliffs while sitting on the couch. We were both pretty out of it what with the joints and alcohol. Anyway, I invited her to crash out with me in my bedroom. We had sex. When I woke in the morning, about seven am needing the bathroom, she was gone. I was disappointed because I'd hoped it was the beginning of relationship with her. I knew she wasn't with anyone and neither was I. Anyway, I didn't think too much of it, but on Monday morning I was called into my Course Tutor's office. The girl had made a complaint against me saying she'd crashed out in my bed and woke to find me having sex with her and when she asked me to stop I wouldn't. It was bullshit. She was awake when we both went into my room and that's when we had sex. Not *after* we'd fallen asleep. Once I conked out, I didn't wake until the morning.'

'Had she taken her complaint to the police?'

'No, she'd only made a complaint to the university at that point but was talking about going to the police.'

'Could anyone else have come into the room and sexually assaulted her while *you* were asleep?'

'We talked about that possibility. But there was an old bolt on my door and I remember shooting the bolt home when we went into the room to prevent any drunken fools staggering in there. So, no that couldn't have happened unless she left the room, returned and didn't bolt it again. But she claimed she didn't. I was suspended from my course pending investigations. I sat at home shitting myself for days, expecting the police to turn up. They never came. It turned out that she had little memory of the night apart from her claim that she'd been raped. She said she fell into a drunken sleep soon after the so-called attack and woke later feeling terrified. She admitted it could have all been a dream as I was sound asleep when she woke but later, she worried that the 'dream' had been real and I'd just conked out after the sex. I had, but not as she described.'

'What happened then?'

'Other party goers were questioned – including her friends. They all backed up my account of how we'd been together at the party. She withdrew her allegation. I don't think she returned to Uni the following year and I avoided drinking heavily at any more parties I attended.'

'Were the police involved in the investigation?'

'I don't know. If so, they never questioned me. I gave a written statement to my course tutor.'

'What was the girl's name?'

'Eleanor Rigby. Not a name I could ever forget. Her parents were Beatles' fans. But we all knew her as Ell.'

'And the course tutor's name?'

'Um … Morgan, if my memory serves me correctly. I

don't recall his first name. I think it began with a J. I have this visual image of Mr. J. Morgan on his office door. He was an okay bloke but when he first questioned me, he kept going on about how the police could test her clothes for DNA and match it against my DNA. DNA was still quite new then. It freaked me out, because my DNA would have been all over her clothes from when we were dancing.'

'Okay, I can understand that and it explains why you are reluctant to provide your DNA. But I can assure you, we're asking for this DNA for *elimination* purposes.'

'Huh. So, you're saying I'm not a suspect?'

'All men are potential suspects until we eliminate them.'

'Right. Fair enough – but some more than others, eh? Okay, I'll give you a sample. It's possible you'll find some of my DNA on Carrie's clothes after what happened at Finn's. But certainly not on any of the other victims. I've never been near them.'


'Well done for persuading him to talk and to give us a sample. You're such a liar though. Elimination purposes only, my foot,' Ayesha said.

'It's true. We are looking at eliminating people. I just didn't add – or ruling them *in* as a potential suspect. Right. I think we need to call it a day. Can you drop his sample in to the labs on your way in tomorrow? Don't come in too early. The chief said nine. You've got an excuse to be a little later.'

'Sure boss. Anything you say boss.'

Ayesha sometimes called her 'boss' around other

members of the squad or uniforms, rather than calling her Rachel. It was a bit of a joke between them these days. As Rachel was a rank above Ayesha, she was technically her boss, but they didn't actually work that way. They usually agreed, before going to interview someone, who would take the lead but neither minded if the other jumped in. She did, however, often delegate tasks.

'I hope Andy's not feeling frisky tonight, I'm shattered and just want to conk out.'

'Way too much information.'

'You're just jealous.'

'As if.'

# 21

**Sunday**

Cien Murphy was parked in a small trading estate in Georgetown opposite the flats where the woman had been murdered. On the news the previous night, Detective Chief Superintendent Mitchell had given a statement to the press saying the woman had been another victim of the serial rapist who had carried out four brutal attacks on women in Newcastle. He was wrong about that. There had been another one. Roisin. They'd watched as the cameras had shown images of the police going in and out of the woman's flat.

'I know that place,' he'd told Conor. 'I've done a few jobs there.'

'Maybe we should check it out. If this rapist is now killing people, we need to devise a plan to make sure Roisin is protected.'

'What did you have in mind?' Cien had asked.

Now he was sitting here with his prized binoculars and a clear view of everything that was happening. The binoculars were a pair that Jess had bought him last

Christmas after he'd dropped and broken his old pair while bird watching up in the mountains.

People in white forensic suits had been walking in and out of the flat, which was on the left-hand side of a horseshoe shaped layout of the small complex. They were loading small packages into a van. Forensic evidence, he assumed. Besides the van, there was a couple of other vehicles parked in the complex. He didn't know if they belonged to the residents or the police. When he'd done jobs there in the past there had only been a couple of vehicles parked in marked spots outside the flats and he'd made the assumption that not many of the residents owned their own transport.

Earlier he'd seen a car pull up and a young aboriginal-looking woman and a man had gone into the flat of the dead woman. They hadn't come out since.

There was a man he thought might be a plain clothes cop knocking on doors. Either that or he was a journo, but he couldn't imagine the police allowing a journo to walk around knocking on residents' doors. He must be a copper. Earlier he'd seen the man invited into one of the flats. Now he was talking to a woman at her door. After a couple of minutes, he moved on to the next flat.

Cien watched as the woman shut the door and then he noticed the vertical blinds in the front window moving. All the flats had the same vertical blinds, obviously provided by the landlord. He trained the binoculars on the window and could see the woman who'd been at the door a few minutes earlier. She seemed to be talking to someone beside her. Moving the glasses slightly he spotted a young male sitting there with what looked like a notebook. He looked as though he was an older teenage boy. Cien registered the slam of the van doors and watched as the boy jotted something down in his notebook. A few seconds later the forensic van reversed out and left the complex.

Was the boy keeping tabs on everything that was happening?

When a police patrol car pulled into the complex a few minutes later, Cien trained the binoculars back onto the boy. The kid was writing in his notebook again. Cien was sure he making a note of everything. That could prove very useful.

The woman he'd seen entering the dead woman's flat walked out with the same man he'd seen arriving with her. Instead of getting into his car, she got into the patrol car which left soon after. The man, who Cien assumed was another cop, went up to speak to the younger man who'd been knocking on doors before returning to his car.

Once again, he could see the kid writing in his notebook as the cop's car pulled out.

In his own notebook, Cien jotted down the number of the flat and what he'd seen.

He was about to raise the binoculars again when he heard a door slam and an engine starting. He looked to his right and saw that the van which had been parked beside him was reversing. He quickly raised his mobile phone to his ear to make it look like he was chatting to someone in case the driver noticed him. Once the van was gone, he put the phone back on the dashboard, raised the binoculars and did another scan. The man he thought might have been a copper was climbing into a car and looked as though he was about to leave.

Cien suddenly felt uncomfortable and had the impression someone was watching *him*. The kid? He brought the binoculars back along to the kid's flat but could see he was busy writing in his notebook again. Perhaps noting down the time the copper left. Something made him turn to his right and he noticed a woman with long dark hair sitting in a car a few bays over. He couldn't see her clearly and was tempted to train his binoculars on her – but she was also holding a pair of binoculars and looking his way. She lowered her binoculars and fired an imaginary gun at him. It sent shivers down his spine. A few seconds later the woman donned a pair of sunglasses, started the car and reversed out. Taking a leaf out of the kid's book, he noted down the colour, make and model and attempted to catch the rego plates but only managed the first few letters before the car turned left and disappeared.

Why had she been checking out the action at the flats? Was *she* a journo? She looked too glamourous to be a cop. Had her gun action meant, 'gotcha' or 'you're dead'? He hoped she hadn't taken any photos of him. If he drove here again, he'd have to come in a different car.

He looked at his watch. Conor would be leaving home about now. He was only working a half day today and then heading over to the golf club where he hoped to bump into Chief Superintendent Mitchell – who happened to be an old golfing buddy of their father's.

They knew from their father's regular habits of reporting back on his matches, that Mitchell played Golf every Sunday morning and then his wife joined him for lunch in the clubhouse. When he lived in Newcastle, their father had played with Mitchell and a couple of other men each week.

After his golf match, their father would have a quick schooner of beer and then return home for the Sunday roast which his mother cooked every week even in the height of summer. The Sunday meal was a big event in the Murphy family. If Conor was working a weekend shift on a rush production job, he'd have to drop in later where a plate had been put aside for him.

Cien didn't play golf – he'd never been bitten by that bug. But Conor had and played as often as he could. And he knew Mitchell still played every Sunday.

Cien packed away his binoculars and started the car. He was due to collect some boxes from Mairead and Roisin's place and take them over to Conor's. Aisling had persuaded the girls to move in with Conor until the rapist had been caught.

# 22

By mid-afternoon no reports had come in from the public about anyone being attacked on the Saturday night. Frank knew that didn't necessarily mean anything. Melody Hudson's attack had been reported quite late the day before. And Rhonda Newland hadn't been discovered for several days. Victims one and four still hadn't come forward either.

The Chief Super was giving him a hard time, pressing him to make an arrest. He'd told him there was insufficient evidence on anyone to do that. He'd mentioned one potential suspect but stressed they were waiting on forensic reports to see if there was enough to bring the man in for questioning. He'd asked his team members to go over all the information they had so far to check that nothing had been missed. He was about to start doing the same thing himself when his desk phone rang, breaking the ominous silence. He felt inclined to ignore it in case it was bad news. His stomach was telling him it was.

Sighing, he picked up the phone, 'Bailey here,' he said.

*'A report has just come in of a young woman who has been found dead in her home, sir. Possibly another victim of the serial*

*rapist. Early reports suggest she's been beaten and raped,'* the desk sergeant told him.

'Where?'

*'Waratah.'*

'Who found her?'

*'I don't know sir. Sergeant Rooney is waiting for you at the scene.'*

'Give me the address. I'll be there as soon as I can.'

Frank walked out of his office and looked around. Paul Lowry had just walked in. He'd do. He beckoned him over. 'We have a report of a death in Waratah which fits the pattern of the serial rapist. We need to head over there now.'

'Oh Christ. Do you want Tyler to join us? He's still over at the flats in Georgetown.'

'No, is Rogers here? I thought I saw him earlier?'

'He's up in the canteen grabbing sandwiches for both of us. I bumped into him on my way in.'

'Tell him to follow us over. You can message him on the way. Here's the address.'

'This one wasn't so lucky,' Rooney said when Frank and Paul arrived.

'Who found the woman?'

'The victim's sister, Sarah. She'd been away overnight attending a friend's wedding up in Pokolbin. After we approached them, the next-door neighbours, a Mr. & Mrs. Morton, kindly offered to let Sarah wait in their place and are plying her with tea. I've got one of our constables in there. The older brother is on his way, but you might want to have a word with her first.'

Frank nodded. He could see Hale was in the bedroom examining the body.

'The victim's name is Becky Wheeler. She's twenty-seven years old. She works at the university dealing with student intake,' Rooney said.

'Okay, thanks. Have you got any uniforms checking with the neighbours?'

'Yes, a couple. The problem with this property is that it's not overlooked. You have the school on one corner and those trees opposite obscure the line of sight from properties there. And with two streets running off Station Road, houses in those roads don't have a clear view onto this property. But someone may have seen or heard a vehicle. The next-door neighbours both retire early and so they heard nothing. I'd say our murderer didn't pick this place at random.'

Frank had to agree. It wasn't looking promising. They just couldn't seem to get a break on these cases. Frank walked to the door of the bedroom, stepping carefully on the metal plates placed there by the techs.

'Good afternoon, Doctor Hale. Sorry scrap that. It's not a good afternoon. What are your initial findings?'

'She has received a severe blow to the head, much like Carrie Ross, as well as indications of having been beaten. But I'd say that this time the cause of death was definitely strangulation. Time of death I would estimate between eleven and twelve last night.'

'Has she been raped?'

'I can confirm it looks that way.'

'Right. When can you do the post-mortem?'

'I know it's urgent. Let's say nine am tomorrow?'

'Thank you. I'll see you then,' Frank said turning away. He asked Paul to remain in the house until the techs finished and to arrange for crime scene photographs to be sent to him. 'Tell Rogers to come next door. And don't eat the sandwich he brings you in the house. Go outside.'

Thankfully Frank hadn't had any lunch, otherwise he might have been at risk of losing it about now. He'd seen countless dead bodies over the years, but bodies of children and young women always hit him hard.

The front door to the neighbours' house was open, but the fly screen door was locked. Frank could see it led into a hallway and judging by the crying he could hear; the living room was one of the front rooms off the hall. He rang the bell and waited. An older woman he judged to be in her 60s answered the door.

'Detective Chief Inspector Bailey,' he said holding up his identification. 'I'm here to speak to Sarah Wheeler.'

'Yes, come in. I'm Jenna Morton.'

'Before you take me to Sarah, Mrs. Morton, I just need to confirm that you and your husband didn't see or hear anything unusual last night?'

'No. That's right. I'm so sorry. Our bedroom is at the front on this side,' she said pointing to a room off to the left of the hallway. 'Apparently Becky's room is on the right-hand side of their house, facing Harriet Street. There's no way we'd hear anything from our room. I have a hearing problem and normally wear aids. Keith is such a deep sleeper the house could fall down around him and he'd sleep through it. We went to bed around ten and were asleep within minutes. This heat exhausts us so much.'

'Okay well thank you anyway. And thank you for taking Miss Wheeler in today.'

'Oh, it's the least we could do. Would you like a cup of tea?'

Just then Rogers tapped on the door. Frank could see he was chewing. Presumably finishing the last mouthful of his sandwich if the crumbs around his mouth were anything to go by. Frank gestured across his own mouth and picking up the message, Rogers pulled out a tissue and wiped his lips.

'That would be very nice thank you. This is Detective Senior Constable Rogers. He'll be joining me while I speak to Miss Wheeler.'

'I'm so sorry for your loss,' was the first thing Frank said to Sarah Wheeler. She'd stopped crying now and was busy wiping her eyes, then her nose. The Morton couple had retreated discreetly to the back of the house.

'I believe you were away last night?' When Sarah nodded, he continued. 'Do you know if Becky had made any arrangements to meet up with anyone, or have any visitors over?'

'No. She hadn't planned on seeing anyone. Some of her friends were going out to a bar, but Becky decided she didn't want to join them. She said she always spends a fortune when they're out drinking. We bought this house off the landlord just last year and we're saving up to re-do the bathroom. Boring I know. But it's an investment of sorts. At least it wouldn't be money down the drain like a night out would be. That's what Becky said.'

She burst into tears again. Frank waited for her sobs to subside before asking his next question.

'Was Becky seeing anyone at the moment?'

'No. She broke up with her boyfriend Arlow a little over a year ago. Not long before we bought this house. That's what prompted Becky to come in with me on the purchase. She'd had hopes of her and Arlow getting a place together but it didn't work out.'

'What about yourself? Are you seeing anyone?'

'Yes. Dan came with me to the wedding. I dropped him back at his place before I drove home.'

'We'll need all those details from you.'

'Why? We had nothing to do with what happened to Becky.'

'I don't imagine you did. It's simply to ensure we dot all the 'i's' and cross all the 't's. Setting up a time frame of events.'

'Oh. Okay.'

'You mentioned you were planning to do up the bathroom. Have you had any other tradesmen in the house carrying out repairs in recent months?'

'We had to get a plumber in last month when we had a leak in the bathroom.'

'Do you have the name of the plumber who came?'

'Um … not really,' she said shaking her head. 'Becky dealt with it. But I know it was an older man Keith knew. Someone who'd retired but did it as a favour for Keith.'

'Keith?'

'Mr. Morton. My neighbour who lives in this house.'

'Oh, yes,' Frank said nodding. With the plumber being a senior, it was unlikely he was the man they were looking for. But he'd ask Keith Morton for his contact details all the same.

'You've had no other work done?'

'No. Becky and I tackled all the painting and floor sanding ourselves.'

'Right. Have you noticed anyone hanging around the neighbourhood? Anyone behaving suspiciously or sitting in a parked car for a long time? We don't believe your house was chosen at random. We think the person who attacked Becky must have been watching the house.'

'Oh my God. Do you mean he was stalking Becky? Or me? Waiting for one of us to be in the house at night alone? You think he watched me leave?'

'It's possible.'

Sarah remained silent seemingly digesting all he'd said. Perhaps searching her memory. Finally, she said, 'No, I haven't seen anyone. No-one who stands out at all. The roads around here are busy during the week because of the school. Kids are being picked up or dropped off. At weekends it's much quieter. If the school has evening events on it can be difficult for me to get a parking spot outside the house, which is a bit of a pain. Thankfully we only have the one car. Becky doesn't drive but I drive my car every day. Where I work is not well served by public transport and because I often work into the evenings, I like to know my car is there for me to get home quickly. Especially when it's dark.'

'Can I ask what you do?'

'I manage the tennis club over at Broadmeadow.'

Mention of the club triggered a connection for Frank that was eluding him. Hadn't Rachel talked about the tennis club in relation to one of the people she'd interviewed? Ah, he'd got it. Robbie McDonald.

'Do you know a member called Robbie McDonald?'

'Why yes. He's one of our better players.'

'Have you ever mixed with him socially?'

'Robbie? No, not really. He's attended some Cup ceremony awards where I've been present. Cups that he's won that is. That's about it.'

'Would he have known Becky? Has he ever been to your home?'

'No, he's never visited me here. And Becky? She didn't know him. Not as far as I know. She's never mentioned his name. Why are you asking about Robbie? He's such a nice, quiet guy.'

It's often the quiet ones who commit these terrible crimes, were Frank's thoughts. The link might be tenuous, but McDonald was now connected to two of their victims. He'd also attended Newcastle University where the victim worked.

'How long has Becky worked at Newcastle University?'

'Since she finished her degree there. So about six years or so.'

'She did a degree at Newcastle University?'

'Yes. In Media. What she really wanted to do was work in television. But while she was at uni, she volunteered to help other students with issues they experiencing – through the student's union. She also worked on the student newsletters. A paid job came up working with student intake just as she finished her degree and she applied for it – always planning for it to be a temporary job. It pays quite well and although she's applied for other jobs in the media field, she was never successful and so stayed on.'

Another link with McDonald. Becky Wheeler might well have been a student while he was still there; they could have known each other. All circumstantial though. Concrete evidence that McDonald knew Becky would need to be found.

Frank was about to thank Sarah when he heard a knock at the front door. He sent Rogers out to investigate and soon after a man he judged to be in his early thirties stalked through the door. Sarah Wheeler jumped up and ran into his arms sobbing. He was either the brother or her boyfriend. Frank raised his eyebrows at Roger who quickly introduced the newcomer.

'This is Jeff Wheeler. Becky and Sarah's brother.'

Releasing Sarah, Wheeler turned to him and said, 'And who might you be?'

Frank introduced himself.

'Isn't it about time you caught the bastard who's been committing these crimes? From what Sarah described when she called me, it sounds like the same twisted mongrel who raped or murdered those other women. How many is that now? Five?' Wheeler almost spat the words out. Frank could see he was almost incandescent with rage.

No. Seven, Frank thought. *If* Becky Wheeler was another of his victims, which wouldn't be confirmed until the post-mortem tomorrow.

'We are following many lines of inquiry,' Frank said.

'The problem we've encountered is no witnesses and little evidence.'

'With all this bloody modern technology, CCTV and everything, surely you must have some clue who this bastard is?' Wheeler said.

'Unfortunately, there haven't been CCTV cameras where these crimes have been committed.'

'What about the school over the road? They'd have security cameras.'

'Rest assured we'll be checking with them. Any cameras they have are likely to be situated at the front or rear of the building which *could* be helpful. Now I'm afraid we need to be making a move. Thank you for your time, Sarah.' Turning to Jeff Wheeler he added, 'Can you provide Detective Rogers with your details in case we need to contact either of you?'


It was almost 10pm when Frank arrived home. Beth was still up reading in the lounge. She'd arrived home from Sydney earlier that evening. They'd had a quick catch-up on the phone before she'd left Sydney. They'd planned to have a quiet evening at home over a meal. But then the call had come in about Becky Wheeler. Beth jumped up to greet him with a warm hug.

'You look as though you've had another gruelling day,' Beth said.

'It certainly has been rough. Since I last saw you, we've had two more cases of rape with one of the victims murdered.'

'Do you think one person is responsible?'

'It's very likely. Our problem is a lack evidence,' Frank sighed.

'I know it's easy to say, but you're home now. How about switching off and relaxing? Do you need anything to eat? I suspect you haven't had a proper meal today – again.'

'We had another pizza delivery around seven. I'm not hungry thanks. I could do with a whisky though; it's been a rough day.'

'Put your feet up then, I'll make it for you,' Beth said.

# 23

## Monday

It seemed as though Frank only been asleep for five minutes when Beth woke him.

'There's a call for you on the land line. They tried you mobile but couldn't get through.'

'What time is it?' he asked feeling quite fuzzy headed.

'Three twenty am.'

Frank groaned and rolled out of bed. Surely it wasn't another one? He staggered out to the kitchen and picked up the phone. He listened as the operator gave him details of another suspicious death with injuries similar to Becky Wheeler. He noted down the address and said he'd be there as soon as he could.

Beth was standing at the entrance to the kitchen, a summer robe wrapped around her. What he wouldn't give to be able to tumble into bed and cuddle up with her again.

'Is it another one?' she asked.

'Sounds like it. I need a quick shower first to help wake me up.'

'Can't you send other members of your team?'

'I could, and I will call at least one of them. But as SIO I need to go.'

Beth nodded. 'I'll make you a quick coffee then. It will help wake you up. It's a good thing you didn't have a second glass of whisky.'


Rachel Sharp was the lucky team member he chose to call out to join him at the scene. He picked her up outside her house before heading to Warner's Bay. They turned into the drive of a large sprawling detached property set on a large plot.

'This is very different to our other cases,' she said.

'I was thinking the same thing.'

'Could be a copycat.'

'Hmm. Let's see what we've got then.'


What they had was one very dead woman, a thirty-four-year-old housewife named Veronica Graf who had injuries to her face and head, much like several of their victims. A narrow black belt was tied tightly around her neck indicating she'd been strangled. It was Hale's assistant who had been called out to this one. Doctor Hina Goto.

'She died about four hours ago. I'd say between 11 and 12 pm,' Doctor Goto said, anticipating his question.

'Are there indications she's been raped?' Frank asked her.

'She's certainly had some form of penetration. I'll know more when I complete the post-mortem.'

'When will you be able to do that?'

'I know Doctor Hale is doing one for you at nine. I'll do this one immediately after.'

'Okay thanks. We'd better go and talk to the husband,' he said turning to Rachel.


Jonas Graf, the dead woman's husband, was a leading barrister. He explained he'd been away in Sydney working on a case which had concluded on Friday. On Saturday, he told them, he'd met up with family members. Sunday he'd met with friends.

'I wasn't planning on coming home tonight. I wasn't due back until tomorrow,' Graf said. 'But I couldn't sleep. I probably shouldn't have driven home because I'd had a few beers with my dinner the night before. But I got up about twelve thirty and decided to return. I'd been tossing and turning for more than an hour by then. After a quick coffee in my room, I set off. Thought I'd surprise Ronnie.'

Graf made a show of looking distressed then putting his hands over his eyes. Rachel wasn't convinced. It didn't seem genuine.

'Your wife didn't wish to join you in Sydney for the weekend?' Rachel asked him.

Graf hesitated before answering. 'No, Ronnie, that's what I usually called my wife, she didn't get on with my family. Too Germanic and anal for her liking.'

Rachel noticed he was already using the past tense for his wife. 'How long have you been married?'

'Seven years.'

'No children?'

'No, Ronnie had a couple of miscarriages in the first few years of our marriage. After that she decided she didn't want children.'

'Did your wife work?'

'No, she didn't need to. I earn plenty. And she'd inherited a share of her father's estate.'

'How did your wife fill her days?' Frank asked. Even if Beth won the lottery, he couldn't imagine her not wanting to work or do something specific with her time. They had fantasised about what they'd do if they ever won big money in the lotto and she'd said, apart from travelling for a time, she'd like to start a free lawyer service for people who couldn't afford to pay. He couldn't imagine Graf doing that.

'She lunched with friends. She played tennis. She—'

'Where did she play tennis?' Frank asked cutting him off.

'Well, she was a member of Newcastle District Tennis Club and played doubles matches there. She also played on private courts. Many of our friends have tennis courts in their grounds and hold tennis parties.'

'Okay, sorry to have cut you off. What else did your wife do?'

'She liked shopping and remodelling the house. Every year she re-did one or more spaces in the house; one of the living-rooms, a bathroom, or the kitchen for example. She considered herself a bit of a designer and advised friends when they wanted to up-grade parts of their house.'

So she did lots of really useful things, Frank thought scathingly. Graf looked at him in surprise. Had he just voiced his thoughts out loud? He cleared his throat before speaking again.

'Were you aware of your wife's movements yesterday or last night?'

'Yes. Well part of the day. I know she had a friend over for dinner last night. I'm not sure what her day was like.'

'Do you have the friend's name?'

'Yes – I think I have her number in my phone. I guessing I won't be able to stay in the house while your team is busy examining it. I'm pretty tired and need to try and get some sleep soon. Would it be okay if I crashed in the guest house out the back?'

'It would be better if you moved out altogether Mr. Graff. The techs might want to examine the guest house too. But first you need to provide us with that friend's phone number, the name of the hotel you were staying at in Sydney, details of your movements over the weekend and what time your arrived back here.'


'How many hours' sleep did you manage?' Frank asked Rachel. They'd arrived back at headquarters by six forty-five and decided there was no point in going home. They had a full day ahead of them. They'd managed to pick up bacon and egg rolls from an early opening café and were sitting in the squad room munching them and drinking coffee. No one else was in as yet.

'I was out for the count by eleven. So about four and a bit hours before you phoned me. I've had worse. You?'

'Similar. What are your thoughts on the Warner's Bay victim?' Frank asked.

'She doesn't fit. Look at the circle you've drawn on

the map there marking where victims have been attacked and predicting the circumference of where further attacks are likely to happen. Our perpetrator has been operating within a small radius in a completely different environment. Suddenly he goes to Warner's Bay? To a big posh house? I think the switch is too extreme. He's operating in an area he knows and is familiar with. But we'll know for sure from the post-mortem, won't we?'

'Yes. The tattoo. We've never released that information to the public. If it's a copycat killing, they won't know about that. And if Veronica Graf's killer *did* happen to know the victims had been tattooed with numbers, they'd have no idea what number was next. Everyone thinks we've had five victims. A copycat would tattoo six on her. Whereas she would be number eight.'

'We don't know for sure that Becky Wheeler is number seven, do we?'

'No. But I suspect she will be though. Lowry is coming to her post-mortem. You're welcome to join us and then remain for Veronica Graf's.'

'Sure. But we've loads to get on with before then. I'll contact the Sydney hotel Graf was staying in. They're bound to have security footage and should be able to tell us if he left his room or moved his car. Graf said he stopped at the services on the freeway. They'll have cameras too.'

'I'll do the freeway services. You do the hotel. I must say I'm glad we've eaten early. I normally don't eat before a post-mortem.'

'Me neither. But I was ravenous when we left Warner's Bay. Pizzas might fill you up temporarily, but they're really just like having cheese and others bits on toast. I want a decent meal tonight. I haven't had one for what seems like ages.'

Frank new what she meant. It was the perennial problem for detectives while working long hours investigating serious crimes. That's why his stomach had expanded so much over the years. Well, that was his excuse anyway.

# 24

Lowry made the 9am post-mortem for Becky Wheeler by the skin of his teeth. Frank thought he looked as though he'd just climbed out of bed. 'Sorry Chief,' Lowry mumbled as he sidled up to him looking surprised to see Rachel there.

'The victim does have a tattoo. A number seven,' Hale confirmed. 'I checked just before you came in and have photographed and recorded it. I've already given a detailed description of the woman for the recording. You can see her for yourselves so there's no need for me to repeat everything.'

Frank nodded.

'There are two sites of impact on the skull. Both pre-mortem and are unlikely to have caused death. I'd say they might have been enough to render her unconscious or cause bi-lateral sub-hematomas. I'll be able to check them further when I open the skull.'

Frank didn't want to be around to see that. Hale knew he became squeamish when he brought out the electric cutting tools. He was hoping Hale would be able to ascertain cause of death before it came to that.

Hale then proceeded to cut a 'y' section down Becky's body which made Frank wince. 'Although there is bruising on her abdomen, I can find no internal injuries,' Hale concluded after spending some minutes examining the body internally. He moved further down. Frank – and Rachel, he noticed, turned away at this point, looking elsewhere. Lowry seemed to have his head down, also avoiding the bright lights exposing the poor woman. Frank knew Hale had been doing this kind of work for a long time, but he couldn't understand how he managed to remain so detached. When Frank investigated deceased victims, they seemed so real. As though they were still living and breathing human beings.

'There is extensive bruising to the vaginal passage and it's clear she's been raped in a similar manner to the other victims,' Hale continued. 'Once again no evidence of semen deposits.' He moved back up the body lifting the right hand. His assistant had just removed the protective covers from them. 'Aha! It looks as though we might have some skin under a couple of the fingers. Something we didn't have with our previous victim.' Hale scraped under the fingernails and then placed the contents into a small container and passed it back to Goto, who screwed a lid onto it before placing it into an evidence bag. He then moved around to the other side and lifted the left hand shaking his head. 'Nothing here,' he said, disappointment apparent in his voice. 'But there's enough from the right hand for us to get a good bit of DNA from with any luck.'

They waited while Hale examined Becky Wheeler's neck. There had been evidence of extensive bruising before Hale cut her open. 'Yes, as I thought,' he said. 'The hyoid bone is snapped. See that.' He waited for Doctor Goto and then in turn all three detectives to lean over and check it out. 'Extreme pressure has been applied to it. There is no doubt strangulation was the cause of death.'

Lowry elected to remain for Veronica Graf's post-mortem. They all took a ten-minute break outside to get some hot fresh air and allow Lowry to have a quick smoke.

'You want to pack that in,' Frank said. 'I'm sure you've seen the damage—'

'Yeah, Yeah, I know. Tell me about this Warner's Bay death.'

Frank filled him in with the details.

'You both think this is a copycat?' Lowry asked them.

'We'll soon find out,' Frank said.

'There's no tattoo,' Doctor Goto told them before turning the body over.

It was as Frank and Rachel suspected.

'The woman is Caucasian, with dyed shoulder length blond hair, about one metre seventy-two tall. That's five foot seven inches for those who prefer imperial measurements.'

She looked at Frank as she said this.

'Cause of death is strangulation courtesy of the belt found around the woman's neck.'

'That's not our perp's usual method,' Lowry said. 'You could be right about it being a copycat.'

Frank scowled at Lowry and shook his head. Lowry

was far too free with his mouth. He knew they were pretty safe around the pathologists but Frank always erred on the side of caution.

Another few minutes passed as Doctor Goto moved around the table, sometimes bending over the body. Then she spoke again. 'There's another difference between this body and the other victims. This woman has internal *damage* rather than just bruising from non-consensual intercourse. And I'm not talking about her abdomen or face,' Goto said.

That much was obvious from the part of the body Goto was examining.

'I suspect that an unnatural object has been inserted in her.'

'You don't think she was raped?' Frank asked.

'It depends on how you classify rape. To cause so much bruising and damage I'd say she was raped. But with what I couldn't say.'

'Then it could have been done by a woman,' Rachel said.

'Perhaps she secretly got off on lesso sex, and had a dildo used on her,' Lowry suggested.

'Paul, enough,' Frank said frowning at him. He often believed Lowry's comments and language were inappropriate.

'You may be correct Detective Lowry,' Doctor Goto said without blinking. 'With regard to the dildo, I mean. It would have been a large one though.'

Frank and Rachel simultaneously threw their hands over their eyes and groaned. Lowry grinned.

**25**

Cien was parked opposite the Georgetown flats again. This time there was no police presence. The victim's flat had police tape criss-crossed over the front door. He wasn't interested in going in there though. It was the boy he'd seen taking notes that he wanted to speak to.

He was wearing smarter clothes today had brought his contractor's ID card with him which he was planning to flash at the woman, hoping she'd accept it without close scrutiny. Last night he and Conor had watched a breaking news flash about another young woman who had been found dead, believed to be a victim of the same rapist/ murderer. They'd been at his and Jess's place hatching today's plan. He'd checked the news this morning to see if there were any updates and watched the brother of yesterday's victim make any angry statement about police incompetence. He rang Conor to see if he'd seen it; with Roisin and Mairead at his place Cien didn't think he would have put the news on. Conor hadn't seen it, but suggested that the angry brother might be a useful ally for them. Cien wasn't so sure about that.

On his way to the flats, he'd heard the radio newscaster

announce brief details of yet another murder victim; this time at Warner's Bay. This murdering bastard has to be stopped, were his first thoughts. But how they were actually going to do that he had no idea.

'Good morning,' Cien said to the woman who opened the door. My name is Detective Sergeant Richards (using the alias he'd made up on the way). I noticed the other day when I was here with my colleague that your young relative was making notes.' He had no idea whether the kid was the woman's brother or son. He couldn't gauge her age at all. 'I wonder if he would allow me to have a look at his notes.'

'HesmebrotherPenn,' she said smiling. 'Esalwaystakinnotes.'

The woman spoke with a strange lisp which slurred all her words together; Cien had to concentrate hard to understand what she was saying. From what he could make out she'd said the kid was her brother and was called Pen. Was Pen a nickname?

'Comen,' she slurred, a beaming smile on her face.

Sitting at the window, with his head tucked to one side was the kid. He wasn't as young as Cien thought. He was busy tapping away on a small screen. From the speed of the boy's action, he imagined it was some kind of gadget for playing games.

The woman spoke to the kid in a language Cien didn't understand. The boy looked up and smiled, his face seeming to light up in recognition. When Cien had done some work for one of the on-site residents last year, he'd had a beard and couldn't imagine the boy would recognise him. He hoped not anyway. Perhaps the look he was giving him wasn't one of recognition, but simply friendliness.

'Edoesnttalkmuch,' the woman said. 'Esautistic.'

Cien didn't have a clue what the woman was saying, but he gathered she was explaining the boy had some problems. As she seemed to.

She walked over to the boy and removed what he could see was an exercise book from his lap. The boy made loud protesting noises but by speaking quietly to him she succeeded in calming him down.

'It will only take me a minute,' he said reassuringly to the boy.

The woman passed him the exercise book which was open at a page with today's date written in neat handwriting. So, the boy was literate. Cien flipped back to the day he was looking for. Last Tuesday when the woman a few doors along was murdered.

At eight pm the boy had listed the registration of a car then noted 9 with Birdy written beside it. Was Birdy someone's name? Did the 9 represent a flat number? There was a description of the man. Red hair. Male. Tall. Pen had noted the vehicle leaving at ten thirty-three. Cien copied the details into his own notebook. Scanning down the page he saw that at 11.12pm he had another entry. No vehicle this time. 'Red', he'd written. And beside it '4 – key'. Christ, if four indicated a flat number that was the dead woman's flat. Was it the same man who had visited flat nine? Had the murderer gained entry by using a key? Surely that couldn't be right.

'Could you ask your brother about the 11.12 pm entry where he's written Red—'

Before he'd finished talking the boy started making loud noises again. Cien looked over to him and could see the boy was nodding madly and looked very upset.

'YeahhesawRedthatnightIdidn'twewenttobedthen Pennsleepsinhere.' She pointed to a single bed he hadn't noticed over in the corner of the room. 'Ithinkyoubettergo Rhondawashisfriend.'

'Okay. I'm sorry to have bothered you.' He handed the exercise book back to the woman. 'Thank you,' he said nodding to the boy and the woman before turning around and beating a hasty retreat.

When he'd arrived this morning, Cien had parked the car out of a direct line of sight of the flats. He didn't want the boy to make a note of his registration. Actually, not his; Jess's registration. He'd borrowed Jess's car this morning. He clicked the fob key, unlocked the door and was about to climb in when he felt something jabbed into his back.

'Don't move – unless you want to experience thousands of volts coursing through your body. I have a stun gun pointed at your back.'

It was a woman's voice. Cien gave a nervous snort of laughter. 'Is this some kind of joke?'

'I'm deadly serious mate. Now tell me, who are you working for? Are you a journo or a PI?'

'What's a PI?'

'A private investigator.'

'Er… no, I'm not a journalist or a private investigator.

Why on earth would you ask me that?'

'Because you were here watching the flats the other day. And just now you've come out of the kids' place. The one who makes notes of all the comings and goings over there.'

It must be the woman who, like him, had been training binoculars on the flats. Why would she be pointing a stun gun at him? Who was she?

'You're the sheila who was here the other day aren't you? Are *you* a reporter or something? What do you want? This is all a bit dramatic, isn't it?'

'I believe I want the same thing as you. Who are you carrying out an investigation for?'

'My family.'

'Okay. Give me your note book. I know you've written down information that the kid had.'

'No. I need it.'

'So do I. How about we go for a little drive then?'

'How about we don't. I could call the police on you.'

'You're not going to dob me in to the police. You wouldn't be here if you were working with them. Why *aren't* you working with the police by the way?'

'I'm not prepared to tell you that until you tell me why *you* want the information.'

'Right. We need to go for that drive then. Go around to the passenger side. I'll drive.'

'Not in this car you won't. You wouldn't be insured.'

She snorted. 'You really think I give a damn about insurance?'

'My girlfriend would though. I've borrowed her car. Okay I'll drive.'

'Give me your notebook first,' she said. 'So I know you're not going to drive off before I get into the car.'

'How do I know *you're* not going to just run off with my notebook?'

'You don't. You'll have to trust me.'

'Huh. Trust me, says the woman pointing a gun at my back.'

Cien sighed and decided to take a gamble. He was curious to know what her game was. The pressure of the gun was withdrawn and he looked around to see a small woman with long dark hair darting around to the passenger side. She opened the door and threw herself in. 'Get in and drive,' she commanded.

'Where to?' he said looking at her once he was behind the wheel. He couldn't see her eyes for the enormous dark glasses she was wearing. She was definitely Asian though. Chinese, Korean or Japanese he suspected. The elongated shape of her face reminded him of Japanese women he'd met in the course of his work. But then he'd met Korean women with a similar look.

'Anywhere quiet and not too far.'

'I'll go to the Phoenix Sports Club then. They have a huge car park and no one will think it strange if we were to sit in the car and talk there.' He also knew they would have plenty of cameras trained on the car park if anything were to happen to him.

Throughout the drive the woman kept the stun gun sitting in her lap. He knew damn well she wouldn't use it on him while he was driving. But once they parked, he wasn't so sure. She might be small but there was a fierceness about her that sent shivers up his spine. He could still remember the hand gun signal she'd made to him the other day.

Ten minutes later he pulled into the car park, drove over to a fairly deserted spot near the rear and stopped.

'So, who are you?' he asked her.

'I'm number one.'

'I don't understand—'

'The first one he attacked.'

'Oh. Sorry. Shit. Did you report it to the police?'

'No. You said you were collecting information for your family. Was someone in your family attacked?'

'Yes. My sister.'

'And she didn't report it either? What number was she?'

'She refused to report it. I don't know how many women have been attacked. There's been five or six reported now; three of them murdered.'

'What about her tattoo? What number did he scratch into her?'

A tattoo? Aisling hadn't mentioned a tattoo. 'I ... she hasn't told us the details of what he did to her. One of my sisters is a doctor; she examined our younger sister. It happened last Wednesday night when she was home alone. He broke into the house.'

'He did the same with me. So by my reckoning she would have been number four. I know two of the murdered ones were three and seven. Number seven being the one who was murdered on Saturday night. Three others besides me have survived. Your sister makes up the seven.'

'I didn't hear anything about a tattoo. And aren't there three women who have been murdered now?'

'Possibly. The police haven't released any information

about the tattoo. I guess to protect the survivors. They wouldn't want anyone to know they'd been tattooed. And the cops always like to keep something back.'

'Where did he put the tattoo?'

'You don't need to know that. So you're carrying out your own investigations? With a view to doing what?'

'I don't know. But my brother Conor and I couldn't sit around doing nothing. I recognised the flats where the aboriginal woman was murdered last week. I've done a bit of work there. I thought I'd nose around to see what I could find out. My sister won't *be* safe or feel safe until we know he's caught. What were you doing there?'

'Like you, carrying out my own investigation. The cops … they're held back by procedures, rules and regulations. I'm not,' she said putting her hand on the gun to make a point.

'What do you intend to do if you discover who your attacker is.'

'Maybe kill him. I'll have to wait and see how I feel. Maybe I'll just castrate him.'

# 26

Frank called the team back to headquarters for a meeting after he, Rachel and Paul returned from the post-mortems. Stuart Tyler and Phil Rogers had been checking around the neighbourhood where Becky Wheeler lived. They'd managed to have the school opened so they could look at footage from their security cameras. They'd also been knocking on doors. Chris Walker had been doing the same around Melody Hudson's residence. Ayesha had called on the sisters before heading off to the university to check out McDonald's story about the historical allegation and to make enquiries about Becky Wheeler.

'Right. Let's hear what you've found out,' Frank said once they were all assembled.

'The school doesn't have any cameras on the side streets. There are too many trees. The cameras at the rear are only trained on the grounds, the staff car park and the back entrance. There was nothing of interest there. There were a number of cars captured on the cameras along the front entrance on Saturday night and some pedestrians – two different couples passed around the possible time of the murder. One couple were on the other side of the road and turned right into Alfred Street. They seemed to disappear into a house on the right-hand side. The others continued past and I couldn't see where they went after that,' Rogers said.

'Any joy on the door to door? Did you check the couple's house on Alfred Street?' Frank asked Tyler.

'Yes. I knocked on several doors along there. We weren't sure which of the two houses they went into. There was no answer at either of them.'

'You need to go back there tonight then and see whether you can catch them in. We'll put out an appeal for the other couple along with any motorists who passed the house. We need them to come forward.'

'Can't we get some uniforms to help in the door to door?' Tyler asked. 'There's not enough of us.'

'I agree. I have put in a request. We're drowning here and now have another murder to investigate. The one at Warner's Bay. We're not sure if it's the same perpetrator. This one was different. There was no tattoo and we suspect it could be a copycat. Paul, I'd like you to take over that. Find the woman Veronica Graf had as a dinner guest last night. We know that around the time his wife was murdered, the husband was either at his hotel in Sydney or driving back to Newcastle having stopped at a services en route. His alibi checked out. Rachel and I confirmed that this morning – it's all in the system. I want you to look into the husband though. He could have arranged her death. By all accounts she was a wealthy woman and, although he is a higher-than-average earner, money is frequently a motive.'

Lowry nodded, seemingly pleased he'd been given the

case.

'I've thought of another area where the Graf case differs from all the other attacks,' Rachel said. 'It hit me today at the morgue when the pathologist gave us the height of the Warner's Bay victim. All the others are between four foot eleven and five foot one – five one being Tessa Cooper and Carrie Ross's height. Rhonda Newland was five foot and Melody Hudson is four foot eleven. Their overall appearance varies, but they're all very small women.'

'Just like you then,' Tyler said grinning.

'Ha ha! I'm five foot four. Veronica Graf was five foot seven. Quite different to all the others,' she said addressing Frank. Frank appreciated the fact that Rachel always quoted heights in feet and inches for him. She knew he could never get his head around centimetres.

'That's a good point Rachel. Stuart, cut out the teasing. You carry on with the Wheeler case. I'm not saying they're unimportant but as we're so thinly spread, I want more emphasis put on the cases that happened indoors. We've pretty much exhausted lines of inquiry on Tessa Cooper and Carrie Ross's attacks. The murders and Melody Hudson's attack all happened in houses where the techs are likely to pick up more forensic evidence. With any luck that is. I'm going to ask Rachel to look at the Newland case with fresh eyes. Ayesha will move between the cases. The same with Chris. Speaking of Melody Hudson, have you anything to report DC Walker?'

'As you know I spent a lot of time at the nearby oval yesterday afternoon talking to dozens of people and doing door to door around the area today. As Stuart found, there was no answer at some places. I did manage to speak to one older lady who spotted a pick-up truck the night Melody Hudson was attacked. She lives in Arthur Street opposite the oval and it was parked on the oval side. And she's sure she's seen that pick-up before. A white one of course. And no number plate.'

'Did she see the driver?'

'No.'

'What about CCTV there?'

'There's a security camera at the entrance of the oval and one at the toilets. I've arranged for the parks department to send he footage over to us.'

'Okay. The woman's information might prove useful. Enter it into the system. And check out that footage. Ayesha can help you. Anything to report back from the university Ayesha?'

'McDonald's account of the historical complaint checked out. The woman who'd made the complaint withdrew it and the matter wasn't taken any further. There was no police involvement. Becky Wheeler was a much-loved member of staff. She completed her degree two years after McDonald. Although they were in different years, they may have known each other as they had the same tutors for a couple of their modules.'

'Okay that keeps McDonald in the frame. I'll see if Chief Superintendent Mitchell will allow us to put surveillance on McDonald. Becky Wheeler's sister works at the tennis club where McDonald plays. He may have crossed paths with Becky there. Another consideration, given Rachel's point about the women's height, is that Sarah Wheeler may have been the possible target. She's also very small.

'I'm going to check in with forensics to see if they have

anything for me from the Newland, Hudson and Wheeler crime scenes. I'll let you know about meeting tomorrow. Thanks everyone.'

Rachel followed Frank to his office. 'You mentioned you wanted me to look at the Newland case,' she said after shutting the door. 'Is there anything in particular you want me to look at?'

'Everything. Read through the case notes. Look at everything Stuart Tyler has picked up on the door to door. It's a bit thin in places.'

'Okay.'

# 27

Cien gulped and wasn't sure how to respond to the woman's statement. Was she serious? She certainly looked it.

'How about we work together on this?' she said after a pause.

'I don't even know who you are. You could be making all this up. You could be an undercover journo.'

She took her sunglasses off and Cien could see that her left eye was bruised. That's why she'd been wearing the glasses.

'This was one of the little presents he left me,' she said. 'I have a lump on the side of my head where he knocked me out if you'd care to feel it. From all that I've read and heard about the other attacks, I got off lightly. He left me with other marks, but I won't be showing you those. My name is Kaede – that's pronounced Kay-ee-dee – Tenaka is my surname.'

'Where are you from originally?'

'Brisbane, but I've lived in Wickham for some years now.'

'That's not what I meant. I—'

'I know exactly what you meant. You want to know my ethnic origins. Okay. My father was born in Australia to Japanese parents. My mother is a second-generation Australian born with Irish ancestry. My Japanese grandfather was taken prisoner in New Guinea during the Second World War when he was just eighteen years old and moved to a prison camp in Queensland. He remained in Australia for some years after the war ended as his home town was obliterated along with all his family by the Americans. He came from Nagasaki. I don't know if you ever learned about the atom bombs the Americans dropped on Hiroshima and Nagasaki, forcing Japan to surrender. The bombs killed millions. On a memorial trip back home some years later my grandfather met my grandmother. They married and returned to Australia where he had citizenship by then. They settled in Brisbane. My grandfather is dead now but my grandmother, who was quite a bit younger than him is still alive. My parents are both alive and they also live in Brisbane. I have one brother and one sister. Do you need to know anything else?'

'Why did you move to Newcastle?'

'My fiancé picked up a top job down here in the steel industry. Neither he nor the job lasted. I, on the other hand, had started a successful business and decided I wanted to remain. When I've taken revenge on my attacker I might sell up and return to Brisbane. Now tell me about your family.'

Cien paused. Not sure how much to reveal to this woman. She had been forthcoming about her family, but was it all true?

'My name is Cien Murphy, spelt C-i-e-n but pronounced kee-en. My parents are Irish, from Galway and moved out here when my eldest sister was a toddler. The rest of us were born here. There's five of us. I have three sisters and one brother. We grew up in an apartment on the top floor of the hotel that my parents owned. A posh hotel in the city where we often had to work in the evenings and weekends. None of us works in that field now.'

'Wow they *owned* the hotel? How did that come about? Were they from wealthy backgrounds?'

'No. They had a smaller hotel in Galway which my father inherited. They sold that before moving to Australia; the proceeds would have gone towards the one they bought here. And as far as I know, they also borrowed heavily.'

'What do *you* do for work?'

'I'm a carpenter, joiner or cabinet maker if you like.'

'Is there a difference?'

'I can make beautiful things, but all too often I'm hired to make shelves. Occasionally I'm able to put my artistic skills into practise on an architect designed house. I'm familiar with the complex where the woman was murdered as I've made built-in shelving units for a couple of the residents there.'

'She was number three.'

Cian shook his head. 'If you say so.'

'What did you get from the boy?'

'A rego plate from someone who was visiting a resident. The boy wrote that he was tall and had red hair and noted the time he arrived and left. Then after eleven pm he wrote Red with a capital 'R' – I don't know why. And noted that 'Red' entered flat four where the woman was murdered using a key – at least I think that's what his notes meant. I tried to ask him whether the Red he'd written down was the same man who'd gone into number nine. But he became quite upset and his sister asked me to leave.'

'Well we have a rego plate and a description. It's a start. What shall we do next?'

'We?'

'Yes. I think we should work together. Perhaps I should meet your brother. Is he at work now?'

'No, he's working from home looking after Ro … looking after our sister who was attacked. She didn't want to stay in her home.'

'I know what that's like. I've been staying with my cousin since my attack. She tried to get me to report it to the police. I almost did. But decided against it.'

'Our sister still doesn't want to report her attack either.'

'I can understand that. But we can't let him get away with this. He's murdering people now. I'd like to meet your brother. Where does he live?'

'Merewether.'

'A safe zone then. Perhaps I should collect my car first.'

'I can always drop you back,' Cien said wondering what she meant by 'safe zone'.

'Okay, let's go. You can tell me about all your siblings on the way.'

# 28

Rachel spent some time going through Tyler's reports on the Georgetown flats. There were two flats where very little information was entered. Flat number eleven where Billy Jordan lived was one. He claimed to have attempted to speak to the occupant on three occasions without success. In flat six he'd listed the names Kirra and Penn Tiller. Beside Kirra's name he'd typed 'mental health problems'. Beside Penn's he typed 'autistic.'

She could see Tyler was still at his desk and after scribbling some notes on a pad, went across to speak to him.

'Stuart, can you tell me about the Tiller's from flat six in the Georgetown complex?'

'The Tillers?'

'Yes. Beside Kirra Tiller's name you've put 'mental health issues'. Beside Penn Tiller's name you've put 'autistic'.'

'Ah yes. Hopeless. *She* can't speak properly and he can't speak at all. Bloody useless.'

'Did you try to speak to Penn Tiller?'

'No. When I stepped into the flat, he was rocking back

and forth making strange noises. You know how kids with autism do that.'

'That doesn't mean he can't speak. The autistic spectrum is very broad – ranging from those with minor difficulties to those with extreme communication and language difficulties. But they are often very observant and skilled in a range of different things.'

'Yeah well, he's one of those extreme ones I reckon.'

She could hear that Stuart had made a judgement call on the Tillers, believing they could not offer him any useful information. He might be right but decided that she'd have to go over there herself to find out.

'What about the resident in number eleven? Billy Jordan. I can see you attempted to speak to him three times. Did you ask any of the neighbours whether he might be away?'

'Of course I did. They said they didn't know. No one had seen him for weeks. The woman in number twelve said he sometimes went to stay with his son up at Patterson. He lost his job recently – no doubt through too much grog and at the age of fifty-nine, I suspect he's unlikely to land another one.'

'Okay. Did you attempt to locate his son in Patterson?'

'No, because he wasn't around when Rhonda Newland was attacked.'

'How do you know his age?'

'I checked him out.'

'It would have been useful to enter his age beside his name then.'

'Yeah, I know, but we're looking for a murderer here and it's unlikely to be him. There are more important things to focus on.'

It would have taken Tyler a matter of seconds to enter that information. Rachel wondered if he had any further information on Kirra and Penn Tiller he also hadn't entered.

'What about the ages of Kirra and Penn Tiller?'

'They're brother and sister. She's twenty-four and he's nineteen. Neither of *them* will *ever* work and will be supported by us taxpayers. It's the same old story with that lot.'

'If by 'that lot', you mean indigenous people, I would say you're being overly prejudiced. There are care homes all over Australia full of *white* people who have developmental difficulties and who we, as taxpayers, support at great expense. At least the Tiller siblings live independently.'

'Yeah well, much as I'd love to stay and chat some more, I have to get on now,' Tyler said standing and pocketing his keys.

Rachel returned to her desk, grabbed her bag and followed Tyler out of the building. It was time to check the Tillers out for herself.

'So, you're the only one in your family who didn't go to university?' Kaede asked him.

'No, my sister, Mairead, didn't. She studied at TAFE to get her dental nurse qualification. Most of her training was on the job. Like it was for me. I did some courses at TAFE but I also completed an apprenticeship. What about you and your siblings?'

'Oh, a university degree was compulsory in my family. My father's an architect. My sister followed in his footsteps. My mother is a music teacher. My brother studied at the Queensland Conservatorium of Music and is now the lead violinist in the Brisbane Symphony Orchestra. The artistic gene passed me by. I did a business degree.'

'Hence you running a business. What is your business?'

'You don't need to know that. For now, anyway.'

Kaede whistled as they pulled into Conor's drive. 'That's some digs he's got there.'

'Yes, he demolished a run-down old property that was on the site and built this from scratch. It took almost two years to complete as he kept changing things.'

'There's too much of that happening in Brisbane. Many of the old homes are disappearing. Did he hire you to do some of your fancy artistic timber work in there?'

'Oh yes, I've left my touch here and there. By the way, I won't be introducing you to our sister – you know the one who ...'

'That's fine. I wasn't expecting to meet her.'

Conor answered the door and ushered them into his studio on the ground floor, signalling with gestures that Roisin was upstairs in her room and to be quiet. Kaede removed her sunglasses as soon as the Conor shut the door. Cien detected an immediate attraction between the two when he introduced them. They shook hands, lingering over the contact. He almost wanted to step in to part them and warn Conor to stick to business. This wasn't a woman to become entangled with. Not if she had murder on her mind. He was regretting arranging this meeting. He'd made a quick call to Conor before leaving the Phoenix car park and was surprised that he seemed more than willing to meet Kaede.

'I'm sorry to hear about your experience,' Conor said eventually releasing Kaede's hand. 'I understand you'd like join forces with us to track down—'

'Yes.'

'What are you proposing?'

'First of all, I want to show you a map I've marked out. Can I put it up on your whiteboard?'

Conor nodded his assent so Kaede unfolded a map she pulled from her bag and, using Conor's magnets, attached it to the board. 'These marks are where all the attacks have taken place. The only one missing is your sister's. Where does she live?'

'Hamilton,' Conor said. 'Samdon Street, opposite Gregson Park.'

Kaede marked the map with a red felt-tipped pen. 'Okay, well that reinforces some of my thinking. Five of the attacks happened either in a park, or in houses very close to a park. Of the remaining two, one happened near a school, the other in the Georgetown flat. I think the attacker identifies the women he wants and works in a job that enables him to watch them at different times. If he was simply stalking the women, he'd become too noticeable. Both the school and the Georgetown flats have grounds that need maintaining. He could work at both locations. I think our man cases out the homes while he's working. As you will see he also operates within the circle I've ringed.'

'No, what about the murdered woman over here at

Warner's Bay?' Cien said stepping up to the map to point out the mark Kaede had placed there. 'Why is this in black? And not red like the others.'

Kaede waved her hand dismissively. 'It's out of his zone. It's a red herring and probably a copycat. Even the police think that. As they should if they have any sense.'

'Hang on,' Cien said. 'There's some big houses in Warner's Bay. I should know. I've worked in several of them. If, as you are suggesting, the attacker is a groundsman, he could have been working in the grounds of the home where the woman died,'

'He *could* have been, but I don't think he was anything to do with that attack. He operates in his comfort zone. And this will be where he's likely to live as well.'

'How do you know the locations of all the attacks?' Conor asked her.

'After picking up the news on them, I've followed the police and observed what they're doing.'

'How did you know which police to follow?'

'I've identified some who are working on the cases. And in other instances, information has been revealed on the news – the approximate location where the attack took place. I've then driven around until I've seen the press vehicles or streets the police have cordoned off.'

'You really have put a lot of time into this haven't you?' Conor said with admiration in his voice, Cien noted.

'Yes. I have a vested interest in doing so.'

'Understandably,' Conor said nodding. 'You think he's a groundsman? If that's the case, how do we find out his name? We can't just ring up the Council and ask for the name of all their employees who work in the parks.'

'Cien has the registration number of a car that a kid at the Georgetown flats noted down. And we also know he has red hair thanks to the kid. I've watched the police visit a man with red hair in Mayfield twice. We could check out his place tonight to see if he has a car with a matching registration.'

'I spoke to the chief superintendent in charge of the police last week. He said they had a man in their sights. He didn't mention he had red hair or anything about him though,' Conor said.

'Was that Detective Chief Inspector Frank Bailey?'

'No. Chief Superintendent Mitchell. He's the one who speaks to the press. I saw him at the golf club. He's an old golfing buddy of our father's. Who's this Frank Bailey?'

'He's the senior investigating officer.'

'Never heard of him. Okay, what do you think about Kaede's suggestion Cien? Once Mairead's home I could link up with Kaede to do that this evening.'

Cien wanted to avoid Kaede and Conor spending time together.

'No, it's fine. I'll go. If there's any trouble it's best only one of us cops it. Best if you stay out of it.'

'I don't want to stay out of it. And checking whether this bloke's car matches the one the kid saw isn't going to get me into any trouble.'

No but being with Kaede might. Cien didn't trust her. She was a real femme fatal. One with a deadly intent. And he suspected she would use her beauty to manipulate Conor into doing things he shouldn't. But he could see that he wasn't going to dissuade Conor. And it *would* be good to spend an evening home with Jess.

'Okay. You two sort it out then. In the meantime, I'll drop you back to your car Kaede.'

'I think we should have some refreshments before you do that. I haven't been a very hospitable host,' Conor said.

# 29

Rachel knocked at the door of number six, holding her identification ready. A young woman answered, her face beaming with delight when she saw Rachel. She had a beautiful smile.

'Hello, are you Kirra?' The woman nodded. 'I'm Detective Senior Sergeant Sharpe,' she said. 'I wonder if I might ask you and your brother some questions.'

'Morequestionsurecomeincomein,' she said gesturing with her arms open as she stepped back. Rachel had the impression she was looking at an overweight child trapped in an adult body. The woman was dressed in a white frilly blouse and pink gathered skirt that you'd expect to see on a young girl. She was wearing white socks and slippers. Her hair hung in long ringlets down past her shoulders. The woman had a speech impediment and spoke without a defined break in her words. Rachel had come across this before. She knew she'd have to listen very carefully to everything Kirra said.

Rachel stepped into an open plan lounge which had a kitchen sectioned off with a peninsular in the left-hand corner. The place was a little untidy but appeared to be clean. A young man was sitting at the window holding an exercise book and some sort of small gadget. After he'd finished writing in his book, he looked towards her but not at her, with his head turned to the side and smiled.

'Hello Penn,' she said.

'Wastheinformationwegavethismorninghelpful?'

'I'm sorry could you repeat that Kirra?' she asked the woman.

Rachel thought Kirra had just said she'd given information to another detective this morning. That couldn't be right. Tyler hadn't been back today. And he was the only one who had been knocking on doors in the complex. She *had* heard her correctly as Kirra repeated exactly the same question.

'Are you saying you gave some information to a detective this morning?'

'Yes.'

'Was it the same man who spoke to you the other day?'

'Noadifferentone.'

'Okay.' She didn't want to alarm Kirra, but perhaps she needed to make her think carefully about letting strangers in to her home. 'I don't think he was from the police Kirra. You need to check people's identification.' Rachel suspected it was probably one of the journalists from a newspaper or someone from one of the television stations.

'Heshowedmeit.'

'Like this?' Rachel said, showing her ID again.

Kirra shrugged.

'What information did you give the man?'

'PennlethimseehisbookbutthenPenngotupsetsoIasked himtoleave.'

She turned to Penn. So far, he hadn't spoken. He was now frowning and flicking pages back in his exercise book. He stopped and held it out to his sister.

'Can Penn talk?'

'Notreallyalittlebit,' Kirra said as she walked over and took the book from her brother.

'Do you know what upset Penn?'

'Yesthis,' she said pointing vaguely to a couple of entries in the book. There was a car registration and a description of a man who had red hair. Beside it he'd written 9 and Birdy. The numbers must represent flats. The registration was vaguely familiar. Taking out her notebook Rachel jotted down the details, and Penn's word for word description of the red-haired man. Later the same night, he'd made an entry about 'Red' with a 4 and key written beside it. Flat 4 was Rhonda Newland's. This was really incredible. Penn had potentially seen Rhonda's murderer. And she realised why she recognised the car colour and its registration. It belonged to Robbie McDonald. They had him now.

'Can I take a photo of what you've written on this page Penn?'

He nodded, still not looking at her. The boy was clearly able to understand everything that was said to him.

'Rrred,' Penn said with difficulty.

'Yes, I know,' Rachel said. 'Thank you, Penn. This has been very helpful.'

'I need to leave now,' Rachel said turning to Kirra. 'But I will call back tomorrow. Don't let anyone else into your flat please. Only me, or someone with me.'

'Ihavetogoouttotheshopsmostdays.'

'I'll see if I can get a policeman to take you to the shops Kirra. I'm going to have some police in uniforms sent over to watch the place like they did last week. Does Penn ever go out with you?'

'HegoesouttoadaycentreonThursdayshedidn'tgolast week.'

'Okay, well if he wants to go this week, we'll have a policeman take him.'

Rachel was worried that if word got out about Penn being able to identify Rhonda Newlands' potential killer, the killer could pay them a little visit. The fake detective who'd visited that morning could be linked to the killer. The two siblings were very vulnerable.

'You mean I get to ride in a police car to go to the shops?'

'YoumeanIgettorideinapolicecartogototheshops?,' Rachel told her.

As soon as she stepped outside the flat, Rachel phoned the Chief explaining what she had discovered. He said he would organise protection immediately and agreed they had to pick McDonald up for questioning. He arranged to meet her outside the bank where McDonald worked.

'That's Senior Sergeant Rachel Sharp, Bailey's sidekick,' Kaede said pointing to a woman who they'd seen leaving flat six. Intending to drop Kaede off, Cien stopped the car and watched while the detective made a call. 'She's obviously picked up the same information that you did this morning and is organising something. I say we follow her.'

'How do you know her—'

She tapped her nose.

'Quit with your probing questions Cien. I told you earlier I've been following them. And I have contacts but I'm never going to tell you who they are. Okay?'

'Right. Like a reporter who will never reveal his or her sources.'

'Exactly. She's heading off. Follow her.'

Despite feeling like telling her to go to hell, Cien reversed out and obeyed.


The detective stopped outside the National Bank Headquarters; parking illegally. Cien pulled into a meter spot and waited. A few minutes later a couple of squad cars arrived. Several uniformed police officers and a man in a smart short sleeve shirt, tie and trousers stepped out the cars.

'That's DCI Frank Bailey,' Kaede said. 'Looks like we're going to see some action.'

Ten minutes later they watched as the police marched a red-haired man out to one of the cars. He was handcuffed.

'That's the man I saw the female detectives questioning – twice,' Kaede said.

'They're obviously arresting him. He *has* got red hair, just like the kid noted.'

'Duh, you don't say.'

'Hey enough of that. The kid saw him in the dark, he might not have been right.'

'Okay, fair enough.'

'You won't need to meet up with Conor now. They

have their man. And you were wrong about him being a groundsman. Looks like he's an office worker.'

'Hmm. Maybe. I still think it would be useful to meet up with Conor and check out the guy's place. He doesn't live alone. I saw another man going in and out of the house. We could pretend to be reporters. I'll grab a camera to take with us. Joe public usually likes to be featured in the news. The housemate might have some interesting information to give us. I want to know he's definitely our man,' she said pointing to the cars that were now speeding away.

# 30

McDonald demanded the presence of a lawyer before he would answer any questions. They were waiting for the duty lawyer to turn up before they could start. Frank had obtained another search warrant for McDonald's house, car, office and mobile phone. He'd sent DSC Patel and DC Walker to oversee the process which was starting at McDonald's home. Last time, the warrant had only allowed them to search his rucksack and collect the clothes he'd been wearing on the night of Carrie Ross's attack. As McDonald used public transport to travel to work, Frank arranged for McDonald's car to be collected and taken to a police garage. They were hoping to find the photographs the attacker had taken from each victim in one of their search locations.

'We finally have the results from McDonald's clothing. It has Carrie Ross's DNA on it,' Frank told Rachel.

'Don't forget he said Carrie launched herself at him. And she confirmed she'd been *close* to him and some of the others. Do we have McDonald's DNA results yet?'

'No. You know how bloody slow they are. I've asked them to expedite it but they have to send it away to Sydney.

177

I don't see why we can't have labs here rather than using Sydney. The Chief Super said it will happen soon. Not soon enough for me. Waiting for Sydney to get their act together is a pain in the butt.'

Frank's desk phone rang. 'Ah this might be news of the duty lawyer's arrival.'

After going through the legal preliminaries Frank launched into his first question.

'Can you explain why your car was parked outside a flat in Georgetown between the hours of 8pm and 10.33 pm Tuesday 22nd November?'

McDonald looked surprised as though this wasn't what he'd expected to be asked. He leaned over and whispered to his lawyer who nodded at him.

'I was visiting a sick friend.'

'And who might that be?' Frank knew from information Rachel had gathered from the boy's notes that McDonald had visited Bert Mills – known as Birdy to his friends, in flat nine. But he wanted to hear what McDonald had to say about his visit.

'Birdy Mills. We were at Uni together and played on the same league team during our years there.'

'I see. And did you often visit Mr. Mills?'

'No, I hadn't seen him for years. A mutual acquaintance at the tennis club told me Birdy was ill and dying of cancer. I was given his address and decided to pay him a visit straight away. I called around there after leaving the tennis club. His sister, Connie, has been staying with him and can corroborate everything I'm telling you. I've since learned Birdy died in hospital a day or so later. Birdy's sister phoned to let me know.'

Tyler hadn't made a note of the sister's presence. Frank would need to find out why.

'We will be checking with Mr. Mills' sister,' Frank said. 'But we will need the name of the mutual friend from the tennis club.'

McDonald nodded. 'No problem.'

'You left in your car at ten thirty-three but returned at eleven twelve pm on foot. You were seen entering Rhonda Newland's flat.'

'What?' McDonald's eyes widened in shock and he began shaking his head. 'No. I went straight home, had a shower and went to bed.'

'Was your lodger home that night? Could he verify what you've just told us?' Rachel asked him.

'Normally he would be. But he was out when I arrived back home. I don't know what time he came in as I was asleep. I certainly didn't go back to where Birdy lives. Why would I? Rhonda Newland's the woman who was found murdered wasn't she? I had nothing to do with that. I didn't know her and I've never spoken to her.'

'When Detective Patel and I interviewed you, you failed to mention that you had been visiting the same complex of flats on the night Rhonda Newland died,' Rachel said.

'I didn't realise she lived in the same place as Birdy when I read about her murder. It was only when the Herald mentioned the Aboriginal Housing in Georgetown in yesterday's paper that I learned where she lived.'

'Why didn't you come forward then?' Frank asked him.

'I ... to be honest it never ...'

The duty lawyer interrupted McDonald's response. He placed a hand on McDonald's arm and leant across to whisper in his ear.

'On the advice of my lawyer, I'm saying nothing further.'

'I think that would be foolish Mr. McDonald. If you have nothing to hide then it is in your best interests to answer our questions.'

McDonald looked across to his lawyer who shook his head.

'No comment,' McDonald said.


'Don't you just hate lawyers who advise their clients to say 'no comment'' Rachel moaned as they re-entered the squad room and headed towards the Chief's office.

'We need more evidence. He's claiming he drove straight home from the flats on Tuesday night. We should be able to pick him up on at least a couple of CCTVs to prove whether that's the case. I'll get one of the analysts onto it. To get from the flats to his house would have taken about ten minutes. That puts him at say ten-forty-three. He's an athlete. It would have been feasible for him to have jogged back to the flats enabling him to arrive there at eleven twelve pm. The time when the boy noted him entering Rhonda Newland's flat. How reliable would you say the boy is?'

Rachel watched as the Chief pulled his chair out, lowered himself onto it with exaggerated force (which indicated he was not happy) and swung around to face her, eyebrows raised.

'Very reliable. About the times he noted anyway. It's what he seems to do all day when he's home.'

'We need that exercise book to be submitted into evidence. It would be useful to spend time looking through it to see what else young Tiller made a note of.'

'Yes. I've thought about that. I suspect he'll become very upset about us taking his book. We'll have to give him a replacement. I'm not sure that will be enough to placate him though.'

'It's curious that the boy said the man entering Rhonda Newland's flat had a key. How could McDonald get hold of a key? That's the part I can't make sense of.'

'I've been thinking about that. Could Bert Mills have held a spare key for Rhonda? You know, in case she locked herself out. If he did, it might have been labelled with her flat number. Mills' sister might be able to enlighten us on that score. If Bert did have a key, it's possible that McDonald took it. We need to speak to Connie Mills to determine whether McDonald would have had the opportunity. The hospital will have a record of her name and contact details.'

'Okay, you get onto that. I'll check with forensics to see if they found more than one key in the Newland flat and whether they've tested them for fingerprints. It's not listed amongst the evidence that has come through so far from them. Everything is so bloody slow it's agonising. Fingerprints are the quickest and easiest thing for them to deal with for goodness' sake. The Chief Super wants to make an announcement about McDonald. Not revealing his name of course, although I'm sure the press will get hold of it soon enough. I told him I thought it was too early, but he's insisting on doing it. Saying that we need to alleviate the public's anxiety. More like he wants to put a stop to the likes of Jeff Wheeler complaining about police incompetency. We didn't even manage to ask him a single question about Becky Wheeler. I think we're going to look incompetent if McDonald turns out not to be our man.'

'You don't think he is?'

'I don't know. He has links to several of our cases now. But it could be argued that those links are all circumstantial. Newcastle is not exactly a sprawling metropolis. The links through the university and tennis club could quite easily be co-incidental. We need to check his alibi for the nights Tessa Cooper, Melody Hudson and Becky Wheeler were attacked. If his bloody lawyer hadn't told him to clam up, we might have been able to pick up that information today. It could prove his innocence.'

'Hmm. Or guilt. It certainly appears that he had the means and opportunity with Carrie Ross's attack and now Rhonda Newland's. He claims he was with a friend the night Melody was attacked but we haven't verified that as yet or the time they parted company. But you're right. We need to pin down his alibis for all the attacks.'

'If we knew who victims one and four were it would help. In principle anyway.'

'Yes, I agree.'

Rachel would have liked to share her thoughts with the Chief but felt he wasn't in the right frame of mind. He was having doubts and concerns about McDonald just as she was. After arriving at the Georgetown flats this afternoon, which was the first time she'd been there, she'd returned to her original theory about the perpetrator possibly being a gardener or groundsman. But now was not the time to air it. She decided she'd make some discreet calls before she did. There had been nothing amongst the reports from Lowry or Tyler about who managed the Georgetown flats and that was one of the first things she would have expected them to find out.

'There is another way we could check out McDonald's alibis for the attacks. With his lodger, Sam Foley. I don't think they're exactly good mates or anything but they do share the same house. Ayesha spoke to him when we went to McDonald's. I could ask her to call on him with Chris and see whether he can recall the dates in question.'

'Yes, do that,' he said nodding. 'Right, we'd better get cracking then. I'll make some calls and do my best not to lose my temper. We'll have another stab at McDonald at seven pm. I'll get the duty sergeant to warn McDonald's lawyer. We might have some more relevant information by then.'

Rachel slid out of his office and closed the door quietly behind her. She could understand the Chief's frustration. The cases they were dealing with were urgent and the labs should be giving them priority over everything else. The problem with having to send their DNA evidence to Sydney for processing, was that it was a much larger city and would therefore have many more crimes to deal with. Newcastle DNA results would not take priority.

She knew the number of the hospital switchboard without needing to look it up. Picking up her desk phone she dialled it.

# 31

Kaede called for Conor at 6pm as they'd agreed. They decided to travel in his car in case the police had noticed her following them. She didn't think they'd clocked her, but you never knew with the police.

'Drive past the intersection first so we can see if there's any police activity.'

The man's house was at the end of a street on the left and Kaede could see several police cars and a van outside it.

'They're here. Damn. That means they could be here for hours yet.'

'What do you want to do?'

After thinking about it for a few seconds Kaede said, 'I say we call on Jeff Wheeler. He's the brother of the Waratah victim and was interviewed by the press this morning. I know he lives in Whitebridge; the press foolishly gave out his location. I looked in the phone book for Wheelers in that suburb and there's two listed. Only one with the initial J. Well in fact it was listed as J & M Wheeler. The 'J' could stand for 'Jeff' spelled with a 'J' rather that a 'G'. We could see if he's willing to talk to us. He made it clear in this morning's interview that he's not happy with the police.'

'Do we explain who we are?'

'Yes, otherwise he'll just think we're more journos. Your brother thought I was one until I convinced him otherwise. We don't have to give him our full names.'

'He might report us to the police.'

'He might. But somehow, I doubt it. I've got the address on a slip of paper in my pocket. What do you reckon? Shall we do it?'

'I'm not willing to knock on his door if there's loads of press parked outside. They would take photos of us.'


'How do I know you're not journalists?' Jeff Wheeler asked when they explained why they'd come to see him. He'd turned out to be the right Wheeler. Kaede recognised him immediately. He wasn't as tall as she'd imagined from seeing him on T.V. He was only about 1.7 metres. Thankfully there were no press at his house.

'Without revealing our full identities to you, you don't. And we're not willing to do that as you might go the police. I don't want to be another one of their *cases*. Neither does his sister,' Kaede said pointing to Conor. She had introduced herself and Conor as 'Miss K and Mr. C.' 'We're not breaking any laws by not reporting the attacks.' Taking her sunglasses off she added, 'This is one of the souvenirs he left me with.'

'Your sister sadly didn't have the same choice as us,' Conor said.

Wheeler's body seemed to slump at the mention of his

sister. 'I know, and I still have another sister who could be at risk. Okay, you can come in, but we'd better talk in my study. I don't want my family involved.'

Wheeler's study was a room on the left located at the front of the house. Using arm gestures, he ushered them in, invited them to sit and closed the door behind him.

'Okay, tell me what you've discovered so far. Detective Bailey called me a short while ago to inform me that they're questioning a man. What can you tell me about him?'

Kaede filled them in on everything she knew, which was where the suspect lived, where he worked, the number of times she'd seen him being questioned by two of the female detectives in Bailey's team, and the car he drove, including that his number plate matched the one that the boy at the Georgetown flats had noted down.

'The one thing I don't know is his name. We were hoping to speak to his housemate this evening but the police are there – presumably searching the place.'

'My sister Sarah knows his name. She was questioned about a member of the tennis club she manages. He has red hair and lives in Mayfield. Sounds like he's our man then. Let me go and speak to Sarah. She's staying with us at the moment. It's too dangerous for her to be in her house in case he comes calling again.'

They waited while Wheeler left them alone. Conor remained in his seat while Kaede started nosing around the study, rifling through papers on the desk.

'Will you stop snooping,' Conor hissed at her. 'Come and sit back down.'

With some reluctance as there were quite a few drawers she would have liked to look through, she made her way back to her seat. 'Looks like Wheeler has his own company – selling security and surveillance equipment from what I can make out. It would have been handy to have a few surveillance pieces while I was carrying out my investigations. Binoculars and a camera were about all I had. I have a mini tape recorder that I hoped to use tonight on the lodger but I doubt I'll get to use it.'

The door swung open and Wheeler strode back in. 'Robbie McDonald is his name. Sarah doesn't think his full name is Robert as he's registered at the club under Robbie. So, what do you propose to do now he's in custody? Surely there's nothing else to be done.'

'The police can only go ahead with a prosecution if they have enough evidence. What if they don't have that? What if they release him and he carries on raping and killing women? I, for one, am not prepared to let that happen,' Kaede said.

'I would agree with you,' Wheeler said. 'So, is it a case of wait and see?'

'I want to keep gathering information on him. He's not as I imagined. I'd worked out that he was a groundsman or gardener. Someone who worked close to the homes of the women he attacked. But it seems I was wrong.'

'Inspector Bailey told me a man was being *questioned*. They haven't arrested him yet. What does McDonald do at the bank? You said that's where they picked him up.'

'I don't know what his work is. I was hoping his housemate could fill us in on that.'

'I had to do a formal identification of my sister earlier this afternoon at the morgue. I couldn't face driving home straight away so I went up to the hospital canteen for a cup of coffee. As you can imagine we didn't get much sleep last night. While I was sitting there a man approached me. His name was Michael Ross. He's the father of the young woman who was attacked in the park. She's still recovering in hospital. He recognised me from the interview I gave this morning – which I'm now regretting. Those bloody idiots mentioned the suburb I live in and a couple of press cars descended on us a few hours later. I told them to piss off and that there'd be no more interviews. Anyway, Ross isn't happy with the police investigation either and congratulated me on saying something.'

'Perhaps we should meet up with him?' Kaede suggested.

'I don't know if he'd be up for that. He gave me his mobile number in case I heard anything. I could give him a ring.'

# 32

After several phone calls, Rachel managed to track down Connie Mills who confirmed McDonald's story of being her brother's friend from his university days and that she had been there throughout his visit. However, she had no idea whether her brother had held keys for other residents. She told Rachel she'd noticed a number of keys in a small bowl in one of his drawers but didn't know which locks they fitted. She agreed to meet Rachel at Bert's flat in an hour. That should give her enough time to make it back in time to resume McDonald's interview.

'I haven't been back here since Bert went into hospital. I'm sorry but the place is a bit of a mess,' Connie Mills said.

'Don't worry about that. You've had your hands full and then grieving. How long had your brother been ill?' Rachel could see the couch was covered in bedding which was presumably where her brother slept during his last days at home. A glass, half filled with water, sat on a coffee table in front of the couch.

'He received his diagnosis sixteen months ago. But he

was already pretty unwell by that time. He had to stop work and lost his flat. That's how come he ended up here. He'd worked at Bunnings stocking shelves and no longer had the physical energy to do that. Four years of a university degree and he ends up working at a DIY store.'

'What did he study at Uni?'

'He trained as a physiotherapist. Thought that would lead him into the field of sport's injuries. He had a job at John Hunter but he lost that after he got into a fight with a patient. The patient attacked Bert because he didn't want to be touched by a blackfella. Bert was simply defending himself. The hospital administrators chose to believe the whitefella because it was the second time Bert had become involved in an altercation with an abusive patient. That time he defended himself though. Bunnings was the only place he could find work after that.'

'Sounds like Bert had some very unpleasant experiences. Is there always so much prejudice?'

'Yeah. There is. It wasn't too bad when I was at school but after that, things have not been easy. I think men cop the worst of it. I trained as a nurse and there's always a shortage of them. But like Bert experienced with a few of his patients, some people make it obvious they don't want me to touch them. I just shrug it off and tell them they'll have to wait until someone else is available. I see it as their problem, not mine. I took long service leave recently to look after Bert. After his funeral I'll be returning – once I've cleared out this place that is.'

'I assume Bert had treatment?'

'Yeah, two rounds of chemo and a number of radiation treatments. But none of it worked and just made him feel like shit he said. He regretted having the treatment as he said it prevented him from having months of a half decent life before the cancer progressed to its final stages.'

Connie walked into the kitchen and pulled open a drawer. 'This is the drawer where I saw the keys.'

Using gloves, Rachel lifted the bowl out and examined them. There were three sets in there and one single key.

'One set might be a spare of Bert's. Do you want to compare them?' Connie asked, offering the set she'd used to gain entry.

'I'd say these were his spare keys,' Rachel said putting one set aside that matched.

The next set had a cheap coloured tag attached with the word or name DOT written on it in capital letters.

'Do you know if there is a resident here called Dot?'

'Ah yes, she's the elderly woman in flat twelve.'

So, Bert did hold spare keys for at least one of the tenants. The final set of two keys had no tag attached and gave no indication of who or what they were linked to. There was a small key and what looked like a door key.

'That looks like a locker key,' Connie said, pointing to the smaller one. 'Maybe they are an old set to the changing rooms at his Uni. He might have held onto them for sentimental reasons. At one point, Bert had hopes of being able to play professionally. He tried out for various league teams just before he started uni but wasn't taken on. He thought it was prejudice because of his skin colour. He was very good you know. The best in the Uni team. Everyone said that. But in his final year he received a knee injury that put paid to his playing days. Some bastard in the opposing team tackled him unnecessarily hard.'

Connie stopped there, Rachel suspecting the unspoken words being that the tackle which had ended Bert's career had been a racist attack. She wouldn't be surprised. There'd been stories of indigenous league players in Sydney being on the receiving end of rough treatment from the odd white player.

'That single key looks like the back door one,' Connie said after a minute of silence.

Rachel looked up in surprise. 'The flats have a backyard?' Her first impressions of the flats when she'd been here earlier was that they virtually backed up to the surrounding fences.

'A miniscule paved courtyard with one of those long narrow clotheslines. It's accessed off the hallway. The whole layout is a stupid design, especially the bathroom as it's a laundry and bathroom combined. I guess it's better than having the washing machine in the kitchen when there's this open-plan layout.'

'I'd like to see the backyard. But before we do that can I ask whether you noticed Mr. McDonald in the kitchen at any point during his visit?'

'I didn't *see* him in there. I grabbed the opportunity to take a shower while he was here. I left the two of them to reminisce. When I returned, they had mugs of tea in front of them which I know Robbie must have made. Bert wasn't up to it.'

It was highly likely then that McDonald would have opened the cutlery drawer looking for a teaspoon. The bowl of keys had been sitting right in front of the cutlery tray and therefore would have been a simple matter for him to both examine and remove a set.

'Okay. Thanks. If we could see the yard now?'

Following Connie into a hallway she could see it led to first a bathroom and then, after a set of storage cupboards, the single bedroom. Straight ahead was the back door. Connie removed the key and compared it to the one Rachel was holding.

'Yep. As I thought.' She reinserted the key and opened the door, allowing Rachel to move past her.

Rachel stepped out to a small paved yard and saw that each flat was divided off by a slatted fence that had wide gaps. At the end of the fence there was an opening. She walked over and looked. Anybody could walk along the length of the flats. Neighbours could also call into each other's flats without the need of using the front doors.

A narrow wall mounted clothes line above the bedroom window projected out into the yard and held four lengths of line. She noticed a small gas boiler also attached to the wall – the same as she had in her house. It dispensed with the need for a large electric water tank and provided constant hot water.

At the back of the yard were bushes, screening the flats from the next-door premises.

'Who takes care of trimming the bushes here?' she asked Connie.

'The maintenance men. They clean up after themselves also so tenants only have to take care of their yard strips.'

'How often are the bushes trimmed?'

Connie shrugged. 'I'm not sure. I noticed they'd been done one day when I went to hang washing out. Only the once since I've been looking after Bert. They must have done the work while I was out shopping. They do out the front and sides more regularly.'

'One more thing before I leave. Do you know who Bert paid his rent to? I know the complex is owned by NSW Aboriginal Housing, but who manages it on their behalf?'

'I couldn't tell you. Not without going through all his bank statements and paperwork. I know he paid by direct debit. He told me that when I came to nurse him. I'd asked him if there were any financial details I'd need to attend to like rent, rates or electricity. He paid everything by direct debit. I can check through the paperwork if you want, but it might take me a while.'

'No, don't worry, I'm sure you have enough to deal with. I'll phone the Aboriginal Housing office. Okay I've seen enough. Thanks for meeting me here, Connie. I need to return to headquarters. Thanks for your time and I'm sorry about Bert.'

Rachel waved to Penn as she approached her car, knowing he'd be jotting down her details. She looked up and saw him waving back. She was reluctant to attempt to remove his exercise book today. She didn't have a replacement to offer him. Maybe tomorrow morning. She'd deal with that first thing.


Rachel headed straight for the Chief's office when she returned.

'Any joy?' he asked her.

'Yes. Bert Mills had a set of keys in his cutlery drawer belonging to one of his neighbours. The owner's name was on a tag. He might have held a similar set for Rhonda. McDonald made tea for himself and Bert while he was there and would have seen them if he was looking for a teaspoon.'

'Did the label have the flat number on it?'

'No. But McDonald could have asked him who Dot and Rhonda were. Dot is elderly so would have been quickly discounted. Bert may not have thought twice about saying what flat numbers they were in. McDonald could have pocketed a set a set of keys to Rhonda's. This is all supposition though.'

'Yes, but another point to raise with him. The techs found two sets of keys at Rhonda's. They *had* fingerprinted them but only picked up a couple of smudged prints that weren't any use.'

'That's disappointing.'

'Yes. If McDonald took Rhonda's keys that means it wasn't a pre-planned attack. He couldn't have known what she looked like. Unless he'd been observing the flats prior to his visit – or saw her entering her flat as he arrived. I managed to get hold of McDonald's friend who he claimed told him about Bert. I've only spoken to him on the phone, but he backs up McDonald's statement that he only heard about Bert on the day of his visit.'

'It's not looking good for an arrest, is it? Not unless we find something else? Have they found the photographs?'

'No. They're weren't at his place of employment. Or in his car. They haven't finished at the house yet. I had hoped to hear from them before resuming his interview but it doesn't look as though we will.' He looked at his watch and announced 'It's time to resume the interview with our friend.'

# 33

**Tuesday**

The morning brought further relief from the unbearably hot, humid weather they'd been having. Frank could immediately tell, even at 6am that the temperature had dropped considerably. Not that that always meant it would be cooler; it was the humidity that was the killer. They'd had temperatures in the mid-thirties most days over the past few weeks. One day it had dropped to 20° but high humidity remained so it was still deeply unpleasant. He'd known the temperature to soar to the 40s with low humidity and he'd barely break into a sweat, but necessitated drinking lots of fluid to avoid dehydration. Especially if you were exposed to the sun's rays. He opened the French doors and stepped out onto the back veranda, immediately feeling the benefit of a gentle breeze. He was exhausted after days with little sleep. Although he'd been more comfortable last night, he'd slept with one ear on alert waiting for a phone call – which thankfully never came. There were aspects of this case that were puzzling. If Veronica Graf was not one of the serial rapist's victims and there were no further attacks last night, then it was the second week running where their perpetrator had not attacked anyone on a Sunday or Monday. Why those particular days? If it was only Sunday, it might suggest some religious significance. But Monday as well – that didn't fit. Of course, they may not have had any attacks last night because Robbie McDonald was in custody. But he doubted that. McDonald just didn't *feel* right.

They'd questioned him again last night at length but for the better part of the interview he'd repeated 'no comment.' However, when they raised the issue of whether he'd removed Rhonda Newland's flat keys from a drawer in Bert Mills' place McDonald had reacted with righteous indignation.

'I offered to make Bert a tea because I was on the verge of bursting into tears seeing my old team mate so weak and close to death. I knew he'd hate that so moving into the kitchen gave me the opportunity to pull myself together. I made us both a plain green tea leaving the t-bags steeping so I didn't have any need of a *bloody spoon* or anything else from his kitchen drawers!' McDonald had said, his voicing rising in pitch as he spoke.

Frank believed him. Rachel had also.

He was brought back to the present by Beth's arms enfolding him.

'There's a lovely breeze out here this morning,' she said. 'Penny for them?'

'Oh, I was just thinking about the suspect we questioned last night,' he said turning to face her.'

'You think he's your man? I noticed the phone didn't ring last night.'

'I don't know,' he said shaking his head. 'Circumstantial evidence puts him in the frame. But solid forensic evidence is lacking.'

'You've achieved convictions on circumstantial evidence in the past.'

'I know but that was different. We *knew* they were guilty.'

'What is your gut telling you Frank Bailey?'

'That he's not our man.'

'There you are then. There's no more to be said. I'd trust your gut instincts any day. You married me, didn't you?'

Rachel was waiting outside K-Mart in Waratah Village. She'd thought they opened early like Coles, but no such luck. They didn't open until 8am. She'd nipped into Coles hoping to pick up an exercise book but they had none. While she was there, she used the opportunity to stock up on non-perishable items they needed at home and loaded the bags into her car. She still had five minutes until K-Mart opened so began reflecting on this morning's tasks. After collecting Penn's exercise book, she planned to examine it in detail; if she could make sense of it. Then she needed to make two phone calls. The first to the aboriginal Housing Office – she knew they had a branch in Newcastle and a second call to the school near Becky Wheeler's place. When they'd provided her with names and addresses she required, there would be visits to make.

The Chief said he'd call her if anything happened overnight. He hadn't phoned so she had to assume all was quiet. The temperature had plummeted last night and the humidity eased, enabling her to sleep with greater comfort. She wondered if there was any truth in the comments made by the ex-Queensland detective based in Sydney, that the hot humid weather sent people 'troppo' and was likely to be what triggered the current attacks. She knew she found it difficult to think clearly in hot humid weather. She knew the Chief was the same. Her body would feel as though it was on fire and cool shower water only provided temporary relief. Less than five minutes out of a shower and it would be as though she hadn't had one. There was no way she could live in a country that experienced sticky humid weather for much of the year. At least in this part of Australia it came in short waves.


Kirra greeted Rachel with one of her huge smiles and invited her into the flat.

'I'm afraid I need to take Penn's exercise book. It may contain evidence that we need,' Rachel explained. 'I've bought him some new ones.' She'd made sure she selected orange ones to match the ones Penn had been using. She knew that small details like that were important to people on the autistic spectrum and Penn was sure to be the same.

'Hewon'tbehappyaboutthatbuthestartedanewone yesterday.'

'He started a new one? Oh, that's great,' Rachel said with relief, hoping that would mean Penn would be okay with her taking his old one.

Penn finished scribbling and, turning his head to the side, gave her one of his huge smiles and a wave which she reciprocated. She wasn't sure if he saw her wave as he wasn't looking at her. He'd picked up a small electronic gadget and started tapping on it, his attention totally focused on the screen in front of him.

Kirra spoke to him in what Rachel assumed was their indigenous language. Penn ignored her. She moved closer to him and repeated herself. Penn stopped tapping his screen.

'It's so we can catch Rhonda's killer, Penn,' Rachel said moving towards him. 'We need your book. You've been very helpful in recording important information. I bought you some new books.'

She held the books out for Penn who with a sideways look, viewed them suspiciously. After putting his current book, pen and electronic gadget on the window ledge, he stood and took wary steps towards her. She was startled by Penn grabbing the exercise books and moving with lightning speed across the room to a bed. She hadn't been sure about Penn's mobility as she'd always seen him sitting down in the window but he certainly had no problem with movement. He sat on the bed and after examining them in great detail he nodded and, pulling aside a makeshift curtain, he placed the exercise books on the shelf of a bookcase revealed behind it. In the brief glimpse she had of the bookcase before he dropped the curtain back into place, Rachel saw that it was full of exercise books. Penn's life.

Penn remained sitting on the bed, his head facing the floor. She waited. After what seemed like an eternity he stood and moved to the other side of the bookcase, pulled the curtain aside and retrieved an exercise book from a long line of them he'd propped upright. She hoped it was the one she needed. He walked back across the room and without making eye contact, handed her the book.

A quick glance at the last few pages confirmed it covered the dates she needed. What was strange was that, after the last entry dates, which was the day of her visit, he'd filled the remaining pages with Red, written over and over again. Looking at Penn she said, 'Thank you.' He didn't raise his head.

'Pennmustlikeyouhewouldn'tdothatformostpeople.'

'Is everything okay with your police escorts?' Rachel asked, pointing to the patrol car sitting outside the flat. The chief had arranged 24-hour protection, insisting that the siblings remained together and needed to be driven anywhere they needed to go. 'Have you had a ride in a police car yet?'

'YesandPennhecamewithusyesterdayhestayedinthecar whileIwentintotheshops.'

'That's good. Until we catch Rhonda's killer, they'll be here every day,' she added.

'R..r..red,' Penn struggled to say.

'Yes, thank you,' Rachel said. 'I have to go now but I'll see you soon.'

# 34

Back in the squad room the Chief's office door was closed
and she could see the outline of a couple of people in there.
She'd catch up with him later. After making herself a coffee
she went to her desk and started leafing through Penn's
exercise book from the beginning. It looked as though
he'd made a note of every single vehicle that had entered
the block over a period of several weeks. He'd also noted
visitors who came on foot, which flats they had entered
and the times of arrival and departure until approximately
11 pm most nights. That must have been when Penn went
to bed. She smiled. This was serious surveillance.

'What are you smiling about?' Tyler asked, appearing
at her shoulder and disturbing her concentration.

'I'm reading through Penn Tiller's notebook. He's
logged, with times, details of vehicles and people he's seen
coming and going at his complex of flats. I was thinking
we could do with a Penn in neighbouring houses at all our
crime scenes.'

'Huh. How do you know if it's accurate? With someone
like that he could be scribbling anything.'

'Did you want something Stuart?'

'The Chief wants to see you.'

'For a full briefing?'

'No. Just you and Paul.'

'Okay, I'll be there in a second.'

She waited until Tyler had turned away before putting Penn's exercise book in her top drawer and locking it. She didn't trust Tyler. If she left it on her desk, he was likely to remove it and start rifling through it himself, making fun of the entries.



'You wanted to see me sir?'

'Yes, to let you know Paul's progress on the Graf case, as you accompanied me to the scene and were at the post-mortem. Also, to let you know my decision on Robbie McDonald. Paul over to you first,' Frank said.

'I've interviewed Nicole Royce. She was the guest at Veronica Graf's on the night of her death. She claims to have left Veronica at ten pm. Neighbours at Royce's place confirmed seeing her car arriving back there at approximately ten fifteen pm. She lives in Belmont so that would be about right. The next-door neighbour saw the car return plus a neighbour a bit further down the road, who was walking his dog, was able to give us the time he left his house. On his return the same dog walker saw her leave the house at approximately ten forty on a bicycle. We've taken her bike in for testing and believe its tyres are a match for tracks outside the Graf house.'

'Do you believe she killed Veronica Graf?'

'Yes. And we have a motive. On closer examination of the footage from the hotel in Sydney where Graf was staying, we picked up Nicole Royce entering his room two nights prior to him returning home. She didn't leave until the morning.'

'So, they're having an affair. You think they plotted the murder together?'

'That's what we believe. We're keeping an eye on their movements. But with any luck we'll have enough forensic evidence to be able to charge her with murder. Whether he was behind it will no doubt be revealed once we question her.'

'As you know, we've been given a pool of uniforms to help us with these cases. A number of them are on surveillance duties with the couple,' Frank said.

'Plus, uniforms are searching the property and the surrounding neighbourhood,' Lowry added.

'So, we were right in thinking it was a copycat.'

'Yes, it would seem so. Now to our number one suspect in the other cases. I'm releasing McDonald. We don't have enough evidence against him. That might change but I'm doubtful. The searches of his house, office and car have yielded nothing. The analyst has come back with her CCTV report. McDonald's car was picked up returning home from the Georgetown flats as he told us. There is no sighting of him returning on foot. *If* he returned on foot, he's likely to have used the Hughes Street pedestrian railway crossing. He wasn't picked up there or on any of the other cameras on the roads. His lodger can't say with one hundred percent certainty that McDonald was home on the nights of the other attacks but he *believes* he was. We simply don't have enough on him. I've asked Paul to let Rhonda Newland's daughter know. I've spoken to Michael

Wheeler. It's just the Ross's who need to be informed right away. I would go over there myself but I've been called to a meeting. Can you pop over to the Royal and see if Carrie Ross's parents are there. I've tried reaching them by phone at home and on their mobiles. There's no answer at home and I think their mobile phones are switched off. If they're still at the hospital they'll have them switched off following hospital rules. I don't want them hearing about our suspect's release on the news. I'm confident neither of you will reveal McDonald's name and will be discreet, but under no circumstances are you to answer any questions anyone raises with you about him.'

'Yes, sir,' Rachel and Lowry chorused.


Michael Ross was furious when Rachel imparted the news that their suspect was being released. He plied Rachel with questions, his anger increasing as she gave him the usual pat answers that their investigations were ongoing and hoped to have more positive news soon. She listened to his tirade for as long as she could stand it then made excuses to leave.

As soon as she returned to the office, she made a call to the Aboriginal Housing Office. Yes, they had a man who carried out the maintenance work at their flats. She was given the name and address of the man who held the contract. A Duncan Doyle. She was about to phone the school near Becky Wheeler's when Ayesha walked into the squad room.

'Morning. What have you been working on this morning?' Rachel asked her.

'Chris and I have been working around Becky Wheeler's neighbourhood at Tyler's request. I've got to report back to him in a minute. Has he been swanning around here all morning?'

'I don't know. He appeared at my desk after I arrived. I think he'd been in with the Chief.'

'Hmm. He said he had a meeting with him which was why he couldn't join us.'

'Did anything positive come of your morning's work?'

'Maybe. I called into the college – or I should say school, and they've given me the name of the man who is in charge of maintaining their grounds. They have a caretaker who does some things but a company comes in every few weeks – at this time of year at least, and mows the bits of lawn and tends to the garden beds at the front.'

'Oh. Let's compare them. I've managed to find out the name of the man who does similar exterior maintenance at the Georgetown flats. Mine's called Duncan Doyle.'

'Ah, not the same. The one who does the school is called Patrick O'Malley.'

'Irish then.'

'Irish name. Doesn't mean he's from Ireland. Look at me,' Ayesha said.

Rachel was looking at her. And Ayesha looked very Anglo Indian. It wasn't until she opened her mouth that anyone would know she was Australian born and bred. Her name alone suggested otherwise.

'Right. Fair enough. Our suspect is being released by the way. The Chief doesn't think he's our man. So, it's back to the drawing board. It might be worth looking at these two maintenance men. How about you and I pay them a visit?'

'You're on. What about Tyler though? He thinks he's got control of me today.'

'I outrank him. Fill him in and tell him I want you with me this afternoon. I thought Rogers was in charge of the Wheeler case anyway?'

'He was, but his wife has given birth prematurely. He had to rush her into hospital early this morning.'

'Oh. I hadn't heard. He's not taking his paternity leave now, is he?'

'I don't know.'

'Right, well I'm going to see if the Chief is back from his meeting and then we can head off when you've finished with Tyler.'

'I wouldn't mind something to eat before we go. I slept in this morning and didn't have time for any breakfast. How about we pick up some sandwiches from the canteen and eat them down at the beach. It's a lovely day, now that hideous humidity has gone. We're allowed a short break, aren't we?'

'Okay. Why not.'

As soon as Ayesha moved away from her desk, Rachel realised the chief hadn't mentioned being in touch with Lisa Tomlinson or Tessa Cooper. She made a quick call to Tessa, whose pessimistic attitude about them ever catching her attacker left Rachel feeling guilty. Next Lisa Tomlinson. As far as she knew Lisa and Melody had returned home against advice. The techs had scoured their house for prints but had found nothing. Their house was in a vulnerable location. The attack on Melody proved that. The chief was worried about a possible revisit from the perpetrator so he'd organised a patrol car to remain outside the house at night. Lisa Tomlinson was adamant they'd be fine and claimed they didn't need it. She'd promised not to take any sleeping aids and was planning on having Melody share her bed until the police made an arrest. Rachel knew the women were aware that they were questioning a person of interest. It had been all over the news anyway. But she needed to let them know about his impending release. She logged back into her computer to find the relevant details and dialled the landline number. Lisa had told her that she was taking leave from her job to be with Melody, who she claimed couldn't go back to work until her black eye had completely healed.

Lisa answered after three rings.

'It's Detective Rachel Sharpe here. I'm ringing to let you know we're releasing the man we've been questioning. Without charge. Our investigation will therefore be ongoing.'

*'Is that because you don't think he's the man who raped Melody or because you don't have enough evidence?'*

'I'm afraid I can't discuss that with you Lisa. Is everything okay with Melody? How's she doing? And, how are you?'

*'We're both fine, thank you. Being careful.'*

Catching sight of the chief returning to his office Rachel made her excuses and said goodbye.

'Is everything okay?' Rachel asked him popping her head

into his office.

'I think it's best if I don't answer that question,' Frank said. Mitchell had bawled him out after he revealed they didn't have enough evidence to charge McDonald. He reminded Mitchell of his request to have DNA testing facilities established in Newcastle and how that would speed things up. He'd then told Mitchell that he didn't think McDonald was their man.

'You and your bloody gut instinct,' Mitchell had yelled at him and went on to say Frank was taking risks with people's lives. He tried to insist that Frank formally charged McDonald, but Frank had remained adamant that it would be impossible to build a case against him. Finally, Mitchell had relented and dismissed Frank with a warning. Mitchell had done this before. Saying he was going to bring someone else in to take over the investigation if Frank didn't get his act together. And threatening to have him transferred out to the back of beyond. Mitchell was largely all bluster but Frank *had* seen him transfer members of the squad to remote outback stations since Mitchell had taken over the post.

'Did you speak to Michael Ross?'

'Yes, he wasn't very happy.' Rachel proceeded to recount what happened.

'Let's hope he doesn't bad-mouth us to the press like Wheeler did. We do need to be looking elsewhere now.'

'On that note – we have the names of a couple of men who are responsible for the maintenance at Georgetown and the school near Becky Wheeler's house. Ayesha and I are going out to interview them this afternoon.'

'Good-oh. Did you pick up the notebook from the Tiller

boy?'

'Yes. I was almost halfway through checking it when Stuart asked me to come in and see you.'

'Pass it to me then. I'd like to see it for myself. I'll finish checking it.'

'Okay. We're going to take a quick sandwich break before we head out. That's okay, isn't it?'

'Of course.'

# 35

'Red hair is common among Irish families,' Rachel said on their walk to the beach. 'Did you know it was because of Irish fighters on the goldfields back in the mid-nineteenth century that red-heads are called Blue, or Bluey?'

'No, I didn't. But I assume that's because when they were fighting, they were considered to be having a 'blue'? Such a funny word for a punch-up, isn't it?'

'Yes. And you're right. It was about the 'blue' or fighting. Apparently, it was common for Irishmen to take part in bare knuckle matches where loads of money changed hands. The fights were called a 'blue' and as many of the Irish participants were red-haired, observers started calling them 'Blue' or 'Bluey'.'

'It's typical of Australians to come up with such crazy labels.'

'Well most of them wouldn't have been *Australian* as such then. Some of them might have been first or second generation who were born here. But many of the immigrants who came out to the goldfields were from the UK. And I suspect it was Englishmen working those goldfields who wouldn't have had a high opinion of the Irish and who originally used Blue or Bluey as a derogatory term. The English considered themselves a cut above the Irish. But as the mix of immigrants widened, and the numbers born here increased, attitudes began to change. The label became an affectionate term and less derogatory; possibly in appreciation of the money that lined their pockets from their wins.'

'And no doubt after spending some of that money on booze,' Ayesha said smiling.

'You're probably right. Shall we sit here?' Rachel said pointing to a bench that looked out across the park to the sea.

They sat and started eating their sandwiches. Ayesha broke the silence saying, 'Isn't that breeze lovely?'

'Hmm,' Rachel said closing her eyes.

'Hey, look over there. Isn't that Becky Wheeler's brother? The one who gave that interview on television bad-mouthing us?'

Rachel opened her eyes. 'Where?'

Ayesha pointed to a picnic bench where she could see three men and one woman sitting around talking. Rachel couldn't make out their facial features as the sun was blinding her. Cupping her hand over her eyes, she scrutinised the group.

'Yes, it is. And the man with the dark hair sitting next to him is Carrie Ross's father Michael. I wonder what they're up to.'

'So, who are the other two?'

'I don't know, but let's move out of their line of sight where we can see *them* more clearly but they can't see us. There – behind that tree,' Rachel said.

Moving off the bench they scuttled over to stand behind a large palm tree. 'I wish I had my camera. I left it in my bag back at headquarters.'

'I don't have mine either. Do you want me to run back and get it?'

'No. We're too far away to capture them in any detail. The other two are probably journalists. I don't recognise them as locals so I'd say they're from one of the Sydney papers.'

The woman who was with them removed her sunglasses and pointed to her left eye. From their position Rachel and Ayesha couldn't see her face clearly or the eye she was pointing to, but after a few seconds Carrie Ross's father nodded and she replaced the glasses.

They looked at each other. 'Are you thinking what I'm thinking?' Ayesha said.

'I'm thinking she was showing Michael Ross a black eye,' Rachel said. 'The woman looks South-east Asian to me. The question is, was she showing her eye to Michael Ross as an example of an assault she's experienced, or is she one of the victims of our serial rapist who hasn't reported it? You know numbers one and four are missing. I can't gauge her height from here but she looks pretty small to me.'

'She seems to be doing a lot of the talking. The other guy with fair hair is nodding to everything she says,' Ayesha said. 'Why don't we go up and speak to them?'

'And say what?'

'I don't know, but I wouldn't mind getting a closer look at the two we don't recognise.'

'No. I think we should return to base and I'll report our

sighting to the Chief. If anyone is going to approach them, I think it should be him.'

'Michael Ross and Jeff Wheeler?' Frank asked. 'And you think the woman was showing Ross a black eye?'

'Yes, and we wondered if she could be one of our missing victims.'

'If she was, that doesn't sound good. It's bad enough that two relatives of our victims are meeting. Hmm. Leave it with me. I'll have a word with Michael Ross. Or I might even stroll down there myself now.'

'Do you want me to come with you?' Rachel asked.

'No. You head off and question those two maintenance contractors.'

Donning a pair of sunglasses Frank grabbed his keys and walked briskly down to the beach, following Rachel's instructions as to where to find the group in question. He was out of luck. The picnic table was empty. They'd gone. Damn. That meant confronting Ross at the hospital. He couldn't face doing it now and the hospital wasn't the best environment to speak to him in. Especially if Ross was planning a verbal assault on the police in cahoots with Jeff Wheeler. If he spoke to Ross at the hospital, Ross's temper might erupt, as had happened when Rachel spoke to him. No, it was best to keep it away from the hospital. He knew Ross returned home most evenings, leaving either his wife or daughter behind to be with Carrie. Rutherford, where the Ross family lived, was only about a 20-minute drive beyond his own house. Frank decided he'd call up there this evening before returning home.

215

# 36

Ayesha grumbled about the pool car they'd been left with that afternoon. It smelt of sweaty male bodies and was littered with empty cartons and food wrappers. 'Probably from members of the drug squad who've been on a stake out,' Rachel said as they did a quick clean up. 'I had use of my favourite one this morning. I think I'm going to have to persuade Andy to let me buy a car. As I live close to work, he claims we don't need a second car. But it's moments like this I'd say we do. The chief has the right idea – always using his own car.'

They'd agreed to approach the Irish contractor first. His headquarters were in Lambton. The odds were that he would be out working on site somewhere and they'd have to wait hours before he or any staff returned but they thought it would be useful to examine his set-up.

O'Malley Maintenance Contractors occupied a large building on the main road into Newcastle. It was a steel-built warehouse with space for several vehicles to pull in off the road. As they parked on the forecourt Ayesha said, 'Note the white pick-up vans. A white pick-up was spotted near Melody Hudson's place and there was that one at the petrol station in Islington near where Carrie Ross was attacked.'

'The one at the petrol station didn't have any writing on the side of it. And the witness who saw the truck near Melody's didn't mention any writing on that either. The one parked at the front here has the name of the company on it. Still, they could have others that don't.'

The shutters were open and they could see another pick-up parked inside. As they walked into the building a man opened an office door to their right and stepped out. He had flaming red hair.

'Help you?' he asked.

'Yes. Police,' Rachel said introducing herself and Ayesha and pulling out her ID. 'Are you Patrick O'Malley?'

'Yes.'

'We'd like to ask you a few questions.'

'Best come into my office then.' He led them past an open office and lounge area where a young woman was busy typing at a desk then through to an office at the rear. He waited until they were both in the room before shutting the door.

'What did you want to speak to me about?' he asked walking behind his desk and taking a seat. He signalled for them to sit on chairs opposite his desk.

'We obtained your name from the Christian School in Waratah and understand your company maintains the grounds there.'

'We do lots of schools across the whole region. Not the state public schools. All the Catholic and other independent ones.'

By Rachel's reckoning that would be a hell of a lot of

schools.

'Do all your work vehicles have the name of your business painted on them?' Ayesha asked.

'The ones owned by our company, yes. When we use a sub-contractor, they use temporary removable ones which attach to the doors of their pick-ups or vans. It's good advertising and I like the public to know who is responsible for the work being carried out at any given site. And people then know who to approach should there be any complaints.'

'Do you get many of those?' Rachel asked.

'No. We've had the odd one over the past eleven years that we've been in business. On some properties there are trees or bushes that overhang public footpaths. When they're trimmed, we have to make sure that everything is cleaned up satisfactorily. We've had a couple of occasions when that hasn't been the case and there has been a complaint. But they are rare.'

'You must have quite a few employees if you work in so many schools,' Rachel said.

'Not that many. We don't need to attend to each school every day. It's a cycle. We have nine full time employees, including me and three sub-contractors.'

'How many of them have red hair?'

'Ah, it's a red hair thing. All of them. It's a prerequisite to working here. You know how red-heads are often bullied and teased at school. Well, we discriminate against other hair colours here to get our own back on them,' he said, keeping his face blank.

Rachel couldn't tell if he was being serious.

'I'm joking of course. Almost. As you can see, I have

red hair. My three brothers and two cousins are red heads as well. Two of our sub-contractors have red hair. So that makes a total of eight out of twelve workers who have red hair. I'm including Sam out there in the office – who doesn't have red hair as you would have noticed.'

'How many of your employees are men?' Ayesha asked.

'Ah, it's only male red-heads you are looking for. Well, that discounts my two cousins then. Six of us including one of the sub-contractors are males. Why do you ask?'

'You may have heard or read about the series of rapes and murders that have been happening in parts of Newcastle?'

'Yes. I have,' he said frowning.

'From evidence collected and eye-witness accounts at the scenes, we know the perpetrator is a red-headed male.'

'I see. There must be many red-heads in Newcastle. Why approach us?'

O'Malley folded his arms and leaned back in his chair. He was taking a defensive stance and Rachel was concerned he might become difficult.

'There are grounds, parks and, of course, the school I mentioned located close to the where each attack took place.'

'We don't do parks or sport's grounds. Unless they're in the grounds of a school which are our main focus. I can't see that you've got much to justify approaching us.'

Arms remained folded with a belligerent look now.

'We're investigating any people we can trace connected to any of the attack sites. The Christian school in Waratah is one of those.'

'Right. And you'd like to collect what from all of us?

DNA I presume for starters. Fingerprints?' O'Malley's voice had taken on a sarcastic tone.

'No. In the first instance, we'd need to know people's movements; their whereabouts on particular dates and times. If they are able to establish solid alibis for those particular dates then we wouldn't need to take DNA or fingerprints. But we would be checking everything out. If for instance someone was unable to provide us with alibis then we'd want to collect DNA and fingerprints.'

'Okay that's fair enough I suppose.'

He unfolded his arms and sat forward.

'I'll have to have a word with my brothers – and the sub-contractor to see if they will oblige you. I'd be willing to provide you with all that you need as long as you give me your assurances that once I'm eliminated you will destroy anything I've given you. That my name won't be held on any police data base.'

'We can assure you that would be the case.'

'And how much time will it take you to for you to collect all the information you want?'

'It would depend on whether each individual has a recollection of their movements on each date and whether they can be corroborated. We're talking about a two-week period. Up to and including last Saturday night.'

'Okay. Well as a married man I can account for my whereabouts. I'm either at work or at home with the family. But two of my brothers aren't married and live alone. They might not be able to provide you with alibis for each of the dates in question. Does that make them suspects then? Would you be hauling them in for more detailed questioning as you did with the poor bugger who was taken into custody yesterday and was splashed all over the news? I know his name wasn't mentioned, but it's only a matter of time before someone leaks it and it's in the papers. He'll probably lose his job and his life will be hell. Presumably you don't have enough to charge him or you wouldn't be here. I don't think my brothers would be happy about attending the police station where reporters might be lurking around to take photographs. I wouldn't be happy about it for that matter.'

'If they provide alibis for *any* of the dates, they will not become suspects,' Rachel assured him. 'We could interview them here, rather than at the station. As young men they might have met up with family, friends or girlfriends.'

'I don't know the intimate detail of their lives outside work. But yes, my brothers should be able to recall Friday and Saturday nights. They are sociable guys. I can't speak for the sub-contractor though. You can go through anything you want with me now. I'll give you my brothers' details and you'll need to make contact with them. I've no idea what time they'll be returning today.'

'My god that was hard work,' Ayesha said as they finally left the O'Malley premises almost ninety minutes later. One of the unmarried brothers, Sean had turned up while O'Malley was going through his diary with them. After they'd explained their presence, Sean was co-operative and willing to provide them as much information as he could remember. On the night of Tessa Cooper's attack, there'd been a family gathering which went on into the small hours. Patrick O'Malley lived in Hamilton South where the party took place. He provided them with his address and his wife's contact details.

Sean O'Malley lived in a flat rental at Bar Beach. He'd had his girlfriend staying over on the Friday and Saturday nights of each weekend in question and had willingly given them her details.

The other unmarried brother, Declan, had returned to the company's headquarters shortly before they left and became obstreperous, refusing to co-operate, ranting about 'fucking pigs'. It took some time for Patrick and Sean to calm him down. O'Malley explained that Declan had been pulled over on his way home the previous week because of a broken tail light on his car. He claimed the policeman in question treated him with disrespect and issued him with a fine even though he had no idea the tail light was broken. He'd been enraged about it ever since. It did seem a little over the top in Rachel's view but perhaps Declan had not given his brothers the full story. O'Malley said he'd talk to Declan about his movements for the dates they required and pass the information on to them that evening. Rachel was inclined to take Declan O'Malley back to the station for questioning. They needed to talk face to face with him to gauge his honesty. His reaction to the request for information was suspicious and his aggressive behaviour was in keeping with a man who might attack women. He did appear to have large feet that might match a size 11 shoe also. Each of the O'Malley brothers had large feet. However, Patrick O'Malley had assured them Declan crashed out at his home the night Tessa Cooper was attacked and had not left the house at any time. There didn't appear to be any connection to Rhonda Newland or the flat complex where she lived either. Declan O'Malley would remain on their radar though, especially as his red hair colour was similar to the one described by Melody.

# 37

Duncan Doyle operated his business out of his modest home which was also in Lambton. The single storey weatherboard house had a large carport at the side with an extension behind it and they could see a white van parked there.

'This is a far cry from the O'Malley business, isn't it?' Ayesha said as they walked up to the front door.

An indigenous man Rachel judged to be in his 50s answered the door. 'Hello we're looking for a Mr. Duncan Doyle.'

'That's me,' he said stepping outside. Rachel noticed he had a limp.

After introducing themselves she asked him to confirm that he maintained the common grounds at the Aboriginal Housing units in Georgetown.

'That's correct. Been taking care of them for close on twenty-five years now.'

'Is it just you or do you have any employees?'

'There's only me and my son, Ronnie. Although he hasn't been able to do the work with me for a while now. He fell off a roof and broke his pelvis and his leg.'

'Ouch. That must have put a strain on you.'

'Yeah. It's been hard with my gammy leg. Got busted up in a car crash five years back. I've had to find some extra help. I don't only do the Georgetown flats. I have several other sites as well.'

'You wouldn't by any chance have hired someone to work with you who has red hair?'

'Yes, that's right. Red. He's been working with me since shortly after Ronnie's accident. I've struggled to do all the work on my own.'

Rachel and Ayesha's eyes met. Rachel could feel her heart thumping. Penn's entry in his exercise book mentioned a single word Red. With a capital letter. He'd been using it as a *name*. Not a description. This could be the man they were looking for.

'Do you have his full name, address and a phone number?' she asked. 'I assume Red is a nickname?'

'Yes, it is. He always goes by that name though. Said it was the better of the two evils what with his red hair and then his given name. I have his information in the office. I'll just get my keys.'

While Doyle was in his house Rachel turned to Ayesha and said, 'I think this might be our man.'

Ayesha opened her mouth to reply when Doyle returned.

'If you'd follow me. My office is behind the car port.'

Doyle stepped off the front veranda and began walking past the van towards the building behind it.

'Red's not been up to anything has he? I know he's a grumpy bugger, but he gets the job done.'

'How long has he been working for you?' Rachel asked.

'Oh, as I said, shortly after Ronnie's accident. About five weeks now. One of the blokes over at Wickham Park put me on to him.'

'Do you work in Wickham Park?'

'No. But I know people who do. Red has part-time work with the Parks.'

This was sounding better and better. Some of their attacks were in or near parks. This Red was certainly a person of paramount interest.

Doyle stopped outside the office door. 'That's funny. It's open and it looks as though the lock has been tampered with,' he said. 'I didn't notice that when I got home this afternoon.'

Ayesha stepped around him and looked. 'It has. Don't touch the door handle Mr. Doyle.' She pulled a pair of gloves out of her pocket, put them on, then carefully pushed the door open.

'Does it look as though anything has been touched?' Ayesha asked him.

'No. That's strange. I kind of expected to find drawers open and paperwork everywhere. That's what happened last time we had a break in. I think it was kids hoping to find lots of cash. The only cash we kept in here was a bit of petty cash for odds and sods. They took that of course. Ever since I've kept the petty cash tin in the house.'

'Can you show me where you keep the records for the man you call Red?'

'In that filing cabinet,' he said pointing to a large old green cabinet to the left of the door.

'I'm going to ask you not to come in sir. We're going to need to get forensics out here to check for fingerprints.

Can you direct me to the correct drawer?'

'In the top one. In a file right at the front.'

Ayesha opened the drawer and pulled out a file. 'This file?'

'Yes, that's it. He likes cash you see and I need to keep a record for my tax returns. The invoices I insisted he gave me have his full name and address. There should be quite a few of them now.'

Ayesha put the file on the desk, opened it and began looking through sheets of loose paper and what looked like receipts. 'What is his real name?'

'Axel. Spelt A-X-E-L. Not like the axle on a car.'

'Axel what?'

Doyle stood thinking for a minute. 'Do you know, I can't remember. It began with an 'L' I know that.'

'There's nothing here with Axel on it. Does he have a business name he works under?'

'No. And his invoices should be amongst the others in the file.'

'They're not here. There are other invoices for supplies and receipts but not his.'

'That's funny. I know they were in there. That's the file where I keep track of all my expenditure. Then I pass the file on to my wife Betty. She does all our accounts.'

'Betty wouldn't have removed anything would she?'

'No,' he said shaking his head. 'I give her the whole file once a quarter to enter up.'

'Looks like everything relating to him has been removed,' Ayesha said.

'You think Red has done that? Why would he?' Doyle asked looking confused. 'It's not going to get him out of paying income tax on the money he earned because I'm sure the Tax Office will be able to trace him.'

'Let's hope so,' Rachel said. 'I'll leave you my card. If you recall Red's surname, please give me a call.'


Rachel had left a post-it note marker in Penn's exercise book at the point she'd stopped looking at it. Frank flicked through the earlier pages to better understand the boy's entries, then continued from where Rachel had left off. In the second half of the book the name Red caught his eye. The entry was for Thursday 20th October. According to the boy, Red had arrived at 8.05 am. He wasn't listed as entering any of the flats. It showed Red leaving at 3pm. He was there most of the day but didn't enter any of the flats? Was he one of the groundsmen who Rachel had tracked down? A few weeks later Red was there again on 3rd November. This time at 8am. The boy's use of a capital letter indicated it was a name. Not a description. At the same time the boy had entered another name. Duncan 8.01am. He flicked back to the previous entry made with Red's name and there was Duncan listed at 7.54am. Duncan and Red could both be the maintenance crew. He scrolled past other entries that day to find Red's name again. The boy had written "RED key 4" at 2.05pm. What did that mean? That Red had a key to flat 4? Or someone had given him a key? Red then left at 3pm. Duncan at 3.10pm. He looked back at earlier entries that day and found a note of Rhonda 4 leaving at 11.08am. Then Rhonda 4 returning at 1.48pm. Shortly before Red's entry. Did she hand Red her key – or … perhaps she had left her key in her door as he'd done on odd occasions when he was moving a load of shopping or luggage into the house. He'd done the same with his car – left the key dangling from the boot. Thankfully he'd only done that at home where his car was parked safely off the road.

He flicked forward to the day of Rhonda Newland's death and noted the entries the boy had made then. He was sure that the boy meant Red had entered Rhonda Newland's flat with a key. A key that he'd possibly removed from her door the week before. The workmen weren't listed as being on site that day so Red had returned solely for the purpose of entering Rhonda's flat. He needed to get hold of Rachel.

Grabbing the desk phone, he tapped in her mobile number from memory. She answered after a couple of rings.

'Rachel, I've been looking at the Tiller boy's exercise book. Where's he's written Red I'm sure it's someone's name. Not a description.'

*'It is a name. Well a nickname that the man is known by. We're just about to leave Duncan Doyle's place now. Mr. Doyle has the maintenance contract for the Georgetown flats. Has done for many years. Red is a man who has been working with Duncan at the flats while his son is recovering from an injury.'*

'Does he have the legal name and address for this man?'

*'He did have, but it looks as if Red might have broken into Mr. Doyle's office and removed everything pertaining to him. All he remembers is his name is Axel – spelled A-X-E-L and the surname begins with an 'L'. He has his mobile number though.'*

'Okay. Bring it in and we'll look at tracing him through that. I'll see if I can find anyone called Axel in the system.'

'*There's a man who works at Wickham Park who knows him. We're going to head over there first and see if we can catch him before he leaves for the day. We'll be back as soon as we can.*'

# 38

Frank did a search on the system for men named Axel. It came up blank. It always surprised him when a person with a previously spotless record suddenly started committing murders or carrying out some other serious crime. The usual pattern for serial rapists (and he'd come across a couple in his career) was that they'd have charges for sexual offences when they were younger which had gradually progressed to violent rapes. They had often served time for previous offences and were the type of man who women instinctively avoided. But there was one rapist he recalled who they'd caught soon after joining the detective ranks. The man in question had been married for many years and suddenly turned into a rapist after his wife left him. He hadn't even had so much as a parking ticket before that. He was very withdrawn, had no friends and his work colleagues had been shocked to learn he was the serial rapist who was causing fear amongst women in the city. If he remembered rightly, it was something the man's wife had said or done that he'd used to justify his decision to take what he wanted from women. He wondered if they'd were now dealing with a similar situation.

He typed the name Red into their system and immediately found a hit. After skimming the details, Frank could see that this was not their man. It was a man serving time in Sydney for serious drug related offences who was in his late 40s now. His real name was Ronald Kray but he went under the alias of Red Kramer. He could understand the man wanting to change his name – had his parents thought it funny to name him after a notorious British criminal or had they never heard of the Kray brothers at the time of his birth?

He was about to log into the motor registry when Paul Lowry burst into his office.

'I've got it!' he declared grinning from ear to ear. Frank wasn't sure if Paul meant he'd just had a lightbulb moment or had acquired something precious. He waited for Paul to explain.

'She's confessed and dobbed lover boy right in it.'

'I take it you mean Jonas Graf?'

'Yep. We need to arrest him now.'

'How did you get Nicole Royce to confess so quickly?'

'I told her we'd matched the bicycle tyre tracks to her bike, we had a witness who'd seen her cycle off after she'd returned home in her car, and that we had visual evidence of her leaving Graf's room at the hotel in Sydney. But the little beauty that really nailed her was the dildo.'

Paul stood in front of him still grinning madly.

'Enlighten me,' Frank said. 'I can see you're dying to.'

'One of the uniforms we had assigned to us found the dildo covered in Veronica Graf's blood in a neighbour's bin early this morning. The bin was outside on the grass verge waiting for collection. Luckily the neighbour had got the day wrong. He thought the collection was on Monday, but it was today and the garbo truck doesn't collect in that area until late morning. It was wrapped in a pillowslip. A pillowslip which matches one from a set at the Graf house. And Royce's fingerprints are on it. The dildo I mean. You should have seen it – it was a great big—'

'Thank you, Paul. I don't need you to go into graphic descriptions. Well done. The Super will be pleased to hear that the team has solved at least one of the murders.'

'There's been no progress on our other cases?'

'Some. We've ascertained our person of interest is a maintenance man who was working at the Georgetown flats. He's known as Red. The name the boy wrote in his exercise book.'

'Tyler should have picked that up. I told him to question the residents thoroughly. If he had it might have saved … well anyway he deserved that telling off this morning. I think he's still smarting from it.'

'I told him off because his attitude and prejudice towards the Tiller siblings meant he'd missed crucial evidence; because he's lazy when it comes to entering information into the system and finally because he was arrogant enough to think he didn't need any support to improve his performance. We could all do with support at times.'

When Frank had asked Stuart what he, as Stuart's team leader, could do to support him to improve his performance, Stuart had reacted with hostility, insisted he was fine and claimed he needed no support. Frank didn't often lose his temper with team members, but on this occasion he had.

'Take Tyler with you when you go to arrest Graf. Show him how it's done without the macho cockiness. And partner up with him for Graf's questioning.'

'Okay.'

Just then Rachel burst into the office looking excited, followed by Ayesha with a similar look. They were all at it today. 'Did you receive my message?'

Frank groaned and shook his head. He knew she was referring to a message she'd sent him on his mobile phone. He hadn't looked at the phone since this morning. It was in his suit jacket pocket which was hanging over the back of his chair – and no doubt was on vibrate.

'His name is Axel Lowe. Low with an 'e' at the end. Duncan Doyle recalled his surname just as we were climbing into the car.'

'Axel Lowe? Sounds like a rock star's name,' Paul said.

'There *is* a rock star called Axyl Rose. From the Gun's and Roses Band,' Frank volunteered.

'You never cease to amaze me with your knowledge of music,' Paul said.

'What, just because I have a few years on me you think I don't follow music? Besides Rose has been around a while now.'

'That'll explain it then,' Paul retorted.

'There's no one with the name Axel in the system,' Frank said turning to Rachel. 'He might, of course be there under a different name. I was about to try the motor registry when Paul came into my office with some good news. He can tell you. Just keep it brief Paul – they don't need all the details you threw at me.'

Looking like the cat who had just got the cream Paul

said, 'Nicole Royce has confessed to the murder of Veronica Graf. I'm just about to head off and arrest Jonas Graf.'

'He was in on it?'

'Well and truly.'

'Well done,' Rachel and Ayesha both said. Frank sat back and watched as Paul filled them in on some of the details. It was one thing Frank loved about the two female detectives. They never resented their colleague's successes and their congratulations were genuine. Unlike Chief Superintendent Mitchell. He almost choked on the words 'well done' as though he hated the fact that Frank and his team caught suspects. Colleagues had encouraged him to go for the Detective Superintendent's position when it came up last year, but the idea of working with Mitchell's negativity day in day out had deterred him. Amongst other things. The current post holder, Jenkins, seemed to cope with Mitchell okay, but then Mitchell left Jenkins to work closely with other teams and appeared to have insisted that he'd deal with Frank's team himself. Frank had always gained the impression that Mitchell didn't like him and was looking for reasons to have him shipped out. Even if he was seeking it, Frank doubted he'd get a promotion while Mitchell was in post. He had heard a rumour that Mitchell was considering taking retirement next year and he hoped that might be the case. Otherwise, he might find himself being transferred to some god-forsaken remote town.

He waited until Paul left the office before turning to Rachel again.

'Any joy at Wickham Park?'

'No. Staff had already left for the day. But just as we

arrived back here Duncan Doyle phoned me. He's given me the name of another groundsman we could talk to at the oval on Arthur Street. Doyle said he knows Lowe as well. I doubt they'd still be there now though.'

Frank looked at his watch expecting the time to be around 4pm and was shocked to see it was 5.15. Where had that hour gone?

'We have another potential suspect. A Declan O'Malley. We've questioned two of his brothers and if their alibis hold, they'll be in the clear. There's still one more O'Malley brother and a few sub-contractors to look into. One in particular who has red hair. O'Malley is digging out their details for us. They all work for the O'Malley maintenance company. They have a large operation which looks after many schools, including the one near Becky Wheeler's house. However, this Red character looks the most promising person of interest by a long stretch.'

'I would agree. By the way, I didn't catch Michael Ross or Jeff Wheeler at the beach. They'd left. I was planning to call into Ross's house around six. I know he's usually home by then.'

'We can check for motor vehicles registered to Lowe and his driving licence for an image of him if you want to head off.'

'No, I think I should stay. If we have an address for Lowe, we need to head off there right away and bring him in. I'll check the system now.'

A few minutes later Frank had found what he was looking for. 'Axel Lowe's driving licence is registered to an address in Mayfield. Hinkler Street. If my memory serves me correctly that's just a few minutes' walk from where

Melody Hudson lives. Lowe is thirty-four years old.' He went into another section of the registry and tapped a few more keys. 'Lowe has a white Toyota Hilux listed at the same address. Looks as though we've got him. All three of us can go and I'll organise a few uniforms as back up,' he said addressing Rachel and Ayesha.

In two unmarked cars and two patrol cars they descended on the single storey brick house in Mayfield. There was an old Toyota Starlet parked out the front, but no pick-up.

A small, slim, exhausted looking woman with brown curly hair answered Frank's knock. After identifying himself he said, 'We're looking for Axel Lowe.'

'You've missed him by about five minutes. He's just dropped the kids off and returned home. Why are you lookin' for him? What's he done?'

'You said he's returned home. He no longer lives at this address?'

'No, he hasn't done for the past two months – not since we split up.'

'And you're his wife?'

'Ex-wife. We're gettin' a divorce.'

'His Toyota Hilux is still registered to this address Mrs. Lowe,' Frank said.

'I bloody told him to get everythin' sorted. I'm still getting' mail for him here.'

'Would you have his current address?'

'No, he hasn't given it to me. Not that I want to know it really, but as he has the kids stay over with him on a Sunday and Monday night, I told him I need to have it. I've just warned him if he doesn't give me his address, he can't have the kids next week. He wasn't too happy and was pretty abusive. I guess I'm shootin' myself in the foot a bit. I need him to have the kids while I work. All I know is that he lives around Tighe's Hill somewhere.'

There'd been no attacks on a Sunday or Monday night over the past couple of weeks. So, if Lowe was the attacker and he was looking after his children on those days, that would explain it. Could the children be helpful in telling them where Lowe lived?

'How old are your children Mrs. Lowe? Could they not tell you where your ex-husband currently lives?'

'I doubt it. Jake is three and Maddy is five.'

'Right.' Not appropriate then. 'There's a few more questions I'd like to ask you. May we come in?'

'I've got to feed the kids, bathe them and put them to bed. How long will it take?'

'Not too long. And one of our officers can watch the children while we talk.'

'Okay, come in then. But I can't give you too much time. I worked until late last night and I was on duty again at eight this morning. I'm bloody shattered. I'm curious to know why you're lookin' for Axel though.'

Frank wasn't about to tell her that, but she could be helpful in providing them with information about their prime suspect.

# 39

Cindy Lowe was only 5ft, like several of their victims, which confirmed that short women were Lowe's 'type' irrespective of their appearance or age. She was able to provide them with some useful information about her ex-husband as well as a photograph taken of him the previous year. It was better than the one from his driving licence. She told them Lowe had a violent temper which she claimed he wasn't like before or after she'd married him. It had developed after he suffered a head injury at work back in March. A tree surgeon had miscalculated the direction a large heavy branch would fall and it had come crashing down on Axel's head.

'His supervisor had sent him over to ask the tree surgeons how long they'd be. The guy told him to stand back while he finished. Axel did but the next thing he knew he was knocked out by this huge bloody branch. He was in hospital for a couple of weeks then out on compo for a while which is why I went back to working so many hours,' Cindy explained. 'He used to work for the parks full time but he can't do that anymore. Now he does just a couple of days a week for them.'

'And you think this knock on the head changed him?' Frank asked.

'Yeah. His whole personality seemed to change,' she said. 'He would fly off the handle at the slightest thing and started bashin' me. So badly I had to take some time off work once or twice. He'd never done that before. I stuck it out when he cried and said he wouldn't do it again. But he kept doin' it. I know in our marriage vows we agree to stay with someone in *sickness and health* but I thought, bugger that. My kids need their mother alive.'

Cindy Lowe was convinced the injury had caused the change in Lowe's personality she told them. She'd kept hoping he would 'recover' fully one day but he didn't change back to the old Axel and she couldn't take it anymore. The last time he'd hit her, she'd said he'd almost strangled her to death – which is why she insisted he move out. He was becoming too dangerous and she feared for her safety.

Frank agreed and decided he'd leave a patrol car parked outside the house for the night in case Lowe returned. His ex-wife might be his next victim.

Cindy worked a few streets away at the Phoenix Club four days a week; from Saturday to Tuesday. The long hours she put in meant she worked the equivalent of a full week over those four days. Thankfully she didn't need to go into work again until Saturday which meant they could keep an eye on her and the children at home.

She explained that she had to get a sitter on Saturday nights, as Lowe refused to have the children. He collected them Sunday morning and returned them Tuesday evening, and Cindy confirmed that he didn't work on

Sundays, Mondays or Tuesdays. As far as she knew Lowe lived alone.

While keeping the children occupied, Ayesha had gleaned from the eldest child, Maddy, that Daddy's house was up a hill off a main road and the house had a red door. Helpful but not specific enough.

Rachel, Ayesha and Frank gathered outside Cindy's front door for a chat. Rachel suggested, after she and Ayesha left Cindy's, they could do a search around Tighe's Hill before it got too dark, to see if they could spot the house and his vehicle. If they did Frank said they were to call him immediately. He put an all-points bulletin out on Lowe and his vehicle but if he'd driven home and the car was parked, it was unlikely it would be spotted.

He left Rachel and Ayesha to continue gathering more information from Cindy while he headed off to Rutherford to call in on Michael Ross. It was unlikely they were going locate Lowe tonight which was worrying as he might be planning another attack, now he was free of the children. They'd contacted an emergency number for the parks department, but the person who took the call was unable to provide details of any personnel and told them to phone the council offices in the morning. Frank suspected any official records for Lowe would still have him listed at the family address.

There was a white van parked outside Ross's house with Wheeler Security written on it, indicating that Jeff Wheeler was visiting Ross. Frank didn't like the sound of that. They'd been seen talking earlier in the day and now they were meeting again. Why?

He knocked on the front door but received no answer. He thought he'd picked up a waft of barbequed meat as he approached the house and wondered if they were in the backyard where they might not hear someone knocking. He retraced his steps and let himself in by the side gate which he could see led through to the rear. As he turned the corner of the house, there was Michael Ross sitting with Jeff Wheeler, another man he didn't know and two women around a table under a covered patio area. One of the women with long dark hair looked South-east Asian, much as Rachel had described seeing at the beach meeting. She was still wearing the large pair of sunglasses.

They all looked up at him and Michael Ross frowned. 'Inspector Bailey, this is a surprise. Why are you here? If it's to tell me you are releasing the suspect, I already know that. Detective Sharp paid me a visit at the hospital.'

The two women at the table stood and walked into the house. The second woman, whom he didn't recognise, had short straight honey blonde hair and was much taller, about 5'6' he estimated. The Asian woman however, was tiny, much like their other victims.

'I *have* come to talk to you briefly about the man we have released today. And to let you know we've identified a different person of interest. We're close to bringing him in. So, if you were thinking of trying to find out the name of the man we released today and going to the press about him, I wouldn't.'

'We already know his name, Inspector. And we're not thinking of going to the press. Not at this stage anyway,' Ross said.

'How do you know his name? It wasn't revealed at the press conference Detective Chief Superintendent Mitchell gave.'

'Someone saw him being taken out of his place of work, accompanied by you. You also questioned my sister about a member of the tennis club,' Wheeler said. 'The description of the man taken into custody who had red hair fitted the man you enquired about. So, we're guessing that's who you were questioning.'

'We have questioned a *number* of people. Not just the man you're referring to. And we had no evidence to justify holding him. Can I ask why you've been meeting? You were seen earlier today at the beach. Now you're here. What's going on?'

'Jeff is advising me on security systems. I'm considering having them installed both here and at Carrie's house – if she returns there. We're not breaking any laws, are we?' Ross replied.

'And those talks necessitate the presence of another victim – one who hasn't come forward?' he said to gauge the reaction of those present. 'The small Asian woman who was just sitting here with you?'

'She's not a *victim*,' the fair-haired man snapped at him.

'I don't believe we've met,' Frank said stepping forward and holding out his hand. 'My name is Detective Chief Inspector Frank Bailey. Your name and your connection to this little group is …?'

Ross waved him away. Frank withdrew his hand. 'You don't need to know his name. Or anyone else's name who's here tonight. Who I meet with in my private home is none of your business.'

'It is my business if you were thinking of doing something illegal.'

'Now what could we possibly do that would be illegal?' Ross said. 'We're just a group of people talking about security. Now if you don't mind Inspector, we'd like to have some privacy.'

Frank nodded, turned and left, thinking it was a shame that Jeff Wheeler hadn't installed security cameras at his sisters' house. To be fair, they might have been talking about security tonight, but he didn't think that was their only topic of conversation.

He decided to head home next. He knew Beth had prepared a cold buffet meal. One that he could eat quickly before heading back to the station. On the drive he thought about what the fair-headed man had said about the Asian woman not being a victim. He'd emphasised the word victim. Taken at face value a person would think he meant she had not been on the receiving end of an attack. But thinking it over, Frank decided it could be construed differently. He could have meant she did not *consider* herself a victim. Over the years he'd been with the police, many women, and men for that matter, refused to be seen as victims across a range of crimes. As though there was an unpleasant stigma attached to the word. And if he was honest, there was, to some extent. They'd re-phrased 'victim of crime', to say they had been 'a recipient of crime' 'on the receiving end of a crime', 'experienced a crime' to name but a few. There were the few who played up the victim role, sought compensation or used it as an excuse to avoid work. Others genuinely suffered life-altering experiences, especially when it came to violence. Carrie Ross, he suspected, was going to take a long time to recover both physically and mentally from her attack. Tessa Cooper less so because she had been on the receiving end of violence a few times during her years as a prostitute and had told Rachel she had no choice but to 'get on with life'. At what cost to her overall well-being? Although he hadn't been able to see her eyes, the Asian woman he'd seen tonight had a determined and fierce look about her. It sent shivers up his spine.

**40**

The group of five people at Michael Ross's house reconvened after DCI Frank Bailey left.

'What happens with our plan now?' Conor asked. 'If we carry it out that Inspector will guess it's us. We could be charged.'

'So what? If we achieve our objective no jury is going to convict us. It's not as though we're going to kill the bastard,' Wheeler said. 'I say we stick to our plan. What do the rest of you think?'

Three heads nodded their agreement with Wheeler. After hesitating, Conor did the same.


Rachel and Ayesha were driving back to headquarters when Rachel said, 'We were going to take a drive around Tighes Hill to see if we could spot the pick-up you saw at the petrol station. Why don't we do it now? You could turn left at the next lights.'

'Okay, no worries,' Ayesha said indicating as they approached the turning. She was caught at the lights which had turned red.

'Are we going to stop each time we spot a red door? What if there's loads of them?'

'I say we drive past and make a note of the number. Don't forget we're looking for the Hilux as well,' Rachel said.

'A white Hilux with a dented front right wing according to Cindy Lowe. That wasn't caught on the cameras as only the left side was showing.'

The lights changed and Ayesha turned, driving slowly up the street to give themselves an opportunity to glance at houses both left and right. They passed one intersection and Rachel suggested they turned right at the next one and right again into Henry Street.

'Carrie Ross lived in Henry Street. Perhaps he lives in the same street and her attack wasn't random. Perhaps he'd had his eye on her,' she said.

'What number was her house?'

'I don't know. I never visited it; I had no reason to. The address is logged in the system back at base.'

'You could try getting hold of Chris. See if he's still there.'

'He won't be. It's almost seven. Let's just see what we can find,' Rachel said.

They repeated the slow drive along Henry Street until Rachel shouted, 'There's a red door! Pull over a bit further up.'

Ayesha parked the car outside an old beaten-up weatherboard house. The grass in the front yard was overdue for a cut. 'This house looks like a rental,' she said. 'They often don't look after the yard.'

'Mm. Could the kid have considered that a red door?'

Rachel asked. The neglected house had a maroon door.

'She might have. It is a variation of red, I guess. There's a woman working in the front yard next door. Why don't we ask her who lives there? There's no sign of the Hilux. If not, we can stroll back to the other house we spotted with a red door.'

'Okay. But if she says a man with a Hilux and red hair lives there, we're to leave immediately and report it to the Chief,' Rachel said.

'If he has his phone switched on.'

'He promised me he would take it off vibration, leave it switched on and he confirmed it was fully charged.'

'Ah huh. As if that will make a lot of difference.'

Both women knew their boss was hopeless when it came to his mobile phone. They grinned at each other as they climbed out of the car.

The woman they approached confirmed a man with red hair and a white pick-up (she didn't know what make) had moved in next door a couple of months before.

'I saw him carrying mowers and gardening equipment down the side of the house and when I asked him when he was going to tend to his yards, he told me his job was looking after grounds and gardens all day long and he's too tired to do his own after work. But he doesn't work every day. He has his kids here a couple of days a week.' The woman went on and on – Rachel eventually managed to interrupt her flow of words and thanked her. Just as they turned to return to their car, a white Hilux pulled up, the driver took one look at them and then screeched off.

'Shit,' Rachel shouted rushing to the car. 'That's him. Bugger. We've messed that up.'

'Not necessarily. We know where he lives now,' Ayesha said as she climbed into the car.

'But I doubt he'll come back here. And if he heads back to his wife's place, he'll see the patrol car there. Do you think you can catch up with him?'

'I don't know but I'll give it a go,' Ayesha said as she started the car and roared off.

Rachel pulled out her mobile and phoned the Chief. Miracles of miracles he answered after two rings.

'Don't take any risks chasing him. And radio in for back up. If you lose him head back to base. I'm coming in now. Keep me posted,' Frank said before cutting the call.

'That was Rachel. They've found our suspect's house,' he told Beth. 'And are currently chasing him. I hope to God they are sensible. I need to go.'

She nodded. She knew from experience that there was no point in attempting to persuade him to finish his meal first. At least he'd eaten about half of it.

'Take care won't you Frank,' she said as he leaned over to give her a kiss.

'I will. I'm not sure what time, if at all, that I'll get back home tonight.'

# 41

'He's turned left into Maitland Road heading towards Newcastle,' Rachel told the radio operator.

Ignoring the red lights and with a siren blaring Ayesha followed him, swerving around a car that hadn't pulled over. They could see in the distance that Lowe had driven through two sets of red lights. Ayesha did the same with the first set but the second set turned green as they approached it. After calling in for back-up, the operator had called for all cars in the area to attend. So far there'd been no sign of any.

'He's turning left on Albert Street, heading towards Hanwell.' Then less than a minute later Rachel announced, 'He's turned left on Hanwell. Now he's on Industrial Drive. Isn't there anyone else out there?' she shouted into the radio.

'*I have two cars on the way,*' the operator said.

'About bloody time,' Ayesha said. 'Looks like he's continuing on Industrial Drive. I'm sure he went straight ahead at the Elizabeth Street roundabout. Did you see?'

'Yes, I'm sure he did.'

After passing through the roundabout themselves they

lost sight of him on the bendy road. 'Is that him turning into George Street?' Rachel asked.

'Yeah, I think so; I'm going to turn.'

'Turning left into George Street off Industrial Drive,' Rachel told the operator.

Just as they approached the lights, two patrol cars came racing down from the opposite direction. They turned and followed Rachel and Ayesha's car.

At the intersection with Ingall Street, they couldn't see any sign of Low's vehicle.

'Left, right?' Ayesha asked.

'I don't know. He could be heading back to his wife's place. If he does, we have him. It's a dead end.'

'I say we go right and around to Hinkler. We can ask one of the patrol cars to go left. He could have gone back to Maitland Road or doubled back to Industrial Drive. We need to cover both options.'

Rachel put in her request to the operator.

There was no sign of Lowe's car as they turned into Crebert Street and then stopped at the entrance to Hinkler Street where Cindy Lowe lived.

'He's not come down here. Shit, I've lost him,' Ayesha said.

'*We've* lost him. He must know these streets well and he could have woven around any of them to lose us.'

'Do you think he might have headed across Industrial Drive towards the steelworks? There's plenty of abandoned buildings over there he could hide out in.'

'I don't know. But let the patrol cars deal with that. I'll radio in and suggest it. I think we should warn the car outside Cindy's that he's on the run and could head their way.'

'I'm glad you persuaded me to have that sandwich at lunch time. Otherwise, I'd be feeling quite ill. I don't think I could face another pizza tonight, let's see if we can pick up something else on the way in. The Chief wants to meet us back at base. Are you hungry?' Rachel asked Ayesha.

'I certainly am. And I don't want pizza again either. How about we get an Indian take-away? There's a place in Beaumont Street. It's not that authentic but the food's at least edible. It won't take long, they have it all prepared sitting in bain-maries for the public to see and make their selections from.'

'Right, you're on. I fancy something spicy for a change.'

Rachel and Ayesha were just sitting down to eat when Frank arrived.

'That looks good,' he commented when he saw the spread they had.

'Get a plate and help yourself,' Ayesha said. 'We bought extra in case you hadn't eaten.'

'I'd managed to eat about half of my meal when your call came in. I was delayed when I encountered gridlocked traffic as I approached Mayfield West. It was due to a three-car pile-up which I eventually managed to negotiate my way around. Don't worry I checked with the traffic police who were dealing with it that it didn't involve our suspect. It happened before you went on your car chase.'

'Maybe that's why there was a dearth of patrol cars to

come to help us. They'd all gone there,' Rachel said before taking a bite of her nan bread.

'Probably. There were still three police cars at the scene. Have you heard anything back from the patrol cars?'

'No sightings of Lowe's pick-up anywhere. It's like he just vanished,' Ayesha said.

'Fingers crossed that if he's in hiding, he won't be carrying out any attacks tonight,' Frank said. 'I'll just get myself a plate and join you if you don't mind.'


After they'd eaten and cleared up, Frank met with Rachel and Ayesha in his office.

'So where do we go from here?' Rachel asked him. 'Do you want us to keep looking at the O'Malley brothers and their sub-contractors?'

'I'm pretty sure Lowe is our man. But, just to be on the safe side continue checking out your other potential suspects. You could ask O'Malley if he's ever sub-contracted work to Lowe. Becky Wheeler's attack wasn't random. Could Lowe have worked at the school and noticed Becky and Sarah Wheeler? There's a table and chairs out on their front veranda, so presumably they sit out there. Anyone passing would see them. It could be as simple as that.'

'Right. I'll get on to O'Malley. What do we do about Lowe?'

'We have an APB out on him. There's nothing much we can do but wait.'

# 42

Lisa Tomlinson was at the kitchen sink washing dishes when she heard the hissing of a cat followed by an aggressive howl. That signalled their cat, Rupert, was spoiling for a fight with one of the others in the neighbourhood. She'd only let him out a few minutes before. Grabbing his box of dried biscuits, she walked to the back door, turned on the outside light and rattled the box through the fly screen door which usually guaranteed to bring him back inside. She didn't want Rupert to get into a fight with that aggressive black tom from next door. He'd ripped Rupert's ear a few weeks back. Rupert was never one for backing down in a fight, but the black cat was almost twice his size and Rupert always seemed to come off worse.

With the yard lit up she could see Rupert was sitting on top the fence, tail swishing. 'Come on Rupert, come inside,' she said. She rattled the box again. He looked at her and then back down the yard where the light didn't reach. Was that a shadow she saw moving there? She tried once more but Rupert, with a final glance at her, leapt down into next door's yard and disappeared from sight. Well, that was a first! She'd never known Rupert to reject his biscuits. She was convinced the cat was sulking about them being away after Melody's attack. The police said they'd feed him but she wasn't sure they had. Lisa peered into the darkness but couldn't see anything except the vague outline of the shed. Shrugging, she retreated inside, shutting and locking the door behind her. Returning to the kitchen she did the same with the window as a precautionary measure. In the past she'd left the window open because there was a security fly screen. She now realised a determined burglar could remove them easily enough. Since Melody's attack she wasn't prepared to take any chances.

Rachel spoke to Patrick O'Malley who confirmed that Axel Lowe had done a couple of sub-contracting jobs for them the previous month, including the school near Becky Wheeler's house. She returned to the Chief's office to tell him.

'He hasn't given him any further work as one of O'Malley's brothers, Sean, who was working with Lowe the last time they were at the school, said that Lowe was behaving quite weirdly. He'd suddenly shouted at a man who was passing in the street. Sean was concerned that Lowe's behaviour would lead to complaints.'

'That's another piece of the puzzle sorted then. He would have had an opportunity to notice the Wheeler sisters. Lowe is definitely our man.'

Conor was relieved to be heading home instead of participating in Mike and Jeff's plan. He knew the girls were disappointed but he'd convinced them it was for the best. He'd invited them to his house for a meal, knowing Cien had promised to cook a big pot of Irish stew tonight. Comfort food for Roisin. And Cien's Irish stew was superb he'd told the girls.

Conor knew Cien wasn't happy about him spending so much time with Kaede. But he couldn't help himself. He'd fallen head over heels for her. Not that he'd made any moves. He didn't think it was appropriate given what she'd recently been through.

As he pulled into the drive, he noticed Cien's car wasn't there.

'Looks like the chef has departed.'

'He probably didn't want to see me,' Kaede said.

'Nonsense. He's been here since eleven am, he no doubt wanted to get home to be with Jess.'

'Hmm.'

Mairead was in the kitchen serving up a bowl of food. She looked quizzically at their extra guest.

'Mairead, this is Ellie. Ellie, Mairead.'

'Don't I know you from somewhere?' Mairead asked.

Ellie's eyebrows scrunched up. 'Um, I don't think so.'

'Ah, I know who you are. You're one of our patients. My boss is your dentist. Doctor Armstrong.'

'Oh, right. You're the dental nurse. I'm sorry, I didn't recognise you without your mask.'

'No, few people do. How do you know each other?'

'Ellie was a good friend of Becky Wheeler. You know the woman who—'

'I know who you're talking about. I'm sorry to hear what happened to your friend,' Mairead said, addressing

Ellie. 'I still don't understand what—'

'I met up with Sarah and Jeff Wheeler this morning. I've known them for almost as long as I've known Becky. Jeff knew that I once went through what … '

'What I went through,' Kaede finished for her when Ellie hesitated. 'Or something similar anyway.'

'Oh.'

'Jeff asked Ellie to join us today when we met up with Mike Ross. He thought Ellie might be a good person to support Kaede.'

'Okay. Now tell me you haven't done anything stupid,' Mairead said.

'We haven't done anything stupid,' Conor reassured her.

'Well, that's good to hear. I was just about to take a bowl of stew up to Roisin.'

'Roisin's your sister who …?' Ellie asked

'Yes.'

'She's still hibernating in her room?'

'Yes, well not exactly *her* room, but the room Conor has given us to sleep in while we're here. We can't coax her out of it.'

'Why don't you let me take that up to her then? As long as you add an extra bowl for me, as it smells delicious,' Ellie said.

'I don't think— '

'Ellie is a therapist Mairead. One who specialises in working with rape victims.'

'Oh. Okay. I don't know how Roisin will react, but you're welcome to have a go, if you think it's a good idea Conor.'

'Yes, I do think it's a good idea.'

Ayesha had just hung up after speaking to Sean O'Malley's girlfriend when her mobile rang. Looking at the screen she could see it was Sam Foley, McDonald's housemate so answered the call. A semi-hysterical Foley started shouting down the phone at her. She asked him to slow down and repeat what he was trying to tell her. After listening to him she reassured him that someone would be with him soon and rang off. Signally Rachel to follow her, she hurried into the chief's office.

'McDonald's lodger Sam Foley has just phoned me. He was walking home from his TAFE course, earlier than usual as the tutor was ill, and he saw a couple of men dragging Robbie McDonald out of the house, bundle him into a van which then drove off. He insists it was a van, not a pickup – with writing on the side of it, but he couldn't see what it said. Doesn't sound like it was Lowe. It sounds like someone's kidnapped McDonald.'

Frank leapt to his feet. 'So that's what they were up to. The little group at Michael Ross's house. Security systems my foot!' While eating their curries, he'd told the women about the five people he'd seen at the Ross house.

'Do you think they're going to try and force a confession out of him? When Mr. Ross was shouting at me at the hospital this afternoon, he kept saying we should have forced a confession from McDonald.'

'I wouldn't be surprised. Stupid bloody idiots. Check

out Wheeler's business. It's called Wheeler Security. He must have premises somewhere. I know he lives in Whitebridge. His address should be in the system under Becky Wheeler's investigation notes. We need to send a patrol car around there immediately.'

'I'll deal with that,' Rachel said.

'I'll check out his business,' Ayesha said.

'I've got Wheeler's number. I'll phone him.'

Rachel and Ayesha hurried off. Frank scrolled through his mobile to find Wheeler's number. It went to voicemail so he left a message. 'Mr. Wheeler, it's DCI Bailey here. I believe you may have taken Robbie McDonald from his house tonight. He is not, I repeat not, the man responsible for your sister's murder. We know who the man is and are currently searching for him. I would urge you to release Mr. McDonald. If your purpose for taking Mr. McDonald was to force a confession from him, I have to tell you that a confession obtained under duress wouldn't stand up in court. It's a pointless exercise. What you're doing is illegal—'

Frank heard the phone beep – he'd been cut off. These stupid mobile phones didn't allow a person to leave a very long message. He re-dialled Wheeler's number asking him to make contact urgently.

Next, he called Michael Ross, leaving a similar, shorter message. He tried the Ross landline which also went to a messaging service. He left a message asking Ross to call him urgently. Would there be any point in going over to the hospital to see Gemma Ross? Would her husband have told her he was conspiring with Wheeler? He suspected not.

Frank left his office to find out what progress Ayesha and Rachel had made.

'Wheeler's business premises are on Soldier Road at Pelican. Just past Belmont Airport. Do you want me to send a patrol car there? I've already sent one to his home,' Rachel added. 'And one to Robbie McDonald's place.'

'I can't see them taking McDonald to the Ross house,' Frank said. 'It's too built up. And Wheeler has a wife, kids and his sister at his home, so it's unlikely he'd take them there either. Wheeler's business premises are the most likely place they'd use. I'm familiar with that road, it's largely businesses and would be quiet at this time of night. I'm sure that's where he'll be. We'd better head off there immediately. And yes, we need a patrol car there. Preferably more than one. Tell them to hold back out of sight and wait for us. I think we should take two cars.'

# 43

Two patrol cars were waiting for them when they arrived at Pelican. Frank pulled over in his car, with Ayesha following suit. Rachel spotted the friendly face of Senior Constable Casey Sullivan, who had trained with her. She stepped out of the car to speak to her.

After introducing Casey to the Chief, Casey said, 'I walked up to the building in question but it's difficult to tell if anyone is in there. There's no sign of the van you mentioned over the radio, but there's large roller doors leading inside the building. They could be parked there. There's also a single door entrance in the front and another one at the side. It's the third premises along.'

'What do you suggest we do sir?' Rachel asked turning to the Chief.

'Is there a way around to the back?' he asked.

'Yes, on the right-hand side. There's a footpath that ends at the side door. It's gravel after that. I didn't investigate any further. The path isn't wide enough for vehicles. Do you think we'll need arms sir?'

'I hope not. Okay. We approach without lights or sirens and stop before we reach the building. We'll need to cover the side entrance and check out the back to make sure there's no other exits. Then I'll knock on front door. Follow me.'

They returned to their vehicles and followed the Chief, stopping short of their target.

Inside the warehouse Jeff Wheeler and Michael Ross (known as Mike to his friends) stood facing Robbie McDonald, who was tied to a chair. He'd removed the sack they'd put over his head after restraining and gagging him. After they'd bundled McDonald into the van, Mike had told Conor, Kaede and Ellie to go home.

'I wanted to confront him face to face,' Kaede had said. 'And why should you have all the fun?'

'The purpose of this exercise is to get him to confess. Nothing else. As much as I'd love to beat him to a pulp, there'll be no violence. We could be done for GBH. And the fewer of us involved the better. If you're not with us when we call the police, they can't charge you with anything.'

'I agree, Mike,' Conor had said. 'Come on girls, I'll take you back to my place.'

With some reluctance, the women had finally agreed and left with Conor.

Now it was just the three of them. They'd spent some time challenging McDonald about his involvement in the rapes and murders. Wheeler had removed his gag so McDonald could answer. He had repeatedly denied he had anything to do with them and pleaded with them to let him go.

'My daughter doesn't believe you would have attacked

her,' Mike told McDonald when they seemed to be getting nowhere. 'But then she doesn't know your history like we do.'

'If you're talking about the incident when I was at uni, I was innocent of that as well,' McDonald said. 'I've only ever touched a woman with their consent. Who told you about that anyway?'

Ignoring McDonald's question, Wheeler said, 'And do you consider when they're drunk that you don't need their consent?'

'What? No.'

'So, you just go ahead and have sex with them anyway?' Mike said.

'I don't. I could have had sex with your daughter the night she was attacked. She was drunk and throwing herself at me,' McDonald told him. 'She's a very attractive young woman and I *was* tempted. But because she was drunk, I pushed her away. I left the dinner party before her.'

'And hid in the park waiting for her to pass and attacked her there instead,' Wheeler said.

'No! I didn't,' McDonald said, shaking his head. 'Why would I need to do that when she was offering herself to me?'

'Are you suggesting my daughter's a cheap lay, you mongrel,' Mike said moving, towards McDonald with his right fist raised ready to hit him. He didn't know how much more of this he could take.

'No, I'm sorry. I'm just saying that I wouldn't take advantage of a woman who was drunk.'

'You've done it before,' Mike said with his fist still

raised.

'Mike, don't,' Wheeler warned. 'We agreed, no violence.'

He lowered his arm and moved away. Nobody spoke.

The silence was shattered by a pounding on the door and shouts of, 'POLICE. OPEN UP.'

Mike looked at Jeff who shrugged. 'We've done all we can, short of using violence. I'm going to let them in. I don't want my door damaged.'

Before Wheeler could make a move, the door opened and several armed police barged in followed by the Inspector and a couple of his detectives.

'No need for the guns, Inspector,' Mike said.

'You left the door unlocked. Some hardened criminals you turned out to be,' the inspector said, grinning at them.


'Is anyone else here?' the Chief asked Ross.

'No, only us.'

'What happened to the other three friends I saw at your place earlier tonight?'

'I told you, we were talking about security.'

'And the rest.'

Rachel cut McDonald's ties. She noticed that his jeans were damp around the crotch. The poor bugger had obviously wet himself in fear.

'Was it only these two men who removed you from your house?' she asked him.

'As far as I know. I didn't see anyone else. When I answered the door two men launched themselves at me and threw me to the floor. Sam must have left the fly screen door unlocked. I didn't really get a good look at them. It was dark.'

Rachel shook her head at the Chief.

'Search the place anyway,' he said.

'Jeffrey Wheeler and Michael Ross, I'm arresting you on suspicion of kidnapping. You don't have to say anything—'

'We know the drill,' Ross said. 'And there's no need to handcuff us,' he added as two uniformed officers approached both men, their cuffs out.

'It's a formality. Cuff them, take them back to Area Command. DSC Patel, can you follow them, get them booked in and read them their rights.'

'Yes, sir.'

'I need to lock up first,' Wheeler said.

'We'll do that for you when we've finished here.'

'But I need to set the alarm.'

'The alarm can stay off for one night. Take them away. DSS Sharp and I will join you shortly,' the chief said addressing Ayesha.

The chief must have noticed the state of McDonald's trousers as he added, 'I think we need to get Mr. McDonald home first.'


Lisa Tomlinson had kept her word to the nice woman detective about not taking sleeping aids. As a result, she wasn't getting much sleep. Melody dropped off within minutes of hitting the pillow while she could lay there awake for hours. They'd gone to bed early tonight as there was nothing on the TV Melody wanted to watch. It suited her – she needed extra hours in bed to make up for the loss of sleep time. They were both still off work so there was no need to get up so early. She liked the opportunity to sleep in but missed work. Perhaps next week Melody could return to her job. She'd spoken to Melody's supervisor and told him, in confidence, what had happened. He'd been very sympathetic and said Melody wasn't to come back in until she felt ready.

She was lying there planning tomorrow's activities – a trip to the library and then the supermarket, when she heard a sound at the back door. She nudged Melody awake and whispering to her said, 'I think we're going to need our weapons tonight.'

While Mairead was upstairs Conor had offered to put Kaede up for the night. She'd had a couple of glasses of wine and he didn't think she should be driving home. Besides, they were waiting to hear the news from Jeff and Mike.

'I have a spare room or if Ellie wants to stay over, she can sleep there. You can have my room. I'll crash on the couch,' he said.

Kaede didn't speak for a moment. He couldn't tell what was going on in her head.

'I …'

He didn't get to hear what Kaede was going to say as Mairead re-appeared and joined them back in the lounge room. 'Roisin's laughing up there. So that woman—'

'Ellie,' Conor said.

'Yes, Ellie. She must have got through to Roisin.'

'Don't interrupt them then. Leave them to it Mairead.'

'I'd love to know what she said to Roisin. I think I'll have another glass of wine then.'

'You'll need a new bottle. This one's empty.'

Mairead headed off to the kitchen and he turned to ask Kaede what she thought when he noticed her looking up the stairs. He followed her gaze to see Roisin and Ellie descending, Ellie carrying the tray she'd taken up with her. It was the first time Roisin had been out of her room for days.

Conor leapt to his feet. 'Hi Roisin, come and join us.'

When she reached them, he said, 'You two haven't met. This is Kaede.'


The Chief handed Rachel a plastic sheet which she spread across the back seat of his car. 'Sorry,' she said to McDonald. 'It's the Chief's private car. Not a pool car.' He nodded and climbed in.

Apart from the Chief confirming from McDonald that he hadn't been hurt, the drive back to McDonald's house was silent.

'Right, a quick shower, change and then we'll be taking you down to the station for a statement,' the Chief said as they arrived.

They had to ring the doorbell to be let in by the lodger as McDonald had no keys. The Chief returned to his car to make a few calls.

'Are you okay?' Sam asked.

With barely a nod, McDonald disappeared into his bedroom.

'*Is* he okay?' Sam repeated the question to Rachel.

'Yes. It would seem so. He has no injuries.'

'I told the two policemen who came everything that I saw.'

'We'll need to ask you to come in and give us a formal statement,' Rachel said. 'Not tonight necessarily. Tomorrow will do.'

'I'm at work tomorrow. I could come after that. About six. Would that be okay?'

'Yes, fine.'

Rachel took a seat in one of the lounge chairs. There was no sign of the gaming equipment she'd seen the lodger playing with the last time she'd been. Instead he had the television on with the sound muted. A football game. Andy was probably at home watching the same thing.

'Do you mind if I turn the sound back on?' Sam asked. 'I'll keep it low.'

'No, go ahead.'

His mention of the word 'low' made her think of Axel Lowe, and set her wondering if his car had been spotted yet. They'd not heard anything further about him.

Ten minutes later McDonald emerged looking more comfortable and wearing a clean set of clothes.

'Where's your boss?' he asked.

'He's outside making a few calls. Why, what's the problem.'

'I've decided I don't want to press charges.'

'I heard that,' the Chief said walking in the door. 'I don't think it will be as simple as that, Mr. McDonald.'

'I'll just say I went with them willingly. I can understand why they wanted to try and force me to confess. Both have had family members who have been murdered or raped and everything that was said in the press pointed to me. Someone at the police must have leaked my name to them.'

'No, that's not how they knew who you were,' the Chief said.

Rachel's phone buzzed in her jacket pocket. She pulled it out and saw it was Lisa Tomlinson. It was late for her to be phoning. She pressed to accept the call and listened to a hysterical Lisa say, *'You need to come straight away detective. He came back tonight but we were ready for him and I think we've killed him.'*

## 44

Frank was about to argue the case for McDonald to press charges when Rachel cut in and said, 'Sir, we need to go. *Now*.' She walked up and leaning close to his ear said, 'It's Lowe.'

'Right. Well, we'll leave it for tonight then and speak again tomorrow,' he said turning to McDonald. 'I'm glad you're back home safely.'

'If he's not pressing charges does that mean I won't have to give you a statement?' Sam asked.

'We'll talk about it tomorrow,' Rachel said.

They beat a hasty retreat and jumped into Frank's car.

'Where are we headed?'

'Lisa Tomlinson and Melody Hudson's place. And I think we need to call for an ambulance.'

'What's happened?'

'Lisa Tomlinson said *he* came back tonight and they were ready for him. She said she thinks they've killed him. I can only assume they're talking about Lowe.'

Frank groaned. 'Oh for God's sake. Why didn't she ask the blokes in the patrol car outside their house for help?'

'I'm afraid I sent them off earlier to Lowe's rental house

in case he returned,' Rachel said. 'One of the cars who had been helping us had to take off to deal with another incident. There were no other patrol cars available. They said everything was quiet at Lisa and Melody's house.'

'Do you know what happened at the women's house?'

'No, she rang off.'

'I guess we'll find out soon enough. You'd better call for that ambulance. What's the address – I haven't been there?'

'Don't worry, I'll direct you. It's only a few minutes away. Go straight over the lights here into Carrington. Turn left into Crebert as though you were going to Cindy Lowe's place and then next right into Arthur Street. It's the first right off that.'

Rachel left him to find his way from her directions while she called emergency services for an ambulance and also radioed in for a patrol car to meet them at the address.


Lisa Tomlinson had conveniently left the front door open for them when they arrived. Frank almost burst out laughing when he saw two little women sitting on the floor in their nighties, each with a raised fry pan in their hands. A trussed-up man was prone on the floor. He recognised him as Lowe, who had several strips of parcel tape across his mouth. Lowe was conscious but looked enraged at his situation.

'I had to put tape across his mouth,' Lisa Tomlinson said. 'When he came around, he kept swearing. It was good to see we hadn't killed him but we couldn't listen to language like that.'

Frank turned away for a moment to stifle his laughter and noticed Rachel doing the same. He'd love to be able to take a photograph of the scene but of course it wasn't appropriate and besides he didn't think he'd ever be able to forget the image in front of him.

'You can move away from him now,' he said turning back to the women. 'He's not going anywhere with all that rope tied around him. An ambulance is on its way and the paramedics will examine him.'

Once the women moved clear of him Frank walked over and removed the strips of tape. 'Axel Lowe, I assume?'

Lowe started writhing and let forth a stream of abuse so Frank stuck the tape back over his mouth. 'I see what you mean ladies. Did he lose consciousness when you hit him?'

'Yes,' Lisa said. 'That's why we thought we'd killed him. We tied him up and dragged him out here and he was dead as a dodo. But then he came around.'

'I'm assuming he broke into the house? You'd had all the locks changed, hadn't you?'

'Yes, and a good thing too. He'd taken a set of keys. He dropped them when we hit him. It was Melody's set of keys he took. She had a koala on her key ring. He forced the back door. I hadn't got off to sleep when I heard him. I woke Melody and put our plan into action.'

'Using fry pans?'

'Yes. They make very good weapons.'

'I can see. How many times did you hit him on his head?' Frank was thinking about Lowe's previous head injury. Although he was awake now, some of their blows could still prove fatal.

'A couple of times on the head. But we hit him in other places as well.'


The front doorbell rang and Frank asked Rachel to deal with whoever it was. The paramedics had arrived followed by a couple of uniforms. He recognised the senior constable who'd been at Wheeler's warehouse.

'We'd dropped off your two men when we heard the call for this address. I recognised Detective Sharpe's voice so said we'd take it. What's happened here?'

'Two little women caught a strapping six-foot two murderer and rapist,' Frank said. 'Alleged murderer and rapist,' he added, correcting himself.

The sergeant and her partner grinned from ear to ear.

'He's going to require hospital treatment and I suspect they'll want to admit him – at least for overnight observation. We'll need him handcuffed to the bed and a guard on his room.'

'I'll sort that. It will be my pleasure,' the senior constable said.


Frank followed the ambulance to the hospital. As he suspected the doctors insisted that Lowe was admitted as head wounds needed to be treated with extreme caution. Lowe had several lumps on both sides of the head. How the women managed to reach his head was a mystery. He'd left Rachel to take statements from them, where, no doubt, all would be revealed. He'd phoned Ayesha to tell her of the night's events and requested that she organise the techs to go over to the women's' house and then she needed to join Rachel as he'd left her without transport.

# 45

Rachel was sitting in the lounge with the two women waiting for the forensic techs and Ayesha to arrive. The Chief had said he'd sort that. She was waiting, notebook poised, for the women to take her through the events of the night. They were dressed now and Rachel had asked them to leave their nightclothes for the techs to bag up. If their assault on Lowe proved fatal, they'd need all the evidence they could muster to establish the chain of events.

Lisa had made them all a cup of tea.

'So, take me through what happened.'

'Well, I heard a noise coming from the back door. Two different lots of noises to be exact. Melody here was asleep but I was still wide awake. I think he forced the fly screen door open, then started working on the wooden door. I woke Melody and told her to get her fry pan ready. We've each been sleeping with one since we returned home. Because they're our only two fry pans, we had to take them back into the kitchen every day, then back to my room of a night.'

Melody nodded enthusiastically to confirm that was correct. 'I like fried bacon and eggs for lunch some days, so we needed at least one of them in the kitchen,' Melody explained.

'I knew he'd head for Melody's room first,' Lisa continued. 'We had made the bed up to look as if she was asleep in it. Before he managed to break in through the back door, we tiptoed into her room being careful where to step and hid in her built-in wardrobe. We'd cleared loads of stuff out of the wardrobe to make room for us to fit in there.  I'd set up a fishing line wire across the doorway into Melody's room and my bedroom. I knew it would be difficult to see it in the dark. Before we went to bed each night, I'd wind it over a hook I'd put on one side of the doorway. The other side was permanently fixed and I'd just unwind it of a morning so we didn't trip over it during the day. If we needed to go to the toilet of a night, I kept a bucket in the bedroom. I didn't want either one of us to trip over the wire half asleep in the night if we needed to go to the bathroom. Melody seldom wakes up once she's asleep but I sometimes have to pay a visit. Anyway, with the fish wire there, anyone trying to get into our rooms would trip over it and fall. And that's what he did when he entered Melody's room.'

That explained how the women had been able to bash Lowe over the head.

'He went crashing to the floor and Melody and I leapt out of our hiding place, and started whacking him around the head and other parts of his body. When he was unconscious, we tied him up and dragged him out to the kitchen. He remained unconscious for a while and that's when I thought we'd killed him. I didn't want to touch him to test for a pulse or anything. But I had to gag him when he did wake up.'

'Yes, you said,' Rachel said keeping her head down so they wouldn't see the smile spreading across her face. She could just imagine the scene. Disorientated from his fall, Lowe wouldn't have had a chance to get back onto his feet before they attacked.

'I went outside to tell the nice policemen in the car what had happened but they'd gone.'

'I sent them off to wait outside his house,' Rachel said. 'We'd been chasing him in the streets nearby and I thought he might go home.'

'Oh, I would have loved to have seen the car chase,' Melody said.

'I don't think he came here in his car tonight,' Lisa said. 'There was no one parked outside when I went to talk to the policemen. And he came in from the back. Do you think he'll be alright?'

'I don't know Lisa.'

'I mean, we didn't set out to kill him. Just to stop him. If he hadn't been on the floor and he'd come at us on his feet, we wouldn't have stood a chance against that giant. He's huge.'

'Now you know why I couldn't fight him off,' Melody said.

'I didn't doubt for a minute that you were telling me the truth honey,' Lisa said, wrapping an arm around Melody.

'You were both very brave tonight. Many women wouldn't have had the courage to defend their home the way you did.' The problem was that if their assault proved fatal the two would have to prove a case for self-defence or they could be facing charges of manslaughter.

'We were determined women, detective. No one attacks a Hudson woman and thinks he can get away with it twice.'

'Is there anything else you need to tell me? If not, I can type this up into a formal statement for you to sign tomorrow?'

'No, I think we've told you everything,' Lisa said.

'Yes, Lisa's told you everything that happened,' Melody said. 'She woke me up and then we followed the plan as we'd agreed.'

'Okay, thank you Melody.'

'Can I go back to sleeping in my bed now that he's been caught? I sleep better in my own bed cos you wake me up with your snoring some nights,' Melody said turning to Lisa.

'I wake *you* up with my snoring? *I* have trouble dropping off to sleep because of your sniffles, snorting and teeth grinding,' Lisa said.

The women were still arguing about who kept who awake the most when Ayesha arrived, followed closely by the techs. Turning back to the women Rachel said, 'I'm afraid we're going to have to ask you to relocate again for the remainder of the night so forensics can go through the house. I know there's a twenty-four-hour motel on Maitland Road. We can book you in there.'

'I guessed that would be the case. I've already packed a small bag for us, and prepared a bowl of food for the cat to leave outside,' Lisa said.

After seeing the women safely into their motel room,

Rachel and Ayesha returned to the house.

The techs had taken all the swabs they needed from Melody's room, the hallway and the kitchen. They'd bagged up all other evidence they needed and were ready to leave.

'We'll need a DNA sample from the other sister,' one of the techs said. 'We already have the younger sister's DNA.'

'I'll get that in to you tomorrow,' Ayesha said. 'What about the back door? Is it secure?'

'Yes, we've managed to refit the bolts he smashed but the lock will have to be sorted.'

'Okay, thanks. We'll head off too then.'


Rachel couldn't stop laughing as she related the sequence of events that led to capturing Lowe to Frank and Ayesha – which in turn made them both laugh. It was two am and they were the only ones in the squad room. It was good to laugh after such a tense and exhausting night.

'I almost burst out laughing when I saw them sitting beside Lowe. I noticed you were battling to stifle laughter too Rachel. But I didn't dare laugh as the two women looked so fierce and serious.'

'I know,' Rachel said and laughed again.

'I would have loved to have seen it,' Ayesha said.

'On a more serious note. Lowe had a fit while I was at the hospital and lapsed into unconsciousness again. They've stabilised him and he'll be monitored through the night. The doctor I spoke to thought his fit was brought on through a combination of his head injuries, extreme rage and stress. He was attempting to fight everyone off while they were trying to examine him. He's a strong bugger.'

'Yes, I could see that he would be,' Rachel said.

'He's been sedated now to make him more amenable. Well, it's time we headed home. Everything else can wait until tomorrow. I think we've gone above and beyond today and deserve some sleep.'

# 46

**Wednesday**

Frank called a team meeting the following morning for 9am. He was in early after having had only four hours sleep to report to Mitchell who was due to give a pre-planned press conference. He would now be able to announce the capture and arrest of the man believed responsible for the rape and murder of a number of women. Mitchell always liked to be in front of the cameras and Frank was more than happy to be relieved of that duty.

Lowe had been formally arrested and cautioned before they took him to the hospital but they'd have to go through the process again when he was well enough to understand the procedure otherwise his defence would claim that he hadn't been in a fit state to realise what was happening.

Reports from the hospital this morning were that Lowe was making good progress and was being his usual obnoxious self towards staff. It was a relief to get him off the streets and although it wasn't for very many hours, Frank had slept soundly for the first time since Carrie Ross's attack when he realised they might have a serial rapist on the loose.

The news of Lowe's arrest spread on the police grapevine. Frank and Rachel were plagued with questions from members of different teams and uniforms popping in to find out the details. They had agreed to keep schtum until the briefing which would coincide with the press conference. Apart from the two officers involved in taking him to the hospital, no one else knew who Lowe was. Officers who had been taking turns guarding Lowe had only been told he was a criminal who had been injured during his arrest.

The squad room was packed with not only Frank's team but many others dying to know the truth.

'Chief Superintendent Mitchell is at this moment giving a press conference to confirm the arrest of a man in connection with the recent spate of murders and rapes,' Frank said.

A cheer went up in the room. He waited for things to quieten before continuing. 'We discovered his name yesterday but not his current address as he was still registered at his ex-wife's home. It was through DSS Sharpe and DSC Patel's diligent work that we identified our suspect. They later tracked him down but when he spotted them outside his house he went on the run. Some of you might have heard that involved a high-speed car chase, but he managed to elude us having had a good head start. Then, several hours later we received a phone call from the sister of one of his victims. He'd attempted to break into their house again. With foresight, they'd set up traps in the house and because of these they managed to subdue and restrain him. So, thanks to two little middle-aged women, we now have our suspect in custody. He's currently in the Royal being treated for injuries sustained during his apprehension. The good news is that he's stable and we're hoping to have him in for questioning in a matter of days.'

Another cheer went up.

'That's not all,' Frank said once they'd had calmed down. 'DSS Lowry and DS Tyler made a formal arrest yesterday of the two people involved in the murder of Veronica Graf which was staged to look like a copycat murder. So, our recent spate of murders and rapes have been resolved.'

More cheering and clapping.

'Now if you don't mind, I need to meet with my team members. We still have many things to deal with.'

It took a good ten minutes before the crowd dispersed, after much back slapping, and hand shaking. Frank noticed Tyler looked a lot more cheerful. Whilst Tyler had done little throughout either investigation, he had sat in on Graf's interview and arrest so Frank had decided to credit Tyler along with Lowry.

'Stuart and Paul, I'm sure you have much to be getting on with on the Graf case. I'll leave you to do that. Phil, Chris, Rachel and Ayesha can you come into my office.'

Frank had allowed Phil Rogers a couple of day's leave to be with his wife and new daughter, but had asked him to return today – before he knew they'd caught their man. He'd meant to message him this morning telling him he didn't need to come back in but had forgotten.

Once they'd crowded into his office, bringing a spare chair from the squad room, Frank turned to Phil. 'Welcome back Phil and congratulations on the birth of your daughter. You can take your formal paternity leave now. There's no need to stay on today. I'm not giving you any tasks.'

'Thanks sir. And congrats to everyone. I have to say I'm a bit jealous that I missed out on all the action. But well done,' he said nodding to Rachel and Ayesha.

'Congratulations to you to on the birth of your daughter,' Rachel said. 'We'll get pressies sorted as soon as we can.'

Frank waited for Phil to leave before turning to Chris.

'Chris, I want to you get onto the Parks Department to check the dates Lowe worked for them over the past couple of months and which locations he worked at. After that I want you to visit the oval in Arthur Street again. Rachel has the name of someone you need to speak to there. She'll give it to you in a minute. Ask him what he can tell you about Lowe. And look for Lowe's vehicle. It must be around there somewhere given that he broke into a nearby house last night. Don't touch it if you find it. Call me. You can head off and start doing that now.'

'Yes sir,' Chris said, standing and leaving the office.

'Now. About last night's little escapade concerning Robbie McDonald.'

'I noticed you didn't mention it amongst the other announcements,' Rachel said.

'No, I discussed it with Mitchell this morning and he takes the view that if McDonald doesn't want to press charges and will swear that he went with them voluntarily then we should release Ross and Wheeler and drop the whole matter, saying it was a misunderstanding on our part.'

'What do you think sir?' Ayesha asked.

'What I think doesn't matter. We do what the big chief says *if* McDonald doesn't want to proceed. I'd like you two to visit him this morning and see if he's still of the same frame of mind. If he is, then tell him we won't be requiring a formal statement from him.'

'We're not the only ones who know about it. What if McDonald's lodger or one of the uniforms who was at Wheeler's warehouse talks to the press?'

Frank shrugged. 'We follow the party line and say it was a misunderstanding.'

'Now, the next thing we need to do is search Lowe's rental property. I told the patrol car you'd organised to sit outside his place to leave once we had him in custody. We have a set of what appear to be house keys that were found on Lowe and I've organised a search warrant. I've arranged to meet the techs there at 11. I'd like you two to come there once you've finished with McDonald. Before that though I'm going to have one last stab at Wheeler and Ross to see if they'll give me the name of the Asian woman we saw with them. I'm sure she was either victim one or four.'

'We'd have enough with our survivors to convict Lowe, wouldn't we? And then there is last night's break in at Melody and Lisa's house,' Rachel said.

'Lowe could say he was there to commit a burglary. Forensic evidence on the victims is slim. He's been very clever. Apart from Becky Wheeler. We're still waiting on the DNA evidence from her fingernails. The Tiller boy's exercise book gives us more. But he may not make the best of witnesses on the stand. I want to see this man put away permanently. Not getting out in twenty years' time to commit more crimes. We'll hopefully have plenty of circumstantial evidence – but we had that against McDonald. If our missing victims had come forward, we might have had more forensic evidence. Especially if we knew who number one was. It's usually the first one they make their mistakes with.'

'Okay. We need to meet up with Melody and Lisa sometime today for them to sign their statements. And we need a DNA sample from Lisa. Can we let them know they can return to the house?'

'Yes. The techs have finished there. They can go home. Tell them you'll call in to see them later today. Now I'd better get off to speak to Ross and Wheeler.'

# 47

Rachel and Ayesha called on the sisters at the motel first. Melody was spread out on the bed watching a TV program; the volume loud enough for them to hear from outside the room. From the open book on a small table, it looked as though Lisa was trying to read. Until Lisa removed her ear plugs Rachel had been wondering how on earth she could concentrate with the TV volume so loud.

'You have the all clear to return home now. We'll call in to see you later this afternoon with your statements ready for you to sign and to collect a DNA sample off you Lisa.'

'You hear that Melody, we can go home now,' Lisa said.

'When my program is finished.'

'No, we need to go now. Otherwise, they'll charge us for an extra day.'

'I don't mind.'

'You might not mind, but *I* don't want to pay for another day when there is no need. It's only a TV show Melody. I'm going to check us out. Pack up your things.'

'We'll leave you to it,' Rachel said.

Walking back to their car Rachel said, 'They're like an old married couple, aren't they?'

'Yes, I was just thinking they remind me of my grandparents.'

When they arrived at Robbie McDonald's house the lodger Sam and another man were loading what looked like Sam's belongings into a car.

'Are you moving out?' Ayesha asked him.

'Robbie told me last night he's going away and he's arranged with an agent to let the house. He started packing things up last night for Christ's sake. He's putting all his belongings, including furniture into storage. Anyone renting it would have to own all their own furniture, whitegoods, kitchen equipment and so on. I don't have any belongings other than what you can see that we're loading into Tom's car. There's no way I could afford it. My mate Tom here has agreed to let me surf on his couch until I can find other lodgings. My month's rent was due to Robbie yesterday. Fortunately, I hadn't given it to him. So, I took today off from work to move. I'm off now. Bugger him.'

'We may need to speak to you again about last night's events,' Ayesha said.

'That's fine. You have my number. But he says he's not pressing charges.'

They walked into the house to find McDonald busy packing up crockery in the kitchen.

'What's going on Robbie?' Rachel asked him.

'Who let you in? Sam, I suppose. What does it look like? I've had it with this place. I'm leaving.'

'What about your job at the bank?'

'I was only on a fixed term contract until the end of

December anyway. I doubt they'll renew my contract seeing as you virtually *arrested* me. I don't think I could face them all anyway. I phoned in this morning to say I wasn't returning and they sounded relieved.'

'Where are you planning on going?'

'I don't know. But as far away from here as possible. I have no family ties here anymore. Maybe I'll head off to Europe. Or the US. Depending on what visas I can get.'

'I gather you still don't want to make a statement about what happened last night?'

'No, I don't. I just want to forget about it all. I heard on the news that you arrested the *right* man this time.'

'That's correct. We have arrested him, whereas you *weren't* arrested Robbie. We just took you in for questioning.'

'It amounted to the same thing and has destroyed any opportunity for me to have a normal life here in Newcastle.'

'Your name wasn't released to the media.'

He snorted. 'You can bet they know my name and if not, someone will leak it. I'm sure it's going to appear in the papers at some point.'

He was probably right. Someone would leak it. Perhaps even one of his colleagues from the bank.

'In case we might want to talk to you again, how long before you leave?'

'I hope to be off in a couple of weeks. However long it takes for me to pack up my life here. And why would you want to speak to me again? I've told you I'm not making a statement.'

'Well, I can only apologise for everything Robbie and wish you all the best for the future.'

McDonald snorted again.

Kaede and Conor watched events unfolding at McDonald's place from the nearby park.

'Looks like the lodger is moving out. That could be handy,' Kaede said.

Conor frowned at her, unclear of her meaning. They'd heard from Jeff's sister early this morning that he and Mike had been arrested. They didn't know anything else, but presumed that as McDonald was back home, there'd been no confession. And it didn't look as if the police were here to take McDonald into custody. The phone in his pocket rang and, pulling it out, he could see it was Cien. He put the speaker on so Kaede could hear what he had to say.

'What's up bro?' he said putting on a fake American accent.

*'I tried to reach you earlier. Mitchell gave a press conference this morning saying they have arrested the man they believe is responsible for all the rapes and murders. He's currently receiving treatment after being injured during his arrest or something.'*

'That's what they said about McDonald.'

*'No, they didn't. When Mitchell spoke to the press after they took McDonald in, he said 'A man was being questioned in connection with the rapes and murders. Now he's saying they have arrested a man.'*

'Okay, thanks. Any news about Jeff and Mike?'

*'Not yet. They're still being held. Don't know if they've been charged. I'll phone you again if I hear anything further.'*

'You heard all that? The man they've arrested is not

McDonald.'

'Hmm. How about we follow the lodger? I'd like to ask him a few questions.'

Frank walked around Lowe's house in disbelief. It was very sparse and he didn't think that was due to Lowe being a minimalist. In the living room there was an old sofa, a T.V. and a manky brown carpet on the floor. The room was dark, largely due to the heavy gold curtains closed across the window. He pulled them open to reveal dirty nets. The place might have been rented unfurnished but landlords usually provided the curtains and/or blinds. It was as though an elderly man who hadn't cleaned the place for years had lived here before Lowe and most of the previous occupant's personal belongings had been shipped out without the landlord cleaning the place up or replacing the curtains. In the kitchen there was a small, old fridge freezer with very little in it. The cupboards weren't much better. It appeared he only had one saucepan, one fry pan and little in the way of crockery or cutlery. And they all looked like an assorted jumble of odd bits he'd picked up from a charity shop. There was no table or chairs in the whole house. The front bedroom, which again had dark curtains closed across the window, had a mattress on the floor with boxes and bags strewn around the rest of the room. The linen looked and smelled as if it been on the bed for the entire time Lowe had been there. A pile of dirty clothes was heaped in one corner. Lowe's standard summer wear. Black singlets and khaki shorts. The other bedroom which the children must have slept in, held bunk beds and a few toys. No cupboards. In the bathroom there was an old shower fitting over the bath and a dirty patterned plastic shower curtain. The bath itself was an old one with enamel chipped all over it, as though someone had taken a chisel to it and exposed the black metal underneath. It was at least relatively clean, like the sink, but there were years of mould accumulation all over the old yellow and red tiles that Frank knew dated from the 50s. The toilet looked original and didn't look like it had been cleaned in years it was so black inside the bowl. A sour unpleasant smell permeated through the whole house. It was a far cry from the clean, cluttered, but comfortable house where Cindy Lowe and her children lived. Its sparseness would certainly make searching the property easier but it saddened him. Although he'd seen worse, it always shocked him to see the conditions some people lived in. The perpetual poverty trap where unscrupulous landlords believed they didn't have to provide low-income working-class people with a decent standard of accommodation. And from interviews with suspects or victims in the past, he knew they believed they had little choice; they either accepted their situation or would be on the streets. After all it was nothing new and was all they could expect according to them. It angered Frank to realise the wide gulf between the haves and have nots. He'd brought the subject up time and time again at police conferences, suggesting they should work with the shire councils to introduce laws for any property that was let where a minimum standard had to be met. Heads would nod and comments would be made about how terrible it was but nothing was ever done about it. It was as though the powers that be preferred to keep the status quo. He felt a stab of pity for Lowe until he remembered what he'd done to all those women.

The two techs were late arriving. He briefed them on what they were looking for; photographs of all the women Lowe had attacked. Or anything else that looked like a souvenir. He also asked them to collect the dirty clothes in the bedroom. With any luck they might find DNA from their victims on some items.

Rachel and Ayesha arrived soon after the techs.

'McDonald is adamant he's not pressing charges. We found his lodger moving out and McDonald packing up to clear out himself. He reckons his life has basically been ruined by our actions.'

'He's maybe right about that if his name leaks out. But that's pretty quick, isn't it? A touch suspicious.'

Rachel shrugged. 'We thought much the same. We can't compel him to stay, can we?'

'No. He's free to go where he wants. Did he say where he was planning to go?'

'Overseas by the sound of it. He hasn't made up his mind.'

'Hmm. The techs are here. It won't take them long. There's so little in the house. Give me a hand moving this couch, will you?'

'It's really bare and smelly in here, isn't it?' Ayesha said looking around and twitching her nose.

'The rest is much the same.'

'I'm not touching that thing without gloves,' Rachel said, promptly pulling a pair out of her bag. Ayesha followed suit.

'I've lifted all the cushions off. Nothing there except food crumbs. I want to be able to see underneath it. We can move it out into the middle of the room then I'll turn it over.'

With some grunting on his part, Frank and the women moved the couch. There was nothing underneath except more crumbs and dust mites. Once they'd turned it over, he could see the base fabric was torn. A good examination of its underside revealed nothing but rusty springs.

The techs walked back into the room carrying bags of clothes. 'No photos anywhere,' they said.

'Damn. They must be in his pick-up then. Where the hell did he leave it?'

# 48

Frank learned the answer to his question within minutes of voicing it. His mobile rang and he saw it was Chris Walker. He listened then said, 'Right. Stay with the vehicle. We'll be there in a few minutes. Don't try to open it. I have the keys.'

'Chris has located Lowe's vehicle,' Frank said after disconnecting the call. 'It was parked inside some garage down at the oval in Arthur Street. We all need to go there.'

Wearing a new set of gloves, Frank unlocked the driver's door to Lowe's pick-up which released the locks on all the doors. One of the techs started searching the front passenger area, and opened the glove compartment. 'Plenty of condoms in here,' he said. 'And packets of surgical gloves.'

A second tech had opened the left rear door and was searching the back. 'There's what looks like a balaclava here,' she said.

'Bag it all up,' Frank said.

He leaned down peering under the driver's seat and

spotted a plastic carrier bag. It was rolled over at the top and when he tapped it with his gloved hand it felt as though it contained a number of flat items.

'I think I might have found the photos,' Frank announced. 'Can one of you get a decent shot of it while it's still under the seat?'

Frank waited until one of the techs took a few photos, then slid the bag out and placed it on the driver's seat. After unrolling the top, he opened it and peered inside. The first photograph was of a very attractive, young, Southeast Asian woman whose large brown eyes stared back at him. Although he'd never seen her eyes, he recognised her immediately.

'Yes, I knew it!' He cleared his throat when he noticed the techs were looking at him. 'This bag contains all the photos Lowe removed from his victims. This is more than enough evidence to nail Lowe now. I'm going to take these photos back to headquarters, if you can give me some clear evidence bags, we'll deal with them,' he said addressing the techs. 'We'll get them over to you later to see if you can pick up fingerprints. You carry on looking to see what else you can find. Chris, you stay here. I'll leave you the keys. When they've finished, arrange for the vehicle to be impounded.' To Rachel and Ayesha, he said, 'Back to base for us.'

Frank cleared all the files from one side of his desk to make space for the photographs to be laid out. They placed them one by one into separate sealed evidence bags. There were seven in total and Lowe had numbered the back of each photo in the order of their attacks.

'Our unnamed victim number one,' Frank said laying her photograph down. 'Ross and Wheeler refused to give me the woman's name.'

'Number two. Tessa Cooper,' Rachel said, placing Tessa's photo down next. It was a booth image of her with her young daughter.

'Number three, Rhonda Newland,' Ayesha said.

'Mystery victim number four,' Frank said. The photo showed a young woman with shoulder-length chestnut brown hair sitting on a rock in a rainforest setting.

'She's beautiful,' Ayesha said quietly.

'She has a fragile look about her though,' Rachel said. 'Perhaps it was just too much for her come forward.'

'Maybe,' Frank said.

'Victim five, Carrie Ross,' Rachel continued. Like Tessa Cooper's photo, it was taken in a photo booth with her sister.

'Victim six, Melody Hudson,' Ayesha said.

'And finally, victim seven, Becky Wheeler,' Frank said, placing the last photo down on the desk and sighing. It depicted Becky Wheeler on her graduation day.

'We've got enough on him now, haven't we?' Rachel asked.

'I hope so. As long as Tessa, Carrie and Melody will testify. Apart from these photos we have nothing to link Lowe to Tessa and Carrie. Unless forensics comes up with something from Lowe's clothing. Like a transfer of DNA. We need to continue building our case though and send as much as we can to the Crown Prosecution. These photos need to go over to the lab. I'd like you to drop them off then you can go and have the statements signed by our heroic women and collect that DNA sample. I have to go and release Ross and Wheeler.'

'We definitely have the right man,' Frank told Wheeler and Ross outside the station. 'We have solid evidence against him. We're hoping to find more that will ensure he'll be imprisoned for the rest of his life.'

'And it wasn't McDonald?' Wheeler asked.

'No. Definitely not. You're lucky McDonald doesn't want to pursue matters and that our Chief Superintendent is happy to release you.'

'What's the name of the man you've arrested?'

'I'm afraid I can't tell you that at present. His name will be released once he's been processed. Just keep away from McDonald.'

'That was Jeff Wheeler,' Conor said after disconnecting his call. 'They've been released. McDonald isn't pressing charges. And the lead detective on the case, Bailey, has told him and Mike they definitely have their perp in custody. They have evidence against him and are looking for more. Are you sure you don't want to go and see Bailey? You have that evidence you mentioned. You could pass it on to him.'

Conor and Kaede were sitting in his car near Bar Beach drinking take away coffees. They'd followed the lodger to his new digs and Kaede approached him with a few questions which the man was more than happy to answer. They'd then returned to McDonald's until Conor persuaded Kaede to abandon their observations. It looked as if McDonald was packing up his house, confirming what the lodger had told her. They'd observed him making several trips out to the bins.

'I doubt they could use my evidence unless I was willing to testify and I'm not prepared to go to court,' Kaede said.

'Even if it meant your testimony could help in keeping the bastard in prison with a much longer sentence?'

'I'll think about it.'


Several hours later Kaede was standing outside the Police Headquarters waiting for DCI Frank Bailey to come out and meet her. She'd decided to pass on her evidence. Conor was waiting in the car out of sight. The last thing they needed was for the Chief Inspector to start questioning him. Although Roisin was beginning to heal, and seemed to have struck up a friendship with Ellie, she still wasn't willing to have anything to do with the police.

'Inspector,' Kaede said nodding her greetings. 'I hear you're looking for more evidence. I was the first one he attacked. I don't know if this will prove useful, but his condom must have broken and he left his DNA inside me. My cousin is a doctor and she carried out a rape kit on me. And photographed the evidence. It's all in there,' she added handing him the package.

The detective looked surprised. 'Er … well thank you for coming to see me. For this evidence to prove useful, we'd need your testimony though. And your cousin's.'

'I can't ask my cousin to testify. It could compromise her

position. When she did the test for me it was on the basis that I would re-consider coming to you with the evidence. You see if you can gather enough evidence without my testimony but if you can't, I'll think about it. I want to see this bastard go down for the rest of his life.'

'That's what we're hoping for also.'

'I'll be in touch,' Kaede said beginning to walk off.

'Won't you give me your name?'

'If, and when you need it. Not right now.'

Kaede had promised her cousin she wouldn't pass her name on to the police. Hina wouldn't have minded Kaede doing so if she had gone to police straight away. But this late in the investigation, she would be placed in a very difficult position and possibly lose her job. As assistant pathologist, she was privy to information she had passed on to Kaede that had enabled her to know more about the other attacks. If Hina was to take the stand as a witness that was bound to come out. There was no way she was going to put Hina in that position.

After receiving the evidence from Number One (as he referred to her), Frank had Chris Walker take it over to the lab. They had Melody and Lisa's statements. Now they were waiting on the results of all the evidence that had been collected. It was going to be quite a few more days before everything was tied up. They had yet to formally question Lowe and process him.

Doctors at the hospital told Frank that Lowe was well enough to be questioned for a brief amount of time. Given that he'd previously sustained a serious head injury they weren't prepared to release him yet. The doctors wanted to keep him under observation for another couple of days. They decided to postpone the formal charges.

Frank popped in to see him with Rachel as a witness that evening before heading home. He said the visit wouldn't take long.

'We found your Hilux, Axel,' Frank said after introducing himself.

Lowe nodded. He seemed very calm and Frank wasn't sure if he was sedated. Had he accepted the inevitability of his predicament? Or was he intending to plead insanity or some other serious medical condition due to his earlier head injury?

'Why, Axel?' The why was always something that bothered Frank if there was no clear motive as in the Graf murder. Yes, Lowe had split with his wife and was feeling aggrieved, but it didn't seem enough of a motive to him.

'I needed to ease the pain of the anger. It festered in me and sex and violence were the only relief I could get. I didn't mean to kill—'

'Okay. Stop there, Axel. Now is not the time, nor the place for you to confess. Wait until you have your lawyer present. No doubt we'll be seeing you soon,' Frank said turning to go. He'd heard enough.

Once they'd left Lowe's room, Frank turned to Rachel and said, 'We'll need expert medical testimony against Lowe for the court case. He's definitely going to use that old head injury to avoid culpability. We need to work on that. And I'd like to know who owns the property Lowe was renting. I'd like a word with them.' Frank planned to send in the local health officer to get the place condemned as unfit for habitation until certain works were carried out.

# 49

**Wednesday 7th December**

Frank's team were in a local pub celebrating. Lowe had been charged formally after he confessed and answered all their questions. Unsurprisingly, Lowe's lawyer claimed his client's previous head injury was the cause of his acts of violence and that they would be presenting evidence in court to this effect. Frank was prepared for this after his brief visit to Lowe in the hospital. Before he was discharged, Lowe was examined by numerous doctors who, while they agreed the previous head injury might have caused a change in Lowe's personality and behaviour, he was totally aware of what he was doing. They concluded he was a sane, but violent and dangerous man.

DNA from Carrie Ross, Melody Hudson and Rhonda Newland were found on Lowe's dirty clothing. His DNA was also found from the scrapings removed from Becky Wheeler's fingernails. The pubic hair they'd picked up from Carrie Ross was also a match for Lowe and his boots matched the prints found at the scene of Carrie's attack. He was going away for the rest of his life.

During his confession Lowe admitted that the women he'd attacked were substitutes for his wife as acts of revenge on her for demanding a separation and divorce. He added that although he'd really wanted to attack his wife, he needed her alive to look after their children so he'd chosen other victims.

Whilst Frank wouldn't have wanted Cindy Lowe to be the recipient of Lowe's anger towards her, the revenge trail he'd left in his wake resulted in the death of two women and who knew what long term physical and psychological damage to five other women. He was under the misguided belief that he had been treated unfairly. An excuse he'd heard many times before from perpetrators of crime.

After one small beer and a couple of soft drinks, Frank left the team to their celebrations and returned home.

Unsure what time he'd be home, Beth had prepared a cold buffet for their meal.

'I decided to wait for you tonight. I didn't think you'd spend long at the bar. Shall he eat out on the patio? It's a lovely evening,' she said, after greeting him with a much-needed long hug. 'Would you like a glass of red wine, or a whisky?'

'Wouldn't mind a glass of red wine. I'll maybe have a small whisky just before bedtime.'

'Penny for them?' Beth asked once they'd finished eating. 'I know you're not that keen on salads but I didn't think it was that bad. You certainly wolfed it down.'

'No, the meal was fine. The honeyed chicken was delicious.' Beth's salads avoided what he called 'rabbit food' and always contained a tasty mix of different dishes.

'So, what was the shudder for?'

She'd noticed that. It was time to tell her what was on his mind.

'I was just recalling the image of Carrie Ross as she lay unconscious in the hospital with all sorts of equipment attached to her. Seeing her like that reminded me of seeing you in the same situation – although with far less sophisticated equipment back in nineteen seventy-five.'

'You saw me when I was unconscious? I thought you only accompanied your sergeant to interview me as I was recovering.'

'So did I until recently when a memory was triggered. After our interview with Miller, the sergeant asked me to accompany him to the hospital to check you out. We needed to verify if what Miller was telling us was correct. That is that you were in a coma and we were unable to question you. I only had a quick glimpse of you when my sergeant asked me to head off and track down the lawyer the couple had visited that day to corroborate Miller's story. As I was heading off a commotion erupted out in the corridor behind me. Your ex, Steve, was there with your father arguing with another PC.'

'Oh. I recall you telling me that my father and your sergeant had to calm Steve down. I didn't realise you were there with them.'

'I wasn't actually with them. I didn't become embroiled in the dispute. My sergeant came out of your room and dealt with that. But I saw you briefly that day, and your father and Steve for the first time – although at a distance. To be honest Beth, seeing you like that – even only for a few seconds I think was a shock. I'd never seen anyone with serious facial injuries like that before. When Sergeant Price asked me to follow up on the solicitor, I was only too happy to leave the hospital. I think the shock completely obliterated any memory I had of seeing you.'

'Seeing Carrie Ross brought back those memories?' Beth reached out and took his hand.

'Yes, and at first I wondered if they were real memories or just images conjured up in my head from what you told me in Bristol all those years later. But after digging into the old brain cells I recalled the scene that Steve Meredith caused outside your room and where I'd been a minute before. I've been meaning to raise it with you but there never seemed to be the right moment while the case was ongoing. And then as soon we caught Lowe, Mitchell sent me off to take charge of the fraud case while Ramsey was on leave.'

'Well you know Mitchell likes to keep you busy – and as you've said many times, to set you up for failure.'

'Mm. I've often thought I'd like to take a break from violent crimes and work in fraud, but I realised while on that case that I'd be no better off there as I'd still be working under Mitchell. I can't seem to escape the man.'

'And you don't have the experience of fraud like you do with violent crimes.'

'No sadly. But it still never fails to astonish me that men can commit such violent crimes. Such as the man we arrested today. Two of his victims died. The count could have been so much higher. Carrie Ross could have died. And you Beth - with the injuries you sustained all those years ago, you might have died.'

'But I didn't. And you're always astonished at these crimes because you wouldn't commit them.'

'According to Lowe's wife, he wouldn't have committed those crimes before he sustained serious injuries in an accident and underwent a personality change.'

'Maybe it's time for you to move away from being so hands on. I know you've said you'd hate what amounts to more of a desk job but ...'

'Hmm. I know. Maybe I will consider applying next time around – if Mitchell retires. Anyway, let's not think about that now,' Frank said squeezing her hand. 'The case is closed. The night is ahead of us—'

He was interrupted by the ring of his mobile phone.

'Leave it Frank. You deserve a night off.'

'I am going to leave it. I wouldn't have a clue where the damn thing is anyway.'

# 50

The two women watched as Robbie McDonald handed a set of keys to a letting agent. They knew he was a letting agent as the name of his firm was plastered over the side of the car he was driving. Earlier they'd witnessed McDonald accepting an envelope which he'd checked before handing over another set of keys. This time to his car. The couple who had bought it then drove off in it.

A removal van had loaded furniture and boxes from the house this morning so they knew he wouldn't be staying there tonight. Information Kaede passed on to them from McDonald's former lodger confirmed he was intending to leave Newcastle. It was time for them to make their move.

McDonald was taking his final black bin-liner of rubbish out when his body went into spasms and caused him to lose consciousness.

'Back the car into the driveway so we can load him easily,' Roisin said. 'I'll get his luggage and lock up.'

'Be careful not to strain yourself, those ribs of yours will still be dodgy.'

'They're fine. They weren't broken, only bruised.'

A few minutes later they were on their way, the radio blasting with a mix of music they'd put together for the journey.


Two mornings later the four-wheel drive pulled into its final destination. Roisin had checked on McDonald a couple of times during the trip, giving him water and a sandwich while maintaining silence. They'd kept him blindfolded and Roisin taped his mouth again each time they moved on. The women popped open the boot to find their gagged guest was awake.

They dragged him into the ruins of an old shack and propped him up against a wall. Roisin ripped the tape from his mouth and removed his blindfold. 'Oh Robbie, I see you've wet yourself again. You have a habit of doing that, don't you? And it smells like you've soiled yourself as well. Yuk.'

'Who *are* you?' he asked her with startled eyes.

'You don't know me, but I think you know my friend here.'

McDonald looked at Ellie in puzzlement, taking a few moments to process her features.

'Ell?' he asked.

'That's Eleanor to you mate,' Ellie said, stepping forward. 'Only my friends get to call me Ell or Ellie. And you certainly aren't one.'

'What are you doing? What's going on?'

'You might remember we had a conversation in the canteen one lunch time – oh it would have been about ten years ago now. I told you that, as a child, I'd camped in the remote outback with my family. We had to rely on bush tucker to survive on that special trip. You said you'd love to do that one day. Well, I'm about to make that wish come true for you. Here you are, in the same place I camped with my family. Only it's a little worse for wear these days. And no one comes here anymore. You'll have the place all to yourself.'

'What do you mean? Where are we? You're not going to leave me here, are you?' he said looking around with a frantic expression.

'Oh yes, we are. I can't tell you where we are. That would be cheating. There's some stale bread and water we'll leave for you. We're also leaving you some of your clothes. You might want to change out of what you're wearing. I think we'll donate the rest of your things to charity. We'll untie you before we leave but not while you're conscious. We'll have to knock you out first so you can't attack us.'

'Why are you doing this Ell? If it's to do with that business at uni, I thought it was all sorted.'

'I told you not to call me Ell. And it was sorted to *your* liking. Not mine. You got away with *rape* and you damn well know it. Making me out to be some drunken slut. I was nineteen years old and a *virgin*. The drinks you kept bringing me were laced with vodka I was told afterwards, whereas you claimed they were just lemon cordial. You *planned* it. One of the other girls in our year told me you did the same thing to her. Only she didn't want to report it because of the shame she felt. When I heard about all the rapes happening around Newcastle I wondered if it was you. Even the police thought you might be responsible for them. And then my good friend Becky was raped and murdered. I hoped they'd finally caught you but it turned out to be some other bastard. Once again you evaded justice. Because you *are* a rapist. I wonder how many more poor women you've raped over the years.'

'I haven't. I didn't … it was just a bit of fun at the time. I don't remember you putting up a lot of resistance. You seemed up for it.'

'*Up* for it. I wasn't capable of being 'up for anything' thanks to you. Once we were in your bedroom and I realised what you were about to do, I kept telling you 'no' but you ignored me. I clearly remember the rape – even though I was too weak and drunk to stop you. I spent the whole of the next day in bed, I was so ill. I suspect I had alcohol poisoning. I wasn't used to drinking like that. I'd only ever had one or two drinks at parties before that night. Your flatmate Mark said you virtually dragged me into your room that night and that I was almost unconscious. You told him I needed to lay down and that I'd had too much to drink. He could tell I wasn't in a fit state to *consent* to anything. But he wouldn't speak out about you. Oh no, all the mates had to stick together. Now while you're struggling to survive out here in the bush, you can reflect back on that night and all the other nights when you raped women.'

'I was just a kid too Ell. I haven't raped anyone … Come on. Don't do this.'

'You might have been a kid. But a nasty narcissistic one. The great athlete. Well let's see how much of an athlete you are now. When you start your trek, you'll find a number of different trails leading off from the shack. Take the wrong trail and you'll be in serious trouble. I'd say 'good luck' but I don't feel generous enough to do that.'

She stepped forward and jabbed McDonald with the stun gun and watched in fascination as his body went into convulsions before dropping into unconsciousness. She waited a few minutes to check whether he had a pulse. Yes, there it was.

She rolled him over and cut through his plastic ties and removed them.

Turning to her friend she said, 'Right. Let's hit the road Roisin. We've a long journey ahead of us. I think we could stop over in a motel somewhere tonight, don't you? And treat ourselves to a tasty meal.'

'Definitely. I could do with a good long shower and a decent kip. Although I napped in the car on the journey, I don't feel like I've had a peaceful sleep since … '

'I know exactly how you feel. I went through months of poor sleep after that bastard raped me. But I'm over all that now. And tonight, I'll sleep even better knowing I've managed to get my revenge on him after all these years.'

After meeting up at Conor's house the two women had struck up an immediate friendship. Ellie's training and experience of working with abused women for some years had worked wonders in pulling Roisin out of her traumatised state. Conor had commented on how much more assertive Roisin had become over the past few weeks. An assertiveness that hadn't been present before her attacks. The only one in the family who seemed disturbed by this was Mairead, who Ellie suspected liked Roisin being a docile, timid woman whom she could manipulate. She could see that Mairead loved her sister but wasn't so keen on her being able to stand up for herself.

Roisin had broken off her engagement, declared her intention of giving up her religion and stated that she wished to live a little before even considering settling down. What that meant was anyone's guess but Ellie was pleased to see the new Roisin emerging. The journey they'd made with McDonald had been Roisin's idea after Ellie had confessed it was a fantasy she'd had for many years to exact her revenge on him.

'Let's do it, I'll help you,' she'd urged Ellie. 'It's the ideal time. Everyone will just think he's gone away.'

When Kaede, who had been with them at the time heard this, she'd offered up the use of her stun gun if the women were serious. Kaede said she had no further use of it now their rapist had been caught. Kaede had passed the gun to them the next day but said she didn't want them to tell her whether they were going ahead with the plan. She seemed to be in an embryonic relationship with Roisin's brother, Conor, and clearly didn't want to be involved in any illegal actions that could cause Conor any concern.

Roisin and Ellie had told their families, friends and employers that they were taking a short holiday break up the coast.

'Do you think he'll survive?' Roisin asked Ellie as they drove away.

'I don't know. I wouldn't like to bet on it.'

Roisin giggled.

## Acknowledgements

As usual I'd like to thank Judy and Laura. They are always my first readers and point out areas that I need to amend.

Also, Thanks to members of the Netherton Writing Group who were subjected to various chapters for comments and feedback.

Thanks to Liat, my typesetter, for her prompt and professional service.

## About the Author

L.E. Luttrell was born in Sydney, Australia and spent the first 21 years of her life there before moving to the UK. After working in publishing (in the UK) for a few years she went on to study and trained as a teacher. From the 90s she spent many years working in secondary education, although she's also had numerous other part time jobs. A frustrated architect/builder, L.E. Luttrell has spent much of her adult life moving house and wielding various tools while renovating properties.
L.E. Luttrell lives in Merseyside England, but also spends time travelling between there, Wales (UK) and Australia.

Follow on:

www.leluttrell.com

 : L.E. Luttrell – Author